Up Harvey's Creek

Karl L. Stewart

Publisher Page
an imprint of Headline Books, Inc.
Terra Alta, WV

Up Harvey's Creek

by Karl L. Stewart

copyright ©2018 Karl L. Stewart

To order additional copies of this book or for book publishing information, or to contact the author:

Headline Books, Inc.
P.O. Box 52
Terra Alta, WV 26764
www.headlinebooks.com

Tel: 304-789-3001
Email: mybook@headlinebooks.com

Cover Photo by Matthew Smith on Unsplash

Publisher Page is an imprint of Headline Books

ISBN 13: 9781946664204

Library of Congress Control Number: 2017957756

PRINTED IN THE UNITED STATES OF AMERICA

Steven King, in his novella "The Body," says that there are no friends we will ever have to match those we had when we were twelve. That being undeniably true, I dedicate this book to my first friend, Dewey Bocook, from Harveytown, West Virginia.

Preface

Isn't it strange how one moment we think we understand how our world is ordered, but then something happens that instantly throws us for a loop and casts entirely different light on what we "know" to be true?

My son is gone, off to the army. It's his turn, he says. "Grandpa fought, Dad fought, and now if I don't go, I'll not be able to look at my face in the mirror." Really, what boy talks like that? But that's just what he said. And then he packed his old blue, beat-up suitcase, the one he used for years at the seminary, and left. Dropped out of college without telling me. Then signed up with the army. And now he's gone. He said he'll write when he gets settled into Fort Knox. At the door I got angry. "You're just like your father," I said.

He stopped for a moment, carefully sat his suitcase down on the stoop and turned up his collar. "Mom," he said, "I've heard you say that a thousand times. And it's always made me mad. But not today. I'm sorry." He looked me in the eyes in a way he never has before. His were watery, but then it might have been the cold wind. "Maybe you're right. But I hope not, at least not like you mean it." He turned away and picked up his suitcase. Then he looked back and my heart felt a flicker of hope.

"I almost forgot," he said. "The only thing I have here that means anything to me is the shoebox full of baseball cards I left under my bed in a cardboard box with some old notebooks. Please put them away and save them until I get back…Good bye."

Before I could say another word, he turned and walked away. He didn't look back. After my son left I cried. He thought when I said that about his father, I was accusing him of something, but

I wasn't, at least not much. He really is so like his father it breaks my heart. Stubborn to a fault, so sure of himself but filled with self-doubt, sensitive and vulnerable, clear but confused, tender and cruel. God knows I miss his father. I lost him, and now I am afraid I've lost my son.

I stood there on the sidewalk until I realized I was freezing and must look stupid without a coat in January. It didn't feel much warmer in the house, though. My arms were all goose-pimpled. I poured a cup of coffee and sat at the kitchen table. He's old enough, I had to admit, to make his own decisions. But he would have made such a fine priest. I sat the cup down with a clink, shivering and sloshing some coffee into and over the saucer. Why does he want to be a soldier? What is wrong with men that makes them think this way? Why do they have to turn everything into a test of their manhood?

Grabbing the dishcloth from the sink to sop up the spill, I felt its cool moisture and remembered what happened just minutes ago. I had just put the coffee on to perk and wiped off the table when I heard Stuart's footsteps on the stairs. A cup, a few words, then he would be off to class at the university.

That's what I thought, but it wasn't to be. He poured himself a cup and awkwardly gave me a little peck of a kiss. Then he sat. I knew something was wrong. Standing at the sink, the dishcloth in my hands, I asked him what was on his mind. Trouble in a class, or with a girl, I thought. I wish he'd leave the girls alone. If he did, maybe he'd recover his senses and return to the seminary. When he spoke, it tore my heart out. It was nothing like I expected. He has left college just as he left the seminary, suddenly, telling no one, asking no advice. I tried to reason with him, but when he makes up his mind to do something, I can never change it. Probably no one can. Now he has gone.

Back in the kitchen, I folded and carefully draped the wet cloth over the edge of the sink. Those stupid baseball cards. The hours he spent spreading them out and arranging them into the teams as he would have assembled them. "What if Hank Aaron was a Yankee and got to bat behind Mickey Mantle? What if Eddie Mathews was a Cub batting ahead of Ernie Banks? On and on he would go. It made me angry, him focusing so much attention on such childish things instead of what he should have been concerned with.

So here I am in the attic. It's colder up here than it is outside. An icy draft pours in through the cracked window rattling at the end of the house. Angrily I toss his box containing those precious baseball cards into a corner. The side of the box hits another box and flips over, spilling the contents onto the dirty boards. Under my breath I curse as I stoop to pick them up and cram them back in.

Beneath the shoebox I spy a number of notebooks, old, faded and worn spiral-bound things filled with writings. His childish penmanship I recognized immediately. They were journals or diaries, and he must have been keeping them for years. But he never said a word about them. So typical. I told him a thousand times we can't dwell in the past. "Your rotten father walked out years ago," I say, "and we have to move on." We have to stop thinking about the past and live in the present. What's past cannot help us. Once it is gone, dwelling on it can only open closed wounds and hurt us all the more.

I stood and kicked the box with the papers and cards behind a large old trunk. The top popped open again, and I saw a flash of a yellow notebook cover. Curiosity got the better of me. Carefully I picked up the entire box and made my way back to the fold-down stairs, backed down them, and carried the box with his notebooks into my bedroom.

My son will probably never return, just like his father. Why should I save these things? I will read the journals then destroy them all, cards included. Why would a person cling to so much pain? I just do not understand. I dug out the faded, tattered notebooks and noticed he had labeled dates on each one and stacked them from oldest to newest. He even gave the collection a name. Inside the cover of the top notebook he had stapled a page torn out of a book of poems. I began to read.

UP HARVEY'S CREEK
by Stuart Carter

'The child is father to the man.'
How can that be? The words are wild.
Suck any sense from that who can:
'The child is father to the man.'
No; what the poet did write ran,
'The man is father to the child.'
'The child is father to the man!'
How can that be? The words are wild.
                              G.M.Hopkins

10

Chapter 1

April, 1958

Why is it that the safest place to be when trouble is after you is up a tree? At least that's so with me. The other night when all hell broke loose I ran out of the house and up the hill into the woods to my favorite tree. I pulled myself up and it was a few minutes before I could breathe and pray and shut all the voices out of my head. Something's broken in our family. I admit I cried a little bit up there in the dark, but smothered it out. Then and there I decided to write down everything that's gone wrong recently. Maybe if I remember everything and put it all down, I can figure out how things got this way. Then maybe I can see a way to fix it so things will work again. So yesterday I lifted this new school notebook from Sissy's pack and tonight I begin my project.

It's just April up here on the mountain so nights can be cool – but the days often bust out glorious as the whole world slowly wakes up from winter and starts unfolding. Up in the woods behind the house the wildflowers are poking up through the cold wet ground. Indian pipe, with its cool stalks, so creamy looking it seems like glass, hides in the deep shade. Trillium splashes itself around in its big blossoms. Sometimes from a distance it looks like patches of snow in the hills. Mom says her favorites are the jonquils because they grow in Wisconsin, where she came from, and when she looks at them she doesn't feel so far away from home. And you don't have to scour the woods to spy the Solomon's seal with the little bell flowers, the Jack-in-the-pulpits with their tiny blossoms tucked inside, the buttercups and the spiderwort. This is altogether my most favorite time of the year.

Everything promises and hopes. Frosts can still kill and shrivel, but beautiful things can be tough too.

Like I said, here I am on the floor of my bedroom. Everybody's asleep now. All the fussing and praying is done, and I'm about as clean as I need to be. Daddy's deep voice is quiet now, as he and Mom have gone to bed. I got a towel tucked up against the door bottom, because sometimes Mom comes by to check on us kids, and if she saw light under the door, well that'd just be an invitation for her to come barging in. This is about the only time I can write without people bugging me, and besides, I'm not all that keen on this room some nights when it is pitch black. These hills get downright spooky sometimes, and once in a while some of the spookiness kind of seeps into this room.

I have awakened some nights with the very hairs standing up on the back of my neck, my heart thumping, scarcely daring to breathe, trying to figure out what it is, but tonight isn't one of those nights. It's so early in the year there ain't many bugs out, so I can open my window without a screen. The night air smells like wet new grass. The spring-peepers down by Harvey's Creek and other new woodsy things just pulse so soft and sweet tonight. And my lamp here on the linoleum floor makes just enough light for me to write by.

I've always wanted to write stuff, stories and poems mostly. They seem easiest and sound the prettiest. One of the oldest things I can remember is one Saturday morning, before I even had my own room, me and Sissy, my big sister, were listening to "Big John and Sparky" on the radio; Mom and Dad were just getting up and jawing about something or other, and we were laying on our bedroom floor, coloring in our books. Sissy's okay. She's usually nice to me, though she is smart and when she wants to, she can usually fool me and make me look pretty silly. Anyway I got tired of coloring – she was shading in her pictures of Mickey Mouse so nice and trying to show me how – but I just liked the strong colors and my pictures didn't seem to turn out so finished-up-looking.

I scrounged up a piece of paper and a stubby pencil and an idea for a poem just hit me. Maybe parts of it came from somewhere else. I think I have heard some of its words in a song once, but I wrote it out there on the floor and asked Sissy to correct it for me; she did and said it was very good and we should show it to Dad and Mom. I wanted to, but ever since that very morning I never show anybody anything I write 'cause they might not like it. But tagging along behind my big sister, I stepped out into the kitchen to Mom slapping around the coffee pot, putting some on to perk. Sissy pushed me forward and I said, "Here, Mommy," and handed my paper to her. Daddy must have come in then but I was so worried about what Mom was thinking as she read my scribbling I thought I would puke and stepped backwards. She read it and gave it back to Sissy kind of quiet like, and Sissy turned to Dad and said, "Read this. Junior wrote it." Dad took it and I thought, now what on earth ever possessed me to do such a fool thing? In a moment he shoved it right back at her, saying, "He never wrote this; he heard it somewhere."

"He did so, daddy, I was right there and even fixed his spelling mistakes. See." But daddy just turned and walked away. I grabbed the paper and ran back into the bedroom. I tore it into as many pieces as I could and promised myself that would be the last time anyone would ever read anything I wrote. I still remember that poem to this very day:

If I rode the wings of
a snow white dove
I'd fly away to God
And never, never come home again
Til daddy and mommy stop fighting.

I am embarrassed now to tell you such a stupid poem. But it's the truth and there it is. I got to remember it all and say the way it was. That's the one rule of my book.

Sissy is three years older than me, and now she wears glasses. She thinks they look smart, so I don't say anything. They're kind of pointy at the corners, and to my mind make her look like an alien. But other girls wear them the same way, so it's the style, I guess. She is about the bravest girl I ever met, always says her mind straight on, let the devil-take-the-hindmost, and smart. She always gets good grades, and the nuns at Holy Jesus School call me Sissy's little brother instead of my name sometimes. Since she's starting high school this fall, we don't hang around much together. And that's okay too. Her friends are mostly other girls, and when they come over now they just shut themselves up in her room and try to find Elvis on the radio. I like Buddy Holly best. And besides, she's got boobs now, and just the other day as I was walking home from the country store eating a licorice wand, Spike Chatham, a big kid I hardly know who lives up by the store, was in his front yard working on his motorcycle, a shiny black and chrome thing, and as I walked by, he mounted up, kick-started it, revved it a bit, and looked at me with a tiny smile, like he knew me. Then, out of the clear blue he asked, "Did anybody ever tell you your sister was good looking?"

Flabbergasted, I said, "Sure."

Slowly pulling away on his motorcycle, he grinned bigger and said, "They lied."

I stood there a second not knowing how to feel – a little angry because he just called my sister ugly, but a little pleased because he included me in a little joke and I knew he at least noticed her. And if you'd ever seen her thinking-mad with her eyes all squinty and her lips all bunched and her round head all squeezed into her brown curly hair, you'd have to admit she was at least a tad ugly. But she was still of my blood – or at least half my blood. She's my sister by Mom, but not Dad.

I was so shocked last year when I learned about it. Dad and Mom were arguing about something or other, I was reading comic books in my room off the kitchen, when Dad up and says about Sissy, "Well, she's not mine anyhow. You didn't tell me you were pregnant when I proposed. And then I shipped out again and come home to marry you. And what do I get? Another man's child."

"Well she's yours now just the same as she's mine, so knock it off, Stu, or she'll hear you."

And there it was, all laying out in the open like that. It made me ashamed and excited, so I went in to tell Sissy. She was sitting on the side of her bed, kind of looking at her shoes, and when she sees me she looks away and says, "I knew it for a long time already." And when I went to think on it a bit, I figured maybe that's why she seemed more settled-like lately, more grown-up, and I left her room feeling lower than when I came in.

In my oldest memories we shared a bed and room, but about the time she started school, Dad and Mom thought I should have my own room. Also, Mom wanted a real indoor bathroom; I guess she was as tired as we were of either running to the outhouse or holding it all night. And I wasn't very good at that. So daddy went to work, and on the back of the house he added a bedroom, a bathroom, and even enlarged the kitchen, all made out of cement blocks.

He did it all himself, and he did a real good job, except when he was shingling the roof in July, putting down as many beers as shingles. He lost his footing and came slipping down the roof on his belly. The eaves might have caught his feet and stopped him - if he had put the eaves up yet. But he hadn't. So like a cussing avalanche, here he came; feet first. Then his backside caught up to them, and he crashed down into the bushes. I ran into the house to get Mom in case he broke something, and she came running. Weird thing was, when we got out there Dad was back up on the roof, hammering away like nothing happened, and when she asked he said he didn't know what I was talking about. If it wasn't for the crushed bush I would have thought I imagined the whole thing. Mom just muttered something, wiped her hands on her apron, and went back inside.

And we sure needed that extra space. Sissy had to make space for Talulah when the baby outgrew the bassinet, and I had this new room with a door to the attic stairs. But then came Wendy, then Tootsie a couple years later. Now Mom's starting to get big again, so expect soon I'll have another ugly sister. And, of course, they all ended up moving into Sissy's room, crowding it up good. Dad made bunk beds for them, so all the girls had to share the same room. But I remember it before and still think of it as Sissy's room.

One day when we were kids, Mom decided me and Sissy needed to do chores. One of them was we two had to take turns washing and drying the supper dishes. Me being so short, I had to balance on a little stool Dad made. We didn't particularly like doing dishes, and especially didn't like washing them. So much water got slopped around, the washer was usually a sopping mess by the time we were through. But we generally got along okay, so I guess it wasn't as bad as we let on. Anyway, I remember it was Sissy's turn to wash. She got it all set up with me up there on my stool with my towel ready to go and do my part, when she has to go to the bathroom.

Right before she leaves, she wags her finger at me and says, "Now, Junior, you just wait right there for me. I won't be but a minute. And don't you dare wash my dishes." Then she prances off.

Well, it don't take but a moment for me to figure out that I could probably get them all done by the time she would get back, and wouldn't that make her mad. So I slid my stool over and launched myself at those greasy dishes. Every second I scrubbed I was petrified she would return and see me at her dishes, so I worked like a fury. Just as I was finishing up the silverware – that was always last – I heard her coming, and with a laugh jumped back to my drying spot. Well, she wagged that same finger at me and scolded me something awful, but I thought I saw her eyes twinkling at the same time.

Later on, when I had the time to study on it, I noticed she had got out of the whole thing and I had done her job as well as mine. I didn't let on or she would of known I was took in and suspicious, but the next time she tried that same stunt, I just stood there with my arms folded, holding onto my towel, hoping I guessed right. When she came back, one look at her eyes told me my guess was on target. Her shoulders sagged. And she never tried that stunt again. But nobody ever could trick me as easily as she could. I admired that and sorely wished I could do the same to others; but that's just a flaw in my make-up, I guess.

Another time she got me good. All us and the neighbor kids were playing a variety of hide-and-go-seek called Ollie-Ollie-Oxen, and she was hunting for us. One thing I can do is hide real good. I'm almost never found out. Grandad once told me if I worked at it, I could just hide in shadows if I did not move an eyelash, or shinny up a tree and be part of a branch. Then when the hunter would go by, I'd fly to home free shouting Ollie-Ollie-Oxen. He was right, as usual. And when I was the hunter, I could beat almost anyone home, even if they had a head start. I loved that game.

After I had got home free, Sissy was having a right-devil-of-a-time finding my best friend in the whole world, my blood-brother, Mooky Campbell. And he wasn't budging from his hidey-hole. So she turns to me right off and says, "You might as well just tell him to come on in 'cause I know where he is anyways. It'd save me the trouble of fetching him in." And before I could even think what was happening, I glance right over to where he was. She sees it and him, starts hopping up and down, cackling like a hen, tags "home" and shouts, "I knew it, I knew it."

I know what she means is she knew she could fool me – and she had. I was so mad at her cheating that Mooky and I left and wouldn't play any more with her for a long time. It's one thing to be made a fool of, but it's another to be made a fool of in public and let down your blood-brother.

The only time I ever felt like I got even a little of mine back from her was once when we got into a fight over my cap pistol. I was running around shooting her and she got mad and yanked it from my hand. I grabbed back for it and in the scuffle she whacked me over the head with the butt of the gun, cutting my skull and sending blood down into my eyes. It really didn't hurt much, but when she started scurrying around begging me not to cry and giving me back my pistol, I knew I had her on the run so I played it for all I was worth. I squealed like a stuck pig. Mom came running; Sissy started begging and a crying. I got babied and Sissy got in a world of hurt. Gee, that felt good. But even that little victory came at the cost of my own blood. And she never did that again.

Man, I wasn't tired when I started this, but I surely am now. Catching your thoughts and making them stay on track and then getting them all down on paper is hard work. I can barely keep my eyes open, much less think to remember straight. Tomorrow's coming quick; I feel all done in for now.

Chapter 2

Dad don't talk to us kids much these days. At the supper table he says, "Kids should be seen but not heard." Not that that keeps us quiet for long, and mostly, when he talks, it's to Mom and it's about work and about money. But sometimes he's surprising and funny. And he used to tell me things that only he knew. I remember once years ago of a Sunday afternoon, after we come home from church not much was happening. The TV show "The Big Picture" was over. It showed our soldiers fighting in Korea. Dinner wasn't quite ready, so I drifted past my folks' bedroom. And there Dad was, all hunched over a bunch of little pieces of a plastic old fashioned ship. He was concentrating so hard on his work that he didn't notice me 'til I asked, "What you doing, Daddy?"

He smiled at me his big handsome smile, and I tell you when Dad smiles it is special. "I am assembling a model ship, J.R.," he announced, "the kind they used back in the olden days, and just to make it harder I'm building it in this bottle." He set the piece down and with his wrist he pushed back at some black strands of hair that were drooping over one eye, studying the hull of the ship in the bottle he had been working on. Then he shook his fingers to loosen them up and went back to work.

While he was daubing some glue to a deck piece, I examined the box it came in. It had a color picture of the ship as it must have looked back when, with its guns rolled out. "What kind of a name is Bon Homey Richard?"

"Actually, it's pronounced Bon Homme Richard." It's a French name means 'Good Man Richard.' He set the model down a minute and blotted up a drop of glue with a piece of cloth... "Its captain was John Paul Jones. He shot a man dead in the British navy, then escaped to America where they made him a captain and gave him this rebuilt French merchantman to fight the British. The French renamed it in honor of a book written by Ben Franklin, rearmed it, and in it," Dad lowered his voice to a tight whisper, "he fought the British to the death."

I knelt on the floor, looking at the construction, envisioning John Paul Jones. I had heard about the American Revolution, but had never heard of him, leastways that I could remember. "Wow, this must have been some ship! Did he win?"

Dad chuckled and pushed his chair back so I could see it all better. "Well, I should say he did, son. The Brits had the biggest and best battleships in the world then, and they fairly shot this old bucket out from under him. When it was sinking and they ordered him to surrender, the cheeky son-of-a-gun shouted, 'I have not yet begun to fight!' Then he ordered his men into the boats and they rowed over to the British flagship, Seraphis, swarmed over the decks, and took over the ship, forcing it to surrender to him and winning the battle."

"Holy Cow!" I looked at the boat with new appreciation. "You must know everything, Daddy. Were you smart in school?"

"Son," he said with a smile, "I was in trouble more than I wasn't. My eighth grade teacher, Miss Purdy, was my last teacher and my only good one. Then The Hard Times hit and I had to quit school and help Pop build sheds and garages for food money. Not long after that, I ran into Miss Purdy on the street. She called my name and asked me why I had not been coming to school lately. After I explained what had happened and that I was quitting, she just told me one thing; 'I'm sorry to hear that. Come back if you can. But if you can't, read everything you can.' She was the only teacher I had who cared whether I lived or died.

"Anyhow, you work hard in school and don't give those nuns grief. I mean it." And then, almost like he was embarrassed at saying so much to me, he reached over and, playful like, ruffed up my hair with his hand. I loved Dad sharing like that with me so I didn't tell him what I was thinking, that he had a model of the wrong ship. He should have the Seraphis. That's what I would've done. But even later on that evening when I got done blessing Mommy and Daddy, Junior, that's me, and Sissy and all our relatives and saying "Now I lay me.." and climbed into my bed, all I could think of was John Paul Jones, the smoke and noise, and him and his men in row boats attacking the mighty Seraphis.

On days and times like that, I felt that Dad and me were as tight as ticks, that he told me things that he told nobody else, and I stored them up safe and sure. Other times he would tell me about 'The War,' about Mac Arthur – a phony, about Ike – a good general for not shooting Monty, whoever that was, and Bull Halsey – a great admiral who I thought sounded as good as John Paul Jones.

But when I asked him if he killed any Japs, he would clam right up. And when I went to Mom to find out more about Dad, she told me, "Your dad is no hero. He never fired a gun at anyone and spent the whole war hiding below decks." She was so down on Dad and the War, I never broached the subject to her again. I felt embarrassed and ashamed for both her and Dad. And I knew she was not telling the whole truth about my dad.

Sometimes of a Saturday morning I would go into Mom's and Dad's room and climb into bed with them. Often my room gets filled up with evil spirits, and it is hard to sleep, so I stay awake in the dark and then have to sleep in the day when it's safer and there are no spooks around. And I learned not to climb in Mom's side 'cause she would smother me up with hugs. Dad would just move over to the middle and give me space. Then I would reach out a toe to touch his leg. It was just perfect and I felt completely safe. I could sleep like that for hours, just keeping contact.

Sometimes though, when he woke up he would ask me to rub his back. I didn't like that very much 'cause he smelled bad and his skin felt slimy. But I did like to fiddle with his moles, raisiny things that he has a number of. He also had a couple hard scars that he didn't want rubbed. I asked him how he got them and all he said was "Jap kamikazes, off Iwo." Nothing more. But I knew about kamikazes from school. When he was sober I learned a lot from Dad about the world but not much about what he did in

'The War.' He kept all that to himself, like it was locked up in a safe – and wouldn't tell me anything. It makes me feel very alone sometimes.

However, just as I say this I remember another time dad did tell me something important and personal, just not about the war. Only last summer on a warm evening, Dad had just gotten home from work installing plumbing fixtures. The handle had broke off our fridge, and Mom had been on his case for days to do something about it, as it was difficult to open with only a stub of a handle. So Dad had gone and bought a new one and brought it home, much to the delight of us kids. However, Mom was not happy and said he had spent too much money when he should have just replaced the handle. He argued that he got a great deal and she should be happy. She wasn't and they carried on all through supper.

Afterwards, they continued the discussion, while I went out on the front porch and slaughtered flies and piled them up like it was a war and they was kamikazes. In a bit the screen door opened and out stepped Dad with his evening snack, a beer and a banana pepper rolled in a slice of white bread. He just looked out across the hollow toward the sunset and said in a low voice, "Never argue with a woman, son. Their minds don't work like ours, and you'll never win." I was so thrilled he had used the word 'ours,' meaning he lumped me and him together that I have never forgot it and am sure I never will.

I don't know how to explain what I am thinking without backing up for a minute. I never read a full book until after fifth grade, last summer. We were in Wisconsin on vacation, I didn't know anybody there, and we were visiting kin on Grampa Teodore's farm on the edge of a town called Mt. Salem. I was bored nearly to tears and it was hot, so when I wandered into town and saw the Public Library sign over a small store front, I just went on in. The librarian, an old lady with grey hair in bangs and a kind smile asked could she help me. I stammered around a minute about looking for a book. She asked what kind of stories do I like, and I blurted out "animals." In fact, I had been worrying some about my dog Reeko and how she was doing. Right away, this old lady showed me a big red covered book and said how it was her favorite dog story.

I sat down at a table and started reading and I tell you now I had no idea how much time had gone by until she touched my shoulder and said she had to close up. I did not want to leave – that book had up and grabbed me by both ears and dragged me in, and I wasn't near done yet. She asked did I have a library card. If I did I could take it with me and read it at home. I told her no and that I had no money for one. She just smiled and said it was free, would I like one. Then I could take out any book I wanted. Likity-split, in a few minutes I had the book in one hand and my new card in the other. I read that book all during supper and most the night. I couldn't put it down. When I tried, it nagged at me 'til I picked it up again. Sometime around dawn I finished it, and collapsed on my bed 'til Mom came in and got me up, teasing me for being such a slug-a-bug, sleeping late. I have read many books since then but none hit me the way "Beautiful Joe" did. It made me feel good, even though it made me cry in parts, because it was so true – people can be so mean to animals it makes me mad, and I missed my dog Reeko and wondered how she was doing.

Now here's what made me think about that book. Everybody in it was either good or bad. I liked that: They were all dependable. And you knew which they were right off, and they stayed that way. Bad people were always mean and good folks were always kind. In a way it was comforting. But in my life it ain't that way. And Dad is the most untrustworthy in that respect. It worries me awful, and it ain't getting better. When I was a kid he was always busy fixing and building and working and doing things with us. And when I got lickings from him they were clean, hard, and short.

He drank a bit, but it only made him jolly and playful, though Mom didn't particularly care for it. He wouldn't even let Grampa Carter come out to the house because as he said, "Pop's a damn drunk. And besides that, he drinks up all my beer." And he laughed. Nowadays, he can still be like in the old days, but more and more, when he drinks too much, you just have to watch out, 'cause he can turn on a dime, and I mean he is then a person to avoid.

Last Friday evening at supper is a good example. Fridays is paydays and often now on Fridays Dad stays out late and comes home loaded, or he doesn't come home at all. On this particular one, he came home but had one too many beers in before he got here. So he was feeling surly. We had just sat down to eat, all in our places and said grace over the food. Sissy was just running off at the mouth as usual, and I could see Dad was getting annoyed, but she didn't notice. When he drinks a lot, he is annoyed very easy and is prone to say and do mean things. She knows this but she was trying to be cute: He told her to be quiet. She said, "Daddy, you send me."

"Shut up and eat or I'll send you to your room!" he barked.

Well, Sissy got her back up, and quicker than she could have planned, she slapped her fork down and shouted, "I'd like to send you straight to hell." Right away she knew she had crossed a forbidden line and was in huge trouble. She shoved her chair back and with a look on her face like a kitten cornered by a pack of dogs, ran from the table into her room, slamming the door. Daddy sat there just a few seconds turning redder from his collar up and nobody else moved or made a peep. The room was choking. Then he slowly stood, and there was death in that place. Before he could take three steps toward Sissy's room, Mom was in front of him, blocking the door. "You're not going into that child's room, Stu."

"Get out of the way, Maggie. You heard what she said. "I'm going to thrash her within an inch of her life."

Mom's arms were gripping the sides of the door. "She was just upset 'cause you were being mean to her. Just calm down a bit. You can spank her later."

All Dad said was, "Later hell," and he cold-cocked her with his left fist. Mom's head jerked back and she crumpled to the floor like she had no legs and laid there sprawled. Dad stared at her like he didn't really see her down there, then turned and stomped out through the front door. The girls and I sat paralyzed. A few moments later, we heard the truck motor revving and gravel spitting as he drove off. Mom slowly pushed herself up, and holding her bleeding mouth, told us to get to bed, and she went into the bathroom. We ran right off to our rooms and never came out. Now here's the kicker. Next morning, Saturday, I woke up, sprang out of bed, and sprinted to their room. There was Dad, snoring away on his belly, and Mom sitting up next to him. She right-away started shaking him to wake him up, but he wasn't quite ready. Then she really shook him hard and said, "Look, Stu. You knocked out one of my teeth last night."

He rolled over and looked at her with the big handsome grin on his face, black wavy hair hanging over his forehead, and said, "Like hell I did, Maggie. You musta fell. Gimme a kiss." And he grabbed her for a hug, and she didn't look so mad anymore either. I left the room, feeling much better that they had made up. I really do believe he did not remember punching Mom. That's about the only good thing comes from him drinking hard – the next day he can't remember what he was mad about night before. So things were good again – for a while.

See what I mean? The same man who would let me take a day off from school so I could travel up to Logan with him in the big green truck and help him install plumbing, and who would build ships and tell me all about them, and who would tell us funny stories about people he met so that we would all be laughing 'til we cried and our sides hurt, that same guy with just too much booze in him could cuss you out or smack you down in a second. It got so that when I saw the green truck coming up the road to park at the bottom of the hill, I would watch everything – how fast he is driving, how he is braking it, how loud does he slam the truck door, how he walks to the house, everything for a clue – should I run to meet him or run away?

And that's what I been doing a lot of lately, running away. Oh, not forever. I tried that but got scared and hungry. So now, after a whipping I got last fall, I don't wait for Dad to grab me, leastways if he is mean drunk. I just run. First time I ran to Mooky's house but I can't do that every time. His dad, Earl, said I could stay one night but then I had to go home. So now I run to the woods.

Mooky and I had built a tree fort in a big oak with powerful branches two summers ago. We hauled up some old shed boards that were left over after Dad rebuilt the garage. Mooky isn't the climber I am, so I had to cup my hands for him to step in to boost him up so he could grab the low branch, even though he is bigger than me. Then when he was up, I passed him the boards and climbed up myself. If I can jump up and get ahold of the lowest tree branch, I then swing a leg over the top and the rest of me just follows. The boards even had some old rusty nails in them, so when we stomped the boards down, they gripped the branches just enough to keep from sliding off the tree. I made very careful not to stomp any nails sticking up. I learned my lesson the hard way a time before, and believe me, I'll never make that same mistake. It came about this way.

Dad was reroofing the garage at the foot of the hill below our house. He first knocked off the rotten old roof boards by walking in the garage and thrusting up with a 2x4, sending them flying every which way into the yard. Then, when they had all been so removed, he would climb up on the ladder and lay down new boards and shingle over them. I thought knocking the roof off looked like great fun and asked to help. Dad put the 2x4 down and walked over to where I was standing. "Son," he said, "look at these crappy old boards. Do you see those rusty nails?" I nodded. "You can drag some of these boards into a pile if you want to. Just you be very cautious not to step on any of those nails. They could infect you and send you on a one-way trip out of this world."

Wow, I thought. There were rusty nails sticking up everywhere. Dad went back inside the garage to continue his demolition while I thought it all over. It would be better if those nails were all pounded out or bent over. I had no hammer to pound them down, but if I was careful, I thought, I could stomp them over so no one would get hurt. I was wearing my old sneakers and they seemed sturdy enough. So I gave it a try and stomped the first nail. It bent over easy, and I was proud of myself so I went for another, and another.

What a team we made, Dad smashing boards off in the garage and me stomping nails in the yard. I'm not sure how it happened, but it did. I misjudged a nail's angle, and suddenly I felt a jolt like I had stuck my finger into an electric socket, only it was my foot and I couldn't seem to make the pain stop. I screamed for Dad and he came running. "Jesus H. Christ, J.R.," and he sized up the scene.

As he had trouble pulling the nail back out of my foot and shoe, what with me screaming and all, he stood me up on the board, and he stood on it too, grabbing me around the waist. One big yank up and I was free of the hated nail. Dad carried me over and sat me down on the bottom step. Then he tore off my shoe. My sock was soaked in blood, and there was a nasty hole smack in the middle of the bottom of my right foot. "Lord, that's ugly. What in the world do you think you were doing? Didn't I tell you to stay away from those nails?"

"I was just trying to help by bending them over, and I missed one," I sobbed.

"Well, we better get you to the hospital before you get tetanus and die of lockjaw or something. Maggie, get out here!" he yelled. "And bring some soapy water, gauze and tape. We gotta get J.R. to the hospital." And he carried me up all those steps like I was nothing, setting me on the front porch step.

Mom came running out with the stuff Dad asked for, looked at the black hole oozing blood, and went back into the house while Dad cleaned it off and wrapped it up. In a minute she was back, hustling Sissy and Talulah ahead of her and carrying Wendy. We all piled into the truck and off we sped, down that red brick road. That foot kept throbbing pain all the way to the hospital and later too, even after the doctor gave me a shot with the biggest needle I ever saw. I cried until the doctor promised me that I would not die, and you can bet I never did anything so foolish as nail stomping again. The funny thing is that at the time it seemed like the right and helpful thing to do. Only when I think on it later do I see what a dummy I was and what it cost me. People can get in a mess of trouble doing what they think is a good idea at the time, and regret it for a whole lot longer.

Anyway, you can see why I was doubly sure to face the boards for our tree fort point-side down before I stomped. The finished fort did not look like my mind's-eye plan for it, but it was good enough for us to sit in and pretend it was anything we wanted. Once we even pretended it was the Bon Homey Richard and sank the whole rotten British fleet from the branches. We don't go much there anymore because Mooky has trouble climbing up, and I refused to build steps as that would mean others could then get up in our tree, which I just won't have.

But at night, when I'm running from Dad, it is perfect. I've got an old jacket with a fur collar I wad up for a pillow, and Mooky found a piece of canvas that we use for a sail or a cover, or a roof or just about anything we need. And that tree holds me up safe and sound every time. Sometimes, when I've run away from Dad and am hiding up in it, I do believe it whispers to me in an old, old voice that things will be okay by-and-by, that what seems all bent now will get straightened and the rips get sewn up again. And by the next morning, when I go down to the house, either Dad is gone to work, which means I'm safe, or he is still asleep, which means I can pretend I was in my room all night. And he's always forgot why he was going to whip me anyways.

Like I said, I never ran from him until last fall. But I couldn't stand the pain of his whippings anymore and figured if I ran and he caught me it wouldn't hurt worse than if he killed me, so when he told me to bring myself over to him and he whistled those switches in the air, I took off for the woods. He started after me, madder than a hornet, cussing a blue streak. I mean to tell you I expected he would catch me and kill me or beat me to a pulp, so I ran like the very wind, trying not to touch the earth, picturing any moment his big hairy arm reaching out and snatching me by my shirt collar, 'til I got to the woods and stopped to breathe.

He had gone back into the house, and then night came. I curled up with my head on the fur collar of my jacket and laid there thinking for a long time. Something had changed, and I knew it could never be the old way again. I now knew I was faster than him, and so if I watched him and where I was, I would not be whipped again, at least not when he was drunk. I just had to be smart and quick on my feet. I might sound like a rotten kid running from my dad like that but if you knew how it was you might think different.

The last time he beat me, before I started running, I can't even remember what it was for. When we misbehave, Mom saves up the details and tells Dad when he gets home and he does the whippings. I think I had pushed Talulah off the slide and she got hurt a bit – nothing serious, but her lip bled and she cried. Well, that and his beer triggered Dad's mean streak; he called me a little bastard and told me to come with him outside. I really didn't want to but was too afraid to disobey, so I tailed him out to the big tree in the back yard. I thought he might just hit me a few times and let it go.

There are three kinds of whippings Dad gives out. The best is when he uses his open hand, usually on your bottom, though you have to watch out you don't get it across the face. That stings awful and sometimes swells up. He used to dish out a lot of those bare-bottomed spankings. The second kind is when he reaches for tools, like a belt or switches or anything handy. They hurt more and that means he's usually been drinking. There's been more and more of these whippings lately. But the worst is when he is so drunk he just hauls off with his fists. You can't brace yourself for a fist to the side of the head or your chest. They always knock you down and hurt for a long time.

But that only happens when he's totally looped and angry. Which ain't that often. Tonight he seemed to still be walking pretty straight, which usually is a good sign, but then he reached up and broke off several young poplar twigs, de-leafed them, and whistled them around in the air, with him grinning a nasty grin like he particularly liked the sound. Then, before I could start in any pleading and crying, he reached down and grabbed me by the muscle of my right arm above the elbow and hoisted me clean off the ground. Man, I mean to tell you it felt like that my arm was being ripped right off.

There I hung in the air by one arm while he scourged my bare legs back and forth with those switches. It felt like a million wasps were all stinging them, but there was no place I could put them he couldn't reach. And my arm felt like it was working loose from my shoulder and my muscle from my arm, so while my legs were dancing and kicking, trying to ward off what felt like flames, with my left arm I was trying to grasp my right arm to keep it from being wrenched off the rest of me.

When he got tired, and not a moment sooner, he dropped me to the ground and turned and stalked back to the house, throwing the switches off to one side. I just scrunched up there, a quivering painful wreck, not even sure I was glad to be alive. Leastwise, I knew I wasn't dead because it hurt too much. I laid there in the dark, hoping he wouldn't come back for a second helping 'cause I couldn't walk right, much less run away. After a while when I hobbled back in, he was gone to bed. Mom teared-up tightlipped, and I cried some more when she picked me up and put me on the counter to rub salve on my red-streaked legs. I wore dungarees for a while after that 'cause my legs were such a mess. It was clear to me that Dad was getting meaner and drunker, so I determined that from now on, when he comes for me drunk – I'm running. He ain't caught me since that night, and I don't reckon he ever will again.

Like I said, most people think of me as a skinny little kid, or a runt. But I can do two things better than anybody I know – run fast, and climb trees. Being up high in some swaying tree doesn't scare me at all. It's exciting and comforting. Once I was chased up the tree in the corner of the schoolyard by a big kid and he came up after me. He really meant to hurt me.

He chased me up as high as I wanted to go, and I started to worry that maybe he was mad enough to not quit. So I went to 'Plan B,' as Dad calls it. I spraddled across a sticking-out branch, like riding a teeter-totter, facing in to the tree so I could keep an eye on him. I just kept lifting and pushing myself out farther, backwards. When he got up to that branch and saw what I was doing, he looked worried but happy. I was now trapped, and he figured he would just come out and knock me off – he started inching out on that branch but then froze. I saw the fear on his face as he looked down, and I just kept backing up 'til I felt the branch give just a bit and start sagging. He saw it too. I wiggled out even a bit more and deliberately rocked the branch, which was noticeably thinner between my legs.

I grinned and taunted him, "So you think you can get me. Come on and try. This'll maybe hold two of us; likely not though. And we'll both crash down. Maybe I'll jump and grab another branch. You'll surely break something or maybe kill yourself. I don't care. I like it here," and grinned at him.

By now he was gripping the branch and thinking about my words and how far away the ground was. In a second he backed to the trunk, then backed down that tree and didn't stop 'til he hit solid earth. I just rode my branch, feeling free as a bird. He yelled up, "You're a crazy son-of-a-bitch," and ran off to join his other thugs. That was my severest test and had passed it easy. I thanked God for making me able to run fast and climb trees like a monkey.

That is why I run to this big old tree. It is more than a play place – it makes me safe. From its top-crotch, even on the hottest days, there is a cooling breeze flowing over the ridge. My tree itself is just over the crest of the ridge to the east of our house. In the fall of the year, when its leaves turn crispy brown and curl up, you can see through them better. Most the other nearby trees lose their leaves first, and from the crow's nest above my platform, I can see maybe a hundred miles; at least it seems so. I know for a fact I can see all the way to the Ohio. You can't see the river proper, but across one low ridge, you can see the low spot, the valley where the river flows and the hazy high ground rising up and stretching away on the other side. That side is a whole nother state, Ohio. There ain't no spot in the whole world can match my tree, and nobody knows about it but me and Mooky, and he'd never tell. This is where I run to and where I'm writing from right now.

Chapter 3

One really great thing about Holy Jesus is that they teach us a lot about music. I don't think my life would be worth a darn if I didn't have music. Ever since I was just a little kid Mom played the piano. She can play most anything but I like it best when she plays the boogie-woogie, like "The Bugle-Boy of Company B." It is the liveliest kind of music ever made. She sort of bounces up and down on the piano stool, and her hands just fly as she pounds the keys. Once she got going so good that a picture fell off the wall. To my way of thinking boogie-woogie, the way Mom plays it, is just about as good as rock-and-roll. Once, of an evening, she was playing in the front room. Dad was kind of slumped over the back of the piano with a beer, grinning at Sissy and me. Sissy said, "Look at us daddy, we're dancing."

He laughed and said, "You kids must get that from your mom. She used to be a hot little dancer. I never could keep up with her."

Mom looked up at him and without missing a beat said, "Now, Stu, you watch what you tell the children. I don't want to give the kids the wrong impression."

"But that's the truth, Maggie. You were a hot little pistol." And he leaned down and kissed her on her mouth. She didn't miss a note. "That's why I married you. And I know why you married me."

"Oh, why's that, Mr. Know-It-All?"

"For my name, you little minx. You just like the sound—Maggie Carter - sounds kind of historical."

"You're crazy. You know that, Stuart? Gertrude warned me—Your mother said the war knocked you loco. I surely believe that now." But she laughed and kept playing.

Even before I started school, Mom had Sissy taking piano lessons. Then Sissy tried to teach me. Sissy got pretty good, but either she couldn't teach me, or I couldn't learn. I realized that for me to play like Mom I would have to practice for years, and I don't feel like I can wait that long, so I gave it up.

What brought this all to mind was that we just finished our annual spring music concert. The boys in my class got to dress up like 'darkies' and shuffle around the stage with a hankie dangling out of their rear pockets and sing a song called "Massa's in de col', col' groun'", a song which made absolutely no sense to me, and when I asked Sister Mary Martha why they had Masses in the cold ground instead of church, she couldn't tell me. Still, it was kind of fun to slouch along and sing together.

These concerts are a really big deal at school, and the nuns get all in a tizzy getting us ready for them. They start in the fall as soon as school commences and somehow they pull everything together for a Christmas pageant and then a spring concert. It's all pretty well organized. Dad says they probably been doing it the same way since Jesus Christ walked the earth, so they should have it down by now. But I don't think the school's been here more than 10-20 years, so I know he's wrong. Still, they do follow their system.

The little kids in first and second grade don't play any instruments, but they sing and act parts in plays. Sometimes they change the scripts a bit too. Like when Sissy played a shepherd girl when she was in second grade: She wanted to be Mary because her friend Lee was Joseph, but Sister Perpetua chose Anny Winchell instead. I hadn't started school yet, so she told us all about what a big snot Anny was while we ate supper. I didn't really care about it all, but I remember it well because her carrying on about it so much gave me the chance to quickly scoop the cold shriveled fish-brained-looking peas off my plate and hide them on a board running under the table top.

On the night of the big play, right before Christmas, we all packed into the upstairs cafeteria to watch the performance. I was so proud of my big sister. I recognized her right away. She was with a bunch of other shepherds when the angels jumped out sang a song, scaring the shepherds so bad that the striped blue and white towel covering her head slipped off and she couldn't get it to stay on. One second it was on the back of her head, then over her eyes so she bumped into other shepherds, causing them to push her back. Sister Perpetua had to step out on stage right during the angels' song to pin it back on. Some people clapped and Sissy smiled. Mom just wiggled in her seat.

The play sailed along with only a few glitches until the manger scene. Then disaster struck. Sissy kept trying to horn in on Mary and Joseph. You could see her edging up to peek in to the manger, squeezing between the holy couple and smiling at Joseph, who returned the favor. The big kids were all standing on bleachers singing "Away in a Manger." Holy Mary tried to keep Sissy out by elbowing her while keeping her hands folded in prayer, but Sissy would have none of it. When Joseph moved over so Sissy could get a better look at the baby, well, that was Mary's last straw. She reached into the manger and grabbed the baby Jesus by the leg and swung him at Sissy.

In the deathly stillness following the end of the song, I could distinctly hear baby Jesus wail "Mama" as he connected with Sissy's tummy. Anny stood up to give her another whack, but Sissy saw it coming and pushed her over. Joseph was still kneeling there with his hands folded as Anny's foot caught the manger when she fell and sent it tumbling. I heard one man sitting behind me say to his wife, "That's not the way I heard it happened," and laughed.

Dad leaned forward in his chair smiling at the scene, and Mom stood up. She would have gone for the stage if Sister Perpetua hadn't stepped out again and grabbed both Holy Mary, who was struggling to her feet, clutching Baby Jesus by one foot like he was a fat, pink flyswatter, and Sissy, standing there with her claws out, dragging them offstage while the choir launched into "Go Tell it on the Mountain." Everybody clapped, cheered, and some even whistled when it was all over. Joseph bowed. I was glad my folks had brought me along. Mom needn't have worried about me falling asleep just because it was past my bedtime. That was a mighty fine play, and I was proud of Sissy for standing up for herself.

Her costume gave her trouble in the spring pageant too. In keeping with the spring theme, the first and second graders were flowers. Their moms had to make their costumes for them and Mom made a doozy. Sissy was a tulip, and by the time Mom was done sewing it all together, and Sissy tried it on, she actually looked like some kind of plant. Mom sews things great, can even make dresses and pants for the family. But she hadn't made many tulip costumes, that's for sure.

Sissy's arms were the leaves, and her body the stem in a long green dress thing that made her walk in short steps. But the petal part kept sagging down. Nothing Mom could do would keep the blossoms from drooping down all around, making Sissy more resemble a green-handled red-headed mop than a tulip. But Mom said it would have to do. And frankly, compared to most of the other home-made costumes, it was great. With the red tulip blossom covering her face, you could hardly tell it was Sissy at all.

For some reason during the play there was a scene where the flowers were playing games while the choir sang, "I'm a lonely little petunia..." – old Sister Mary Martha directing, as usual. On stage, some flowers were trying to jump rope, others play with yo-yos and such. The tulip and an orange thing Mom said was supposed to be a tiger lily were playing jacks. Sissy loved to play jacks and was really good at them. But here, on stage, her baggy green sleeves were always getting in the way of her scooping up the jacks, sending them all over the stage, where they had to be collected by the tulip from among the dancing, playing flowers. Sure enough, one thing led to another. The third time the jacks took off, and before she could collect them, a yellow daisy jumping rope came right down on one with her bare foot, causing her to collapse and cry out, "Oh, shit!" Even though Dad said things like that all the time, it was a pretty sure bet that was a naughty word for a daisy.

Sister Mary Martha stopped directing the choir to eyeball the kid who swore, and the choir stopped cold. The other kids on stage, Sissy included, turned to see what caused this. Sissy kicked her foot out of the green sleeve-like dress, and her jack's ball went shooting out into the audience. Naturally, she took off after it.

Suddenly it was chaos. A rose strode up to the fallen daisy and scolded her for cussing. The daisy, to cover her crime, started crying, and kicked the rose right in her stem.

At this point Sister Perpetua came gliding to the rescue again, clapping her hands to get the flowers' attention, and with a shrug to the audience and a nod to Sister Mary Martha, led the daisy and limping rose off stage.

Sissy was crawling around in the third row, trying to find her ball. Sister Mary Martha cranked up the choir for the grand finale, "Bring Flowers to the Fairest, Bring Flowers of the Rarest." As the song ended, Sissy stood up and shouted, "Don't worry. I found my ball." Everybody clapped. Later on, Dad said Sissy had a flair for the dramatic.

I could hardly wait for the day when I could go to school and be in plays, sing in the choir, and play in the band. Yup, they got a band at Holy Jesus too. The third through sixth graders play in the 'pipes' band. That's okay, but the songs are all so short they are not very interesting. I sat next to Leo in the pipes band, and even though the songs seem ridiculously easy he never seemed to catch on. There were only three short white pipes, looking like fat candles, sticking up from its holder. So we could only play three notes. Still, Leo almost never hit the right one at the right time. You were liable to hear his squawk anytime during a song. He'd look over at me and whisper, "Junior, what's the note?" I never knew what to tell him. To me they looked like tadpoles swimming around there on the page - There were so many. But I did help him once, and I think that's kind of what made him my friend.

After a particularly awful playing of "Toot, toot, toot – toot, toot, toot – We just love to play our flutes," I leaned over and told him, "Look, Leo, at the page of notes here. The higher they climb the stairs, the shorter the pipe we play. Get it?" He stared at the sheet for a minute, like he had never seen it before, real intense-like, and nodded his head slow and thoughtful and smiled at me. It didn't cure him of bad notes, but at least he caught on that the notes are related to which pipe we blow in.

The seventh and eighth graders play real flutes, pipes with holes in them, so they can play songs with more notes. Sissy was in that band last year, and she was real good. She better be. For weeks before the concert, every evening we would hear her in her room practicing "Key Largo," 'til it was making me sick. But the truth is that when the concert was performed, and the flutes did their songs – they were always last – 'cause they are the best, she did real good, with no mistakes or screw-ups. I kind of like 'Key Largo' now.

Chapter 4

They say every family has secrets, and I guess ours is no different from others in that respect. I found out something about Dad entirely by accident yesterday and I been thinking on it ever since. It's been cold and rainy lately here towards the end of April after our first warm spell got us all antsy for summer.

An old navy friend of Dad's dropped in, named Frank Bardo. He called up three nights ago and said as how he was in town for a few days, could he come on over for a short visit? Well, one thing led to another, and here he was invited to come on over for supper and spend the night on the sofa. Dad was real jolly about it, said he had only seen Frank once since they were demobilized but that Frank and Dad really had some times during the war and a lot to catch up on. Their third buddy, a guy named Otis who Dad always talks about, got killed there. Mom made her meatloaf and steak-fried potatoes for supper and even put a tablecloth on the table. Dad bought a case of Black Label Beer. So everything was set – everything but the weather, which stayed locked into cold, grey, rain on the hills.

So it's kind of surprising that when Frank knocked on the front door, it caught everybody off guard. All us kids were in our rooms trying to stay out of Mom's way. She was on a cleaning rampage getting the house fit for company. That all ended when she answered the door. I heard the vacuum shut off and a man's voice, higher than Dad's talking to Mom. She called us all out and introduced us. Frank is a friendly man, shorter than Dad by nearly a half-foot. He was holding his wet hat in his hands, and I could see his hair was thinning, and his grey suit seemed to pinch a bit under his arms. It was kind of funny to think of him in a sailor suit. He seemed older than Dad.

Mom took his hat and his suit coat, which was really soaked about the shoulders, and asked him to have a seat on the sofa. And would he like a beer? He would. "Stu should be home by now. He must have stopped off for something at the grocery store. Why don't you watch some TV while I go straighten up a bit." She turned on the TV, a brown Fada with about a twelve inch screen, handed him a Black Label from the Fridge, and then she disappeared. Frank rolled up his sleeves to near his elbows, loosened his fat blue and red striped tie, and settled down to watch.

I still remember when Dad brought that Fada home one afternoon and set it up. When he turned it on and adjusted the rabbit-ears antenna, who did I see but The Cisco Kid and Pancho laughing on a hilltop before they rode off. It was one of the great moments in my life. Now though, the TV is mainly a Saturday morning and Sunday afternoon thing. Us kids watch Howdy Doody and cartoons while we eat our Cheerios. We learned early on that there ain't no use in getting up too early. The only thing you'll see are the TV test patterns. Anyhow, I was adjusting the antenna to improve the reception while Frank was chatting about nothing, asking about school, which grown-ups do when they don't really care to talk, and the front door busts open in a gust of rain and in steps Dad.

When he comes in Frank leaps up and the two go for each other, shaking hands and holding on to each other's arm with the free hand. "Frank, you old So-And-So, I heard you were coming by so I had to stop and get some cigars. I see you already found the beer. God, it's good to see you! You're staying the night, of course." All the time shaking hands.

"Well, Seaman Carter. It's been a long time, old son, since our paths crossed. Has it really been that long? Seems like yesterday since demob. You don't look a day older. And I just met your lovely wife and kids."

"Frank, you may not have been much of a sailor, but you're still a master bullshitter." And they both laughed. "Sit down. Sit down." And Dad reached into the brown paper bag and withdrew a box of King Edward cigars. "I love these smokes. Remember the ribbing we took about them. Otis hated them so much he was always trying to hide them from me."

"Actually, Stu," Mom chimed in, having reentered the room, "it's no wonder. That is the rottenest smell I can imagine. I wouldn't have hid them. I'd a thrown them overboard." And they all laughed.

That's pretty much how the whole evening went. Supper was great, with Dad and Frank trading tales about their time in the Pacific. They had met at San Diego after the USS Hancock was first commissioned in '43. They were members of her maiden crew, 'Plank Owners' Dad calls them, and stayed with her for the rest of the war. Before that, Dad had been on the Augusta, a battleship in the Atlantic, where he fought the Nazi submarines. They talked of crewmates, mostly of Otis, Dad's best friend, who enlisted with him after Pearl Harbor, of officers they hated and liked, of storms, battles, and lying on the beaches getting some rest and relaxation.

Dad told of a time when he had helped construct a still below decks in the Hancock and using raisins made a potent hootch that landed him in the brig for a while. But he didn't mind, 'cause it got him out of duty during a helacious storm. After supper, we all went back into the living room but did not turn the TV back on. Dad and Frank had such a good time talking that by the time it was half-hour past my bedtime, they still had a half-case of beer to go. After I cleaned up and said prayers, I laid in bed and thought on what a grand adventure the war must have been. I was so sad I missed it.

This morning when I woke up I didn't know what time it was. It was so gloomy outside that it might have been six or it might have been ten. The rain pelted my window glass and ran down in blurry streams. The house felt cold because after the warm spell, Dad shut off the furnace, and with all the cooking and visiting last night, he hadn't turned it back on.

Tip-toeing out of my room, I could see no one was up yet. Frank, pretty much covered by a quilt, snored away in his clothes on the couch. He had carefully draped his suit coat and fat tie over the arm of a nearby chair, with his shoes and Argyle socks on the floor beneath. The room fairly reeked of cigar smoke and stale beer. I knew Mom would have the doors all open today, regardless of the weather, to air it out. She must have been up already because the ash trays, big heavy glass things, had all been dumped, and the beer bottles, all empty, had been put back in the case. Still, I didn't think it would be a good idea to go into the front room and turn on the TV, even to watch Saturday morning cartoons. I know what a bear Dad can be when he wakes up after he's drunk a lot, and I didn't want to have both him and Frank mad at me. So there I stood until Talulah came running out yelling, "Cartoons. Let's watch Bugs Bunny!"

From Dad's room I heard his voice rumble out, "Let's not and say we did." And Frank woke up with a snort and chuckle. I could see I needn't have worried about Dad. He was in a good mood. And that set the tone for the rest of the morning.

He was up earlier on a Saturday than I could remember. He made his special treat for breakfast, French toast, the right way. Now I have seen it where in some homes, French toast is made out of regular bread and served up lathered in syrup or some such silliness. Dad used thick slices of fresh bread, dipped in the egg batter, and dropped in the sizzling frying pan. When it hits your plate, each slice is a good inch-thick golden crusted beauty, with a soft and moist inside. And it's not done then. No syrup on our table. Dad says that's for hicks. The French toast would be buttered and sprinkled with white powdered sugar. The only option worth trying otherwise would be brown sugar on the toast. A couple of those with a side of Dad's pork sausage patties, a cup of coffee and a glass of milk, and I promise you that there is no better breakfast in the world. You can't have a bad day after that.

And it was at the breakfast table, as Frank was finishing off a cup of coffee, that he mentioned a problem he was having. "Stu, I wonder if you could help me out. I wouldn't even mention it but it looks like this rain will continue unabated for a while yet. And my windshield wiper mechanism is on the Fritz. Do you know of a place where I can get it repaired this morning?" I swear to you that is the way he talked, fluffy as a priest.

"Why sure, Frank. I think I do. Smitty's Garage is open 'til two this afternoon. I'll give 'em a call." And he went to the phone.

"Maggie, after a couple days of rain like this, these kids must be getting stir-crazy. On the way through town I passed a YMCA downtown. They have a swimming pool." Turning to us kids, he asked. "Would you youngsters like Uncle Frank to take you swimming today, get out of your mother's hair for a while? Would that be okay with you, Maggie?"

"Why certainly, Frank. That is really kind of you. But you don't have to do this."

"Hush now. Don't be silly. After such hospitality as yours, it's the least I can do. Well, kids, what do you say?" Sissy and Talulah were fairly jumping up and down. I don't care that much for swimming, but getting out of the house for a while sounded great, so I didn't object. So shortly after breakfast, all our swimming gear wrapped in towels, we headed down to Frank's car. Dad got up front to direct Frank to Smitty's. Us kids piled in the back. We had never even been to the YMCA before, didn't even know there was an indoor pool in Huntington.

When we pulled up in back of the yellow brick building by the entrance doors, I decided to make my case. "Dad, I don't really want to go swimming, but I am real curious about the windshield wiper motor. Why can't I go along to Smitty's? I like that place. He's got lots of cool tools."

Dad thought about it for a moment. Then Frank spoke up. "That, young man, is a capital idea. Stuart, why don't you remain here and keep watch on your daughters, while your son directs me to this Smitty's?"

I didn't think Dad would go for it, but after a pause he agreed, and we pulled out while he hustled Sissy and Talulah into the pool. Wendy was too little to come. And I directed Mister Bardo straight to Smitty's. Smitty's really is an interesting place. It's got two bays for cars to be lifted on hydraulics, a mechanic named Jed, who always offers me a stick of Black Jack gum, a radio that is loud, and lots of tools and things to mess with.

Both bays were open, so Jed got to work right away, while I killed time watching him work. Frank hovered, making sure everything was done right and asking a hundred questions. There was one time Jed had to make a phone call to the auto parts store. They hurried whatever it was right over. Then it was done, the wiper worked good as new and we were on our way back to the pool. By now the rain had turned into a steady heavy, cold drizzle. Frank said again as to how thankful he was "that your father knew of a place that could fix the wiper so promptly."

He was just talking like that when we splashed around the corner down the block to the swimming pool. We could see someone sitting in the rain on a bench by the doors. He looked familiar. "Is that your father?" Mr. Bardo asked as we drove up. Dad looked up and stood when he saw us. "Holy Christ!" Mr. Bardo said as he yanked the car to the curb. He jumped out of the car and hurried to Dad. "Stuart, what's the matter? What are you doing out here? Is everything all right? Are the girls okay?"

Dad smiled a kind of sick, sad smile. His coal black hair was plastered to his forehead and water dripped off his nose. "Sure, everything's just great. The girls are fine."

"Well, sit down in the car for a minute and tell me what's going on. Why are you sitting out here in this weather?" They both climbed into the front seat. Dad looked soaked to the bone and was shivering. He didn't look at Mr. Bardo but stared straight ahead, like he was seeing through the rain on the windshield.

"I tried, Frank. I really tried. We went in and I checked the kids through and met them in the pool area." He paused. I sat in the back seat, but I don't think Dad even knew or cared I was there. "Remember off Iwo, the day we were hit by two kamikazes. I was working on damage control after the first when that Jap popped right up over the fantail – we watched him coming like it was slow motion. Body pieces were everywhere, a finger, a foot, a dog tag, every stinking piece of burnt meat or broken bone. I'd collect enough to put in a bag and call it a man." Dad rubbed his leg like it was hurting him.

"My leg was screaming at me. I wrenched it lifting an unconscious pilot out of his Hellcat and diving to the deck before it blew up. To this day I don't know why I lived when all those shipmates died. That's where Otis bought the farm. That second Jap, though didn't slam into us. He flew down the deck over the other men, through the smoke and wrecked pieces of planes. I thought for a second he was going to land. He flew right by me, Frank, nodded his head, banked his Zero, and crashed into the ocean. Why? Why did he do that? I should be dead.

"Then I was told to go below to see the corpsman. I was down there, below the water line when the second bastard hit, came right down through the flight deck, knocked the power off for a while. Frank, it was black as hell down there, and everybody crying and screaming, echoes off the wall, and the water splashing 'cause the pumps were off, the Hannah listing to starboard. I was sure we were all going to die right that day. I was terrorized. To this day I don't mind outside pools and the like, but indoors – the water splashing – screaming – echoing." Dad stopped talking and just sat staring out the windshield. When I was almost sure he was done he said, real quiet-like, "There's too many ghosts, too damn many ghosts. And the nightmares are getting worse." Then he slumped. I never saw my dad look so small.

Frank sat staring at his hands gripping the steering wheel. After a moment, in a quiet voice he said, "Just sit tight. I'll go get the girls." And he dashed out into the rain. Dad and me just sat there in the car, the only noises the hum of the motor and the swipe of the wipers. In a minute they all came squealing and laughing, piling back into the car. Dad had pulled himself together again and seemed to listen as the girls told of the fun they had. By the time we got home, the rain stopped and Dad and Frank seemed back to normal.

When we climbed out of the car, Dad asked Frank if he wanted to come up to the house. Mr. Bardo said he would love to but had to get going soon. When I hung back a bit, Dad told me to head on up to the house: He and Mr. Bardo had a few things to talk about. So they stood by the car, both leaning against it side by side, while they talked. I sure wish I knew what it was they were saying, but I guess I heard more than enough. As I climbed the steps to the house I thought about everything I had learned, and it made me sad. I guess Mom was right. Dad was no hero, just a drunken coward, still afraid of ghosts.

Chapter 5

These woods are so great. When I feel rotten all I have to do is walk in them and they pick up my spirits. People are such jerks sometimes – not Mooky or my friends, but some people, especially guys who are mean to animals. It was a real pretty day today; cool, but good walking weather, scrubbed up blue sky with quick cotton clouds racing west to east, so I hiked home from school. It's Wednesday, and this Sunday is Easter, so we're off the rest of the week. Four days' vacation. Everything looking mighty fine. That is, until I nearly got to the foot of our hill where the rill flows through a culvert under the road into Harvey's Creek.

The creek is pretty full right now, what with spring rains and all, and there was a group of boys from up the road, public schoolers, whose names I don't know but I seen around, clustered on the edge of the bridge looking down into the water. They seemed excited about something, so I kind of edged up to see what was going on. One boy had a fat little brown pup, still with his milk-belly, cute as a bug's ear, all wiggles and licks and whimpers. He would toss that pup into the cold muddy water while all the other boys would laugh as the little guy paddled as hard as he could for the shore. They were doing this over and over 'til that pup was all wore out and begging to stop. But that boy thought he was so smart and such a big shot.

When I saw what they were up to I walked away feeling mad and dirty. I stomped up the steps to our house. Mom was in the kitchen starting up supper. I couldn't help it. I dropped my books on the table and said, "Mom, some people are so mean they should be dead." And I told her what I seen. She just clucked about how some boys are meaner than others and for me not to be that way – like I ever would. Then I said, "I think I like animals better than people. A wild animal might kill you for food if it's hungry, but it won't hurt you just for fun, like those boys with the pup. It makes me really sad." I grabbed my notebook bag and headed up to the woods and my tree fort. My throat felt like it had shrunk two sizes.

Deep in the woods, up here just over the ridgeline, you can see and smell spring all around. The leaves are starting to unwrap on the early trees already, but still the forest floor is as open as it'll be all year. From where I sit writing, my eye keeps catching hold of movement, and I think maybe my dog Reeko has tagged along, or some other small animal is moving along the wet ground. Or maybe a spirit is passing by, on its way to a secret meeting somewhere deeper in the woods. But it is only the windflowers milk-white blossoms fluttering away when a wisp of wind crawls by. Mom calls them anemones, but Granny, who knows everything about plants, calls them windflowers and always puts them in deep woods and in stories about haunts. I just think they're gay little dancers. And today they're wearing their Easter white.

When I was a little kid Easter was, next to Christmas, my favorite holiday. The Easter Bunny, going to Easter Mass, all the grown-ups dressed up in their very best, the women with their fancy hats, the incense and sprinkling in church, the hunt for our hidden Easter baskets with the different candies and all – well, it all just made for a real special time. Mom and Dad still hide our Easter baskets, and that's fun, but actually most of the rest of the business I could do without. Dad doesn't want to go to church anymore so it's a fight between him and Mom to get him going, and then they're grouchy. And frankly, I don't like cold hard-boiled eggs. The only way they are tolerable is with salt and hot buttered toast. Whoever came up with the bright idea that kids would like to eat candy and cold hard-boiled eggs was a moron. Usually, after a day or so of sitting in the fridge, they end up in egg salads or something more tasty.

And the eggs just remind me of other things I don't like about Easter. Years ago one Easter morning Dad surprised us with a baby chicken, a roly-poly little ball of cheeping yellow fluff. Sissy and me just loved that chick, that is until it got bigger and not so pretty or playful. Dad fenced off a piece of the yard and put a crate-like box in it for Chick's house, and there matters rested and Chick grew.

One summer afternoon I was walking back to our house, crossing over from Mooky's yard when I saw Dad sitting on the crate in Chick's yard with the gate to her pen open. He was holding her with both hands. When he saw me he called out, "J.R., come here a minute, son. I want to show you something funny." I didn't see anything funny about Chick but I walked back there anyway and into the pen. "Here, sit on my knee and watch what happens." I plopped myself down, and just then he took a butcher knife he had stuck in the ground beside him, and holding Chick tight between his legs, with one hand he stretched her neck and with the other he slashed off her head and tossed it aside. Then he let her go.

One of Chick's eyes blinked and her beak moved just a bit, like she was wondering where the rest of her was. The rest of her was flapping and falling and getting up and flapping and falling again, all the while spurting blood from the place on her neck where her head should have been, staining her white feathers all red. I couldn't even scream. I just stared, and Dad laughed.

Dad cleaned up that bird and gave it to Mom to prepare for dinner. Mom was none too happy about it, and when it was served up, Sissy, me, and Talulah just stared at our plates until Dad was getting mad. "Eat your suppers, and stop this stupidity. It was just a bird. Now it's meat. That's the way things are. You're not leaving this table until you clean your plates." And he stabbed a big forkful of chicken breast.

I love fried chicken the way Mom cooks it up, and I was hungry, so after a while I gave it a try. Chick's drumstick tasted just like regular chicken, but when I thought about her running around without her head, I almost cried and couldn't swallow but a bite or two. But that seemed enough for Dad, who finished his off, plus seconds, but then left the table in a huff.

Don't get me wrong. It ain't that I don't know where our meat comes from. I've seen the Sather's hen house and all. And I know bacon is pig and hamburger is cow. I guess I just never seen the blood and dying before. And I still think Dad shouldn't oughta have laughed.

The next Easter I guess Dad gave up on the chicken thing, 'cause on Easter morning there was no peep-peeping. What there was in a box were two beautiful grey little baby bunnies, which we promptly named Thumper and Cottontail. We took turns cuddling them, feeling them tremble, and laughing at their wiggly noses and soft pink eyes. As they grew they got pretty smart too. They wouldn't stay in Chick's pen but always found a way out. So Dad built a grand two room rabbit hutch up on stilts, to protect them from foxes and other prowlers.

One room was all cozy wood for nesting. Dad would put fresh straw in there every so often. The other room was made of tight fencing on all sides but the one facing the wooden room. On the top was a hinged door through which we would put their food and water. Those rabbits never crapped in the back room, only in the wired part so it could fall through the floor to the ground below, so their place stayed nice and tidy. Dad even bought rabbit food for them, little green cylinder things that the bunnies loved to crunch on. Often, when Dad would mow the yard, we would gather up handfuls of just-mown grass and pile it into their hutch. Some evenings we would even take them out of the hutch and let them feed in the cool clover. They never ran away, and after a while we would gently pick them up and return them to their house. They never pecked at us the way Chick used to.

I never saw Dad kill them. One October day after school I just walked around back of the house and there they were, dead, hanging from Mom's clothesline, pinned by their ears. I ran into the house screaming and crying, "Dad's killed the bunnies. They're both dead. Why'd he kill them?" The girls were already crying in their room. Mom tried to shush me up, but I felt so torn up I yelled, "I hate Dad!" and ran to my room, slamming the door. When we were all called for supper, I mean to tell you that was one quiet table. You could tell even Mom was steaming. When Dad ordered us to eat, and we knew it was one of the bunnies – without their fur I couldn't tell which – all us kids just sat there with our hands in our laps.

Talulah was the first one to speak up. Looking straight at the food platter she said, "You killed our bunnies, and we're not going to eat them, and you can't make us!" Her black Shirley Temple curls bounced with her anger. And she was only four years old.

Dad ate some. Mom took a small portion, pushed it around with her fork a minute and then said, "I guess I'm not very hungry either." Dad looked around and pointed his knife at everybody in general and cleared his throat like he was about to launch himself into an angry scene. But I think when he saw how it was with everybody, he sort of saw what he had done was wrong and didn't say anything. He finished chewing his bite, sat down his knife and fork across his plate, pushed his chair back, and with his hands leaning on the table looked like he wanted to say something but didn't. Then he got up and went into the front room and turned the TV on.

We looked to Mom for what to do. She told us to go to our rooms for a bit while she tidied up. When she called us back out to the table a bit later, all that was on it was the vegetables and fried boloney slices – no rabbit. Dad was gone. I don't remember anyone saying a single word during that meal. And Dad never brought home another animal – for Easter or otherwise.

Chapter 6

May, 1958

One thing I know is there's good and bad about everything. Almost nothing is clean one way or the other. School's not yet out for the summer, but we already got us our first heat wave and there ain't nothing we can do about it. When summer comes and we were little kids we used to just strip down to our underwear, fill up the two tin tubs with water, and splash around, or else we could walk to the edge of town to swim in the city pool. One day last summer that's what we did, all of us but Wendy.

She's still fragile on account of her getting over polio and being only seven. She used to wear braces on her legs and when she got them off she had to crawl before she learned to walk all over again. Watching her crawl made my throat hurt. She can walk now, but not as far or fast as the rest of us. And she still has something wrong with her heart, a murmur or something. Nobody is ever allowed to hit her or make her cry. But, heck, who would ever want to. She is small for her age, and yellow-haired, and pretty, and never yells. But she sure can talk a blue streak. When she does get her feelings hurt, 'stead of hitting or sassing back, she's as likely to just climb up in a chair and curl up and whimper like a pup. It can break your heart to see. And she's mighty shy around strangers. So she stayed home from the pool.

Sissy, me, and Talulah, along with Mooky and his little brother Andy, all hiked in, nearly three miles. That may seem like a long way for a bunch of kids to walk, but it is always an interesting hike. Heck, on many a nice school day we hike home, which is even farther. Harvey's Creek flows on our left along the west side of the red brick road the whole way in from our house until we're only about a hundred yards from the swimming pool. Then it meets another creek which crosses under the road, and they veer off together to the west. It is shallow and shady in stretches, with a few deeper pools in it where you can almost always find crawdads and tadpoles and skitterbugs. Some folks call them water spiders, which shows how dumb they are 'cause spiders have eight legs and these don't. But they are a very miracle the way they sidle over the water, putting little dents in it but never getting their tiny feet wet.

Mooky and I would study on it, but we never could figure out how they did it. God made them, so we guess He can do it any ways He wants; though He does have a curious way about creating such things. Mooky says He does it just so He can show us how clever He is. I don't know, but I sure wish I could handle water like a skitterbug. Once in religion class at Holy Jesus I said I guessed that if skitter bugs could walk on water, why so could Jesus. The class laughed, but I meant it.

This creek itself is a wonderment to me, where it starts and where it ends. I'd like to track it someday to find out. Dad says it dumps into the Ohio River – that's where all the streams hereabouts go – but he never followed it himself. And I know the Ohio goes all the way to New Orleans, Louisiana, and then fills up the ocean.

I know for a fact that a small piece of that ocean starts up on the hill in the woods behind our place, squeezed out of the base of some low-layered rocks half-way up a ridge where the ground is all mushy until the stream collects itself and bubbles down between our property and Mooky's grandparents' place. Then it dribbles into Harvey's Creek in the holler below. For some reason it is a comfort to think this little rill can get so big and travel so far, starting out the way it does up among the bee balm mints.

Mooky and I always walk side by side, stride for stride. We never tried to; we just noticed one day that we did, and never stopped. This was about five years ago. After that we talked about maybe we were brothers, but his mom Kate laughed like her sides would split when we told her what we thought. Then we figured we would become blood brothers, so one morning I got out my

Barlow knife that we play mumble-de-peg with and pricked the end of my right hand index finger and did the same to his. Then we clasped hands and let the blood mingle. So we sure enough are blood-brothers. I cannot think of a time when he was not my best friend in the world, nor want to think on a time when he wouldn't be.

You can hear the loud-speaker music and the kids yelling from the swimming pool as you come around the bend where the creeks merge. The pool has a big chain-metal fence around it and a small wading pool where Wendy stays when Mom and Dad bring her along. The big pool, which starts at three feet deep and drops to twelve feet at the other end, also has two diving boards on it, a low one and a high one. Everybody has to take a shower when they enter and leave the pool, which we all agree is very dumb, then we meet inside at the pool's edge.

I like going to the pool in the summer because the water is so clean, they play cool music, like 'Unchained Melody,' that seems to float all through the air, and there are just so many people not paying you any attention while you have fun with friends.

Sissy usually goes down to the lounging area by the deep end and looks for any friends to hang out with and tan. She is a fine swimmer and once in a while, when she has baked enough, she will dive off the diving boards, stroke to the side of the pool, lift herself out and lounge some more. Mooky, a year younger than me, doesn't swim well, but he is learning. I really can't swim a lick on top of water but can go like a crocodile underwater.

Sissy and I took swimming lessons together a couple years ago. She finished them. I didn't. I remember it like it was yesterday. Dad and Mom decided we had to take them, so early of a Saturday morning they sent us off to the pool for lessons. I thought someone would teach me how, and when we got there, we all lined up along the side of the pool, standing in the water. It seemed like fifty of us. I made sure I was standing in the shallowest water I could find because I had tried to swim before, but couldn't even doggie-paddle like some of the little kids could.

Then the teacher, a guy who looked to be in high school, told us to push off from the side, pull ourselves forward with our hands digging into the water, and to kick with our feet. Sounded simple. Then he blew the whistle and everyone took off, splashing hugely.

I tried my darndest, but every time I took a couple whacks at the water my feet would drop and touch the bottom of the pool. Then I would stand up and watch the other kids all pulling away across the pool. I would try again for a few strokes and kicks, stand again, and watch the first kids touch the other side.

One more time, and holding my breath 'til I sank, I flailed away until I had to breathe and so came up choking and coughing. There I was, about twenty feet into the pool, standing, while our "teacher" is telling some of the others what a great job they're doing as they hoist themselves out. I guess some people can learn to swim and others can't, me being one of the latter kind. So I just hung back and figured I'd go through the motions and walk across as fast as I could every few strokes.

Sissy and me went again the next Saturday. She was doing swell, but when our teacher told us to go to the deep end and jump in I knew the game was up. Like a prisoner on a pirate ship, I felt condemned to walk the plank. Standing next to the low board, I jumped in. They said we should naturally float if we just held our breath. I am here today to tell you that is a lie.

I opened my eyes under water, and like a leaf drifting down, I just kept sinking, watching the bottom of the pool coming closer and feeling the pressure building on my ears. I figured I was not made to float, so I started kicking and clawing for the surface. Just before my lungs burst, I broke the surface, and there was our teacher, standing with his whistle dangling from his tanned neck and his hands on his hips.

"What in Sam Hill are you doing?" he asked.

"Not drowning," I hacked and sputtered, as I dragged myself out, grabbed my towel, and stalked off to the shower.

Quitting was easy. Keeping quit was another matter. Quicker than I could think, it was Saturday again, and the only way I figured I could stay home would be to claim I was sick and fight it out with my folks. I knew my plan was thin, but it was all I could think of. Mom took my temperature, but it was normal and she couldn't find anything wrong, so she called in Dad; he sat down on the bed and told me I had to go. I said I was sick and wouldn't. He said he would take me because I was just pretending to be sick, and Sissy had already left, but I became desperate and started blubbering. "I won't go. You can't make me. I am so sick. Please, Daddy," I sobbed.

Well, I mean to tell you, he got steamed. He stood up and said in words that cut right to the truth, "Why you're just a little yellow coward." And he stalked out of the room, leaving me feeling dirty with my face burning, but at least I was safe from drowning.

I was ashamed he knew the truth, but happy he would never force me to go to swimming lessons again. And he never did, though once I had a close call when we were picnicking at a shallow spot on the Big Sandy River near Perry's Point. I don't know why the river is named that because at least where we were it is rocky as a wall, and shallow enough to walk across. Compared to the Ohio, it is hardly even a river. Where it sweeps around a wide bend, it lays down a gravel bar that is perfect for wading. The current sweeps farther out toward the other bank and makes a deep hole there. But after it makes the turn it gets all shallow again so you can walk right across the whole thing.

Mom and Dad were setting up the picnic while us kids were finding pretty rocks near the edge in some shallow water. Dad seemed playful, took his shoes off and rolled up his pants. Then he came down to where we were, picked up a small flat rock and sent it skimming across the water. I tried one but it only plopped.

Dad showed me how to choose a stone and the proper way to flick it. Surprisingly, the next time I picked one up and bending sideways, flicked it like I seen daddy do, it skipped a couple time before sinking. Dad chuckled and said, "See, you can learn to do anything you need to," and before I could catch my breath he scooped me up and took a couple steps toward the deep water. I panicked and started to fight, but it was too late. "I'm going to force you to learn to swim," he said. And with that he tossed me in that deep pool.

I did not skip on the water like a stone, but sank like a rock. I thought for sure I was going to die and to this day do not know how I got to shore, but I did, gagging and coughing up dirty water. I wouldn't go near the water or Dad the rest of the picnic. Dad was disgusted with me but he never pulled a stunt like that again. It is true that I am the world's worst coward, especially around deep water. Even today, I keep an eye out for Dad whenever we're near water over my head.

But anyhow we usually have a grand old time at the swimming pool until we're all tired and Sissy wants to go home. And that day we hiked in was no exception, right up until it was time to go home.

I do not like to shower with other people, so I went real slow while Mooky, Andy, and a few others splashed through quickly and then got dressed. There were only a couple big guys horsing around when I went in to take my shower. Then I hustled back to the locker to put on my clothes. There on the locker bench was my towel and clothes. But my brand new swimming trunks were gone. Mom just gave them to me at the start of summer vacation, and now they had disappeared. They may have been a little big on me, but they looked sharp and Mom said I would grow into them.

Losing them made me feel sick and scared. I looked under the bench and in the lockers and garbage can, thinking maybe it was a dirty joke, but they were nowhere. Then Sissy outside yelled to hurry up. I dressed, went out, and told her someone stole my trunks and I couldn't go home without them – I'd get a licking from Dad for not being careful. She said to go talk with the attendants, but she was going to start home 'cause it was suppertime and Talulah was crying 'cause she didn't want to leave yet. Mooky said he'd look for them with me. Man, I was really glad he stuck by me.

We marched up to the counter where a couple teenagers were pretending to work, taking money and occasionally renting out lockers, but mostly just flirting and teasing each other. When I told them my problem, an older girl chewing gum said to go look around in the pool area and see if someone was wearing them. So we did, and just then I saw my trunks, navy-blue with a white anchor and gold trim going up the ladder to the high diving board. I knew that was them. I'd been there all day and no one had trunks like them. But the kid wearing them was a high-schooler with friends.

Mooky and I nervously hiked over to the lifeguard, trying to look cool up on his high chair, and I pointed out the culprit, figuring he had to do something about it. I think he believed me, but he didn't want to side with a kid against one of his own, so he peered down at me from his perch and said, "Prove those are yours," and went back to staring off into space.

I was so angry I wanted to yell at him, but Mooky touched my arm and said, "Let's go. He won't do nothing. He's a big, fat coward." And we walked away. And you know something? That high-and-mighty lifeguard didn't say a thing, and I know he heard Mooky's remark, and that made me feel a little better. We caught up with the others before they got home, and when I told my story at supper I didn't get a licking. I learned three things today – one, thieves can be anywhere and they don't care who they hurt; two, being a big shot don't make you brave; and three, it's great to have a blood-brother.

And while I'm on the subject, I know "Mooky" sounds like a really dumb name, and to be sure, that ain't his given name. His dad Earl, so I heard, thought it would be cute to have a boy named Duke. Now to be honest, I don't remember this part but I've heard it a hundred times so count it as true – when they brought the baby over to show Mom and Dad and me and introduced him as Dukey, the best I could manage was Mooky. I called him that ever since and now so does nearly everyone else. And he don't mind.

Actually, neither of us wears our real name. Junior ain't a name – my name is Stuart Lee Roy Carter, same as Dad's, except for the Roy part. I took that name at my Confirmation. We were supposed to pick a Saint's name, but I wouldn't let go of Roy, because of my hero Roy Rogers, "King of the Cowboys." He can't be a saint now 'cause he's still alive, but I'm sure someday he will die and go straight to heaven. Then I'll be ahead of all the other kids who want to be named after him.

My other middle name, Lee, comes from the greatest general of The War Between The States. Dad says he never liked the name "Junior" and won't call me that; says it was Mom's idea. The closest he comes is calling me "J.R." Usually, he just calls me "son" and when we were at the Kroger store last week I asked what he wanted to be called. He didn't think but a minute on it. Then he told me to call him 'Dad.' He said 'Pop' was what he called his dad, 'pa' sounded too hick, and 'daddy' was too babyish. He said he just couldn't stand the way grown men still called their pop "daddy." So I call him 'Dad.'

Chapter 7

In Holy Jesus School, there are three kinds of kids – the victims, the bullies, and those who play games like basketball at recess. Ever since first grade, maybe because I was small and shy and came from the hills and talked a little different, I got picked on. Even big girls would taunt me on the playground. Once I got beat up by twin girls, the Halstead twins. One sat on me and held my arms. The other danced around and mocked me, kicking me once in a while, but not enough to hurt, except for my feelings. That was hard to live down and I avoided them like the plague after that.

I learned how to create space around me. When a kid would chase me I would climb up the monkey bars, stand on the top and kick at him and try to stomp his fingers. I owned those bars – nobody touched me there. On the swings, the biggest swings with the longest chains I have ever seen, when someone wanted me off, I would stand on the seat, pump it up 'til it was parallel to the ground and the chains were just starting to bounce slack at the top of the swing, then quickly drop down on my seat, rare-back and drive the swing over the top of the bar, looping the loop. It was really scary the first time or two I did it. Only a few of the bigger kids could do it, but it got so I could anytime I wanted. Sometimes I would even stand up and pump, flopping to my seat only when I was about to start the final swing over the top. It scared some of the other kids away and made me feel safe.

In the spring the sixth through eighth graders have track meets. Everyone can compete but only the seventh and eighth graders make 'the team.' Last week Father Doughty, Dad calls him Dough Grabber, asked who wanted to race. I know I am fast so I signed up, and they let me.

First we have a couple mass runs, which I do well in, and it turns out that I'm in the final heat. The other three guys are all eighth graders; but I know the blond haired kid with the flattop, Doug, has the reputation as the best athlete in the school. A hundred yards away, against the church wall stands Father Doughty, along with all the other kids who are out of the running.

Us four step around a bit and take up our positions. I have never run in a real race before, so I glance over to Doug, figuring I would just copy whatever he did. He looks at me and smiles; it don't feel particularly friendly, more challenging – like. Then he crouches down and puts his fingers on the ground and kicks out one leg like he has to loosen it up or something. The others are doings similar such things but not as professional looking. I figure that if I try aping him, I'll get something wrong and look stupid, so I stand there crouched to run like I always do, wondering if I really belong here, and will I look foolish. My teeth are just chattering with the cold and my nervousness and as I'm scanning the field one more time, not really paying attention, I hear Father Doughty yell "GO!" and everybody takes off with me bringing up the rear, feeling foolish for not having paid attention.

In just three steps I catch the last guy, and in ten I push past Doug, who sounds like he's really working, and there's nobody ahead of me. I run like Dad would yank me to hell if he catches me. My imagination almost gets the best of me – I can almost feel his hand nearing my neck. I never ran so fast in my life. Then I see everybody shouting and jumping up and down, and Father Doughty waving his stopwatch and yelling at me.

I can't figure out why until I realize I'm running off at an angle, trying to get away from whatever is chasing me, and not running directly across the field to him like I am supposed to. I turn and take aim at him and fly across the finish line still considerably ahead of everybody else; Doug coming in second, not smiling at me now, and looking shot, is standing all bent over breathing hard with his hands on his knees.

Father Doughty said it was a great run but he didn't get a good time because I didn't run in a straight line. I couldn't tell whether he was upset because I didn't run straight or because I beat the big boys. Anyhow, I felt mighty fine for winning, but stupid for running around the field messing up his stop watch. I mean to tell you, I was even hoping some of the bigger kids might like me more or respect me now they knew I was good for something; that is until I heard an eighth grade girl say to Doug, "That's all right. He only won because he is so little and skinny." I wouldn't race those boys anymore after that. But I know I am the fastest boy in Holy Jesus School. And so does everyone else. I can thank Dad for that. Which just goes to show you that sometimes the littlest and the weakest can still win just because they are too scared to lose.

Another time that shows the same thing was when I was a kid, right before the end of third grade. Mooky and me were playing in my front yard with a microscope his dad had given him to look at small things. But he wanted to show me something else. If you focused it on the sun just right, he said, you could start leaves and dry grass to burning. But he was told that if he started any fires with it, Earl would take it away, so after he showed me that, he turned it on a little red ant, and darn me if it didn't cook right up. We had a hill of red ants, which I avoided, because they stung me, but with this new weapon I figured I could fry them like God. Later, I read how Archimedes of Syracuse did the same thing to the Romans, and I asked Dad how come we didn't just fry the Japs like that. He said we kinda did.

Anyhow, we marched right over to that ant hill. Mooky stood off to one side while I went to war. I fried a number of them, then felt all kinds of prickly stings on my feet and moving up my legs. I was so absorbed in my destruction of the ants by fire, I hadn't noticed they were setting me on fire 'til I was being swarmed. I brushed, and stomped, and finally started screaming. Mooky started yelling too. Mom came tearing out the front door, took one look me, hauled me off the ground by the scruff of my neck and plopped me, shorts, shirt, ants and all into one of the big galvanized tubs full of water us kids would use to cool off in.

The water helped immensely, but my ant problem was quickly replaced with a water problem. It seemed that Mom was trying to drown me. She'd hold me under water for a second, then pull me up for air, rip my shirt off, brush me with her hands a moment, then, smash, back down I'd go. At last she hauled me from the tub, limp as a half-drowned cat, the water's surface fairly covered with the corpses of hundreds of red ants. I was hustled into the house where she rubbed liniment on the bites, and Mooky disappeared to his home with his microscope.

I was such a mess that Mom never did ask what I was doing standing there on a red ant hill, and when later on I told Dad I was just trying to kill the ants, he looked at me kind of odd and just said, "My God, that's dumb. You're lucky they didn't kill you." So you see, I may be bigger than a million ants, but I don't mess with them at all any ways, any time, leastways not the red ones.

Chapter 8

One thing I hate more than just about anything is bullies. Maybe because I am smaller than most kids my age, or a little shy around others, bullies just seem to find me and pick on me. One night, when I was in fifth grade, after a particular bad day on the playground, I asked Mom and Dad at supper what I should do. The subject came up because I had to explain a rip in my shirt I got when a mean kid grabbed and yanked at my arm on the playground. Mom said, "Junior, don't you go getting into fights. Just walk away." She put down her fork and spit on her hand and rubbed it on my hair to try to force down the cowlick. "Next time that happens you tell one of the good sisters. They'll take care of it." I knew that was what she was going to say before she even said it. It was always the same thing, and always just as unhelpful.

"Ever try walking away from Cecil Swishberger? You can't. He'll follow you and push you down and laugh at you. Him and his lackeys. If you tell a nun, that'll just make Cecil mad and he'll lay for you after school. I hate his guts!"

"Now don't you go and say that. You don't hate anyone. You got to pray for your enemies and turn the other cheek."

"Jesus, Maggie," Dad interrupted. "If J.R. does what you say, he'll never get home in one piece. You gotta stand up to a bully, J.R. Give him a knuckle sandwich. I promise you that he'll back down." Dad made a big fist, and Mom just ate her peas.

Well, I found me a third way, and it worked for a while. You see, there are two gangs in our school. Cecil Swishberger is a big seventh-grader, and he runs one of them. Mark Alder is an eighth-grader who hates Cecil's guts, and he runs the other. The gangs are made up mostly of fifth through seventh-graders, though there are a couple moron eighth graders in them as well. You don't have to join, but if you're known to be in one or the other, at least the members of your own gang won't pick on you. The gangs don't do much except fight each other on the playground once in a while. The nuns pretend they can't see it and just glide around in pairs fingering their rosary chains.

Cecil and Mark will set a time, say noon hour, tomorrow right after lunch. Both gangs will then line up on opposite ends of the playground and then on a signal will rush to the middle and try to beat each other up. The other kids just make way and let them go at it. The gangs are pretty evenly matched, and no one is allowed to use anything other than fists and feet. Depending on how many show up, either gang can win on any given day. Mark never knew I existed, but I hated Cecil so much that I joined Mark's gang.

The day of my first fight, I almost stayed home sick, but decided I had better show. If I didn't, I would have both gangs against me. After I finished my peanut butter and jelly sandwich and milk, and stowed my Lone Ranger lunch pail, I headed for the playground, feeling like how a man condemned to be hung must feel. The knot in my gut was so tight, it hurt, kinda like when I'm waiting for Dad to whip me.

Our gang was lining up on the church side while Cecil's gang took position at the fence on the opposite side. There were a dozen or so little kids running around in between, playing kickball or tag or just chasing each other, squealing and laughing. Mark and Cecil lifted their right hands at the same time, and at the same time they dropped them, Mark shouting, "Ungawa," which was his all-purpose command that basically meant "Do what you know I want you to do, or I'll make you pay later." I thought it was kind of stupid, but that's what he always said.

For just a second I wondered what would happen if no one charged but Mark and Cecil. Would they finally fight each other? I never found out. With hoots and hollers to pluck up our courage, we charged to the center of the field, knocking over a few smaller kids along the way. I picked one kid up and kept running. I bellered like a bull and waved my arms and danced around like a nut, making like I was fighting anybody nearby but avoided any real contact as much as possible. Luckily, only one time did a kid from Cecil's gang grab me. I yelled, and swinging my arms and kicking like crazy, broke his grip, and he took off for easier prey.

Then it was over, and Cecil's gang broke and ran for shelter. Most ran for the school, but two boys got trapped beside the church and dodged in there through the back door, hoping to sit out the rest of the lunch hour. But Mark told me and another kid to watch the back door and then led a half dozen of his meanest cronies right down the main aisle in the church.

The two boys were kneeling right in the first pew by the communion rail, I guess figuring that getting so close to Jesus's home there in the tabernacle would protect them. But Mark must of figured that Jesus wasn't in just then, so him and his boys strutted right up there, and kneeling on both sides of those two guys, punched them in their shoulders and sides 'til they were crying.

At times like this I always wished God wore skin. Even though Cecil's gang were mean kids, I felt sorry for them and wished I had the nerve to call off Mark and his gang. Still, Cecil's boys would have done the same to me if they had won and I had hid in the church.

Not everybody in the school is in the gangs. A lot of boys, mostly eighth graders, hang around the front of the school where a basketball hoop is fixed to the wall. They chose up sides and played basketball every day. Once I tried to join in there, and a classmate of mine, a real nice kid named Billy Hammer explained the game to me.

As I remember, you have to keep bouncing the dumb ball while half the guys are trying to grab it from you. While you are doing that, you have to get close enough to throw that thing almost to the top of the school so it goes through the net on the way down. If it goes through the net on its way up it don't count.

One day, when they were a man short, I got picked to play, and let me tell you, playing that game is somewhat different than watching. When our team didn't have the ball, my job was to wave my arms around and try to block the guy I was guarding from the basket. Thank God they didn't give him the ball. But they did make a basket.

Then we got it out of bounds. It was passed to Billy, who quickly bounced it on the blacktop a few times and threw it to me along with a smile. Well, I bounced it a couple times like he did. Some kids yelled at me for using two hands, and not knowing what else to do, I threw it in the general direction of the hoop. It never got close.

A kid from the other team caught it and they were off and running. Somehow, that ball never made its way back to me during the rest of the game, though later I had to admit it had been kind of fun. I thought of it as kind of like playing Keep-Away while scoring an occasional point. The good thing was no one was allowed to foul you while you had the ball.

I told Dad and Mom at supper that night about playing basketball and how hard it was to shoot the ball up so high. Dad said tall guys make the best players, but sometimes even short guys can be great at the game. He talked about a man named Jerry West, who according to Dad, was from West Virginia and was about the best in the game. He may not be as big as some other players, but he is smart and quick and is a dead-eye shot.

A couple days later on Saturday Dad drags out the ladder and leans it against the side of the tree on the south side of the kitchen. Using a tape measure, he climbs up that ladder and marks ten feet. Next, with a big grin, he hauls a new basketball hoop on a board, already netted, up the ladder and after wedging a chunk of wood under the bottom of the basket board between it and the tree, he proceeds to nail the back board to the tree.

Then he backs down and we stand there looking at it. Man, that basket seemed a hundred feet up. Then he goes back in the house and in a minute returns with a new orange basketball. I never seen one like this. The ball at school was all beat and scuffed up, but this was bright orange and even smelled like new rubber.

He stood under the basket, bounced the ball a few times on the packed dirt and tossed it right up and in. Of course, Dad's so tall he didn't have to toss it very far. Then he gave it to me. I was so proud, I really wanted to be good at this. But no matter how hard I tried, the best I could do was smack the ball on the underside of the rim. Usually, the ball would hit the tree and carom off somewhere I wasn't.

It was discouraging to be so pitiful in front of Dad, but I kept trying, and after a while actually got one shot over the rim. Dad told me to keep practicing, and that someday I would get good at it. Then he went in the house. I took a few more shots and chased that ball around the yard. Then I ran off to Mooky's to play Cowboys and Indians.

How could I tell Dad I didn't want to practice basketball? I just wanted to play with other boys and not get beat up. When I was at home I would rather go exploring in the woods or play with neighbor friends. I just don't think I was cut out for basketball, and you can forget about dribbling that ball around in our yard. As soon as I tried, it would find a rock or a root and take off again with me in pursuit. Dad must have sensed it was a bad fit 'cause he never pushed me at it again. Still, once in a while I drag that ball out and shoot it up there, pretending I am somebody named West, and a thousand fans are cheering for me. And if I can pretend enough, it is kind of fun.

Anyhow, I was still in a pickle about being bullied – Mom saying don't fight, and Dad saying I had to or I would grow up to be a sissy.

One evening Dad was sitting on the front steps to the porch drinking a Black Label and seemed to be feeling ok, so I sat down to be near him and screwed up my courage to ask him a question. Of course, I knew he was in The War, but I wanted to know did he ever have to fight anybody with his hands before that. I couldn't imagine him ever being picked on by bullies.

"Course I did, J.R. It was rougher back then. Hard times they were, and I had to quit school after eighth grade to help Pop with his building projects." He took a swallow from the long-neck. "Hard work made me grow tough. One time after we were done working, we stopped in a bar over on Eighth Avenue. Pop asked me to go around the corner to the smoke shop for some pipe tobacco. While I was in there waiting and looking around, this fellow came running in, all excited, from the bar, telling me to hurry up. Pop's in a fight."

Dad stopped talking a moment to drain the beer bottle. Now I'm holding onto my knees. I can just see Grandpa in trouble and Dad rescuing him. "I stuffed the tobacco in my pants pocket and hurried out. It was just next door to the bar, so a few seconds later there I was. A big old boy was in Pop's face, jawing about something, calling him a chiseling cheat about some building job he did. And I could hear Pop's gravel voice jaw him back, though I couldn't see him because the big fellow was between Pop and me. I surely didn't announce myself. I just walked up behind him and swung down as hard as I could with locked fists on the back of that old boy's neck. He went down like a ton of bricks and before he could get himself back on his feet I grabbed Pop and hauled his ass out of there."

He reached for another bottle of Black Label. Then he said, "That's how you do it son. If it isn't a fair fight, sneak in your licks when he isn't looking. But get him good. Then get away." While what Dad said made good sense, hearing him tell me to hit a guy when he wasn't looking and then run away seemed not very brave. I don't think Roy Rogers would do it that way.

All I knew was that I was sick and tired of the gangs at school and I hated being pushed around. Then one Friday at noon hour we were just hanging around when that jerk Mark said, "I have an idea that would really be fun. After school today let's beat up Leo. He's so stupid he wouldn't know what hit him." And he laughed.

Leo wasn't exactly a friend of mine. I had helped him out in the pipes band once, and he liked me. He lived over past the other side of town out in the country, too far away to be friends. He was an only kid and was a bit slow when he talked. In school when he read out loud he always had to tackle each word as though it was the only word on the page. He made sense of what he read after he finished a sentence – so sometimes it took a while. Also, when he read, he had his little quirks. Such as he never said 'the'; he always read it as 'thee'. Still, he could sound out most any word and when we were outside playing at school or at his place, he was never mean, always was friendly and laughing and likeable. He also could run and climb pretty good.

Another thing some kids made fun of with Leo was his looks and voice. His shaggy brown hair seemed never combed, and when he talked through his big buck teeth he almost sounded like most of the words were getting there roundabout through his nose. Still he never did me no wrong.

His daddy had an old barn but no cattle I ever saw. My Dad and his were friends, I guess, and we had gone over there only a couple times. Our dads would sit around, laugh and drink beer, while Leo and myself would run off and play. The first time there, he asked me would I want to see the barn. I said sure and off we went. The big doors upstairs where you drive the hay wagons in were already slid open a bit but I didn't know what I was seeing until we squeezed in.

There, piled up about ten high were stacks and stacks of old tires; there must have been thousands of them, filling up the entire upstairs of the barn, all neatly stacked up about as high as a grown man could throw them. We started down a path between the stacks and after a few steps the path broke off into another. Five or ten curving steps further and it forked again. Suddenly, I realized I was in a maze built of old tires. Off I ran, Leo chasing and laughing. This was like kid-heaven; we could have played all day.

Once, with Leo chasing, I scampered up a pile, and from up there could see the whole barn full and pinpoint him by the occasional sight of a pack of brown hair and his giggle. When he would get a little too close, I slid down inside the stack until he passed. But it was so easy to avoid him that way that I gave it up and played it his way. After awhile Dad called and I had to go, but Leo made it a point to ask me to come back and play again. I liked that a lot.

So here I was listening to these goons laugh about hurting this kid who wouldn't hurt a flea. I feebly tried to talk them out of it, but when Mark turned on me with a "What's the matter? Are you Leo's girlfriend?" and his buddies all laughed, I shut up. Right before class I waited for and grabbed Leo before he went into the classroom. "Leo," says I, "don't hang around after school today. Leave right away. Don't wait and ask to bang out Sister Consuela's erasers."

"Why, Junior, what's the matter?"

"Alder's gang is going to beat you up after school, so just go straight home. You got it?"

"Why?" he asked in a whiney voice. "I never bothered him."

"That doesn't matter. They're just jerks and you gotta go right home, and fast. I can't stand and talk. Just do it – hear?" and I went in to my seat.

When that final bell rang and everybody took off at the end of the day, sure enough, there was Leo carting Sister Consuela's erasers outside to bang on the school wall. Either he had forgot or was paying me no mind. I felt awful 'cause I knew what was going to happen when he went outside.

I followed him, a couple steps back. And sure enough, down to the left of the steps stood Mark and four lackeys, none of which would have had the guts to fight anyone one-on-one. I thought to myself, well, I have done the best I could. I warned him, and he ignored me. Now it is too late, and I started to bypass the group, which by now had surrounded Leo, with Mark-the-mouth starting the action.

First he jawed at Leo, who seemed too scared to do anything. Then he pushed Leo hard so that he bumped into a goon, dropping his erasers. I stopped walking and watched a few seconds. I saw Leo's face. He glanced down and was thinking of picking up those stupid erasers. Once he bent over, I knew he'd be a goner.

To this day, I don't know what got into me. I felt all squirmy inside. I didn't really make a decision – I just had to do something. So I took a deep breath and went charging right at Mark Alder's back, yelling "Run, Leo, run!" just as I crashed into Alder, bringing my fists down as hard as I could on the back of his neck, crashing him to the pavement, face first, with me on his back.

I'm pretty sure I was the second most surprised person there. Mark's henchmen just stood there, nearly as stunned as me, while I gave him another whack to keep his head down. "What's wrong with you, Leo? Run!" I shouted. That seemed to break the spell and he took off. Like I said, he could run pretty good, and he showed me then. Unfortunately, that also seemed to free up the other four, and Mark bucked me off, climbing to his feet, mad as a wet hen, wiping a red spot above his lip. I don't think anyone ever took him down before.

I figured I had done my part, and not wishing to become Leo's substitute victim, I bolted too. As I ran away, I heard Mark yelling at his "Men" to go get me. But I wasn't worried about that because I knew that even if they had the guts to come after me, they wouldn't catch me. And I was right. Within a block I was free of the whole bunch.

I never second-guessed what I had done because I knew it was right, even if Mom would have been furious had she found out. When she asked how my shirt sleeve got tore, I told her it was from playing at recess. But later on I went to Dad and told him kind of what happened, and asked what to do next. He said, "Don't do nothing, J.R. Go to school Monday, and don't run scared. That makes the other guy have to figure what to do. Odds are he is as worried as you are. At least now he knows you'll fight." I doubted that Mark was scared of me, and I prayed that I would get sick Sunday night, but even that thought gave me little peace because I knew that would only postpone my day of doom.

Sunday morning we all got up and got dressed as usual; those not going to Communion ate a little breakfast, Dad buffed my shoes while I stood on a chair, we all piled in the green Packard, and headed for church. Dad found a parking spot about a half-block away and we started walking.

Ten steps down the sidewalk and I could see walking towards us Mark Alder by his big ugly self. I quick-stepped up to Dad's side and grabbed his hand, staring at Mark as the gap closed. No words were spoken. I stared at his face like I could see through his head, looking for some sign of recognition or emotion, but he just stared past my shoulder like he didn't see me. And when he came to pass us, Dad must not have seen him 'cause he didn't even move over one inch for him, so Alder had to step off the sidewalk to go around us.

Mom and the girls walking and chatting away behind us had no idea it was Dodge City at high noon and I had just plugged the bad guy (with a little help from Dad). They may have thought we were going into church to Mass, dipping our fingertips in the holy water and blessing ourselves as we entered, but I knew I was walking into the saloon and cocking the Stetson back on my forehead, then striding up to the bar to order a shot of red-eye.

That look on Mark's face as he stepped to go around us told me all I needed to know. It was the same look that sat on Leo's face when he realized what a mess he was in – fear, plain and simple. I knew then that I would have no trouble with that jerk on Monday or any other day, and I was right. He never spoke to me or bothered me again, and his gang can rot for all I care. Ungawa

Chapter 9

Sometimes, writing this book just ain't very sensible. What I plan to do and what happens are just not the same. I get an idea, but when I put the pen to the paper the idea freezes or a different one pops out. I want to write about something from long ago, but I can't until I unload something that just happened, something I can't talk about, but which my mind won't let me quit. This has been bugging me for nearly two weeks and it's all I can think about – even in school. So today I made up a baloney sandwich, grabbed an apple and a couple chocolate-chip cookies, stuffed them in my Roy Rogers lunch pail, and headed up to the tree fort to get some serious writing in. Things ain't too good at home just now, and I need to get a handle on them before it's too late.

Mom and Dad had a huge fight one night not long ago that got so loud it scared me and made Talulah cry and Wendy whimper. Tootsie is only three and don't notice nothing but hugs. Sometimes she even sleeps in Mom's bed when Dad don't show up. Sissy shushed the girls and told them not to worry, that the fight would be over soon. Our folks were just mad, she said.

That was true, but they never been this mad before. Mom was waiting up for Dad, instead of going to bed like she usually does. And it seemed the longer she waited the madder she got. The creaking floor was fairly singing with her pacing. We heard Dad come in feeling good and drunk and friendly, and right away Mom was after him.

"Where you been, Stu? I been worried sick about you. It's nearly 2 a.m.!"

"Just out with some friends having a beer or two. Leave me alone and go to bed."

"It's payday and we got bills piling up. How much money you have left? Let me see?" a pause, some mumbling, then "Is this it? Ten dollars. How am I supposed to feed this family on ten dollars a week, much less pay the bills? Stu, we're in trouble. You haven't made a house payment in months, and all you can do is stand there and grin like a dumbass."

"Maggie, come here. I love you when you're feisty and I know you can't help loving me."

"You are not getting around me this time. You stink like cheap perfume, and that's lipstick, you sonofabitch. That's where all the money went. You've been whoring around again. Don't touch me. Don't touch me, I said. I'll bust your head. I can't stand it anymore!"

"Maggie, put that radio down, dammit!"

Then a crash, a chuckle, a struggle with grunts, a slap, a louder slap. Her crying voice, "Go ahead, you bastard, hit me again. You're real good at getting drunk and beating up pregnant women and kids. Well, I won't take it anymore. We can't live like this. You've gotten just like your alcoholic father."

"Christ, Maggie, you brought it on yourself. Leave Pop outta this. And why'd you hafta go and get pregnant again?" A quiet pause. "You know when you get on my case so bad, and then you go all frigid, why, you'd drive anyone to drink. And don't lie to me. I know you're running around with your whore friends too. So get off my back."

"Running around? How? How, Stu? Look at me. That's a real laugh. You won't even teach me how to drive a car. I got five kids. How could I run anywhere? You useless, jealous drunk. No! Get your hands off me! Get away from me." Another crash that sounds like a plate smashing off the wall. "I can't stand the sight of you. You don't want me pregnant? That's another joke. You made me this way, so go sleep with your new woman because it's for sure you won't be sleeping with me anymore." Then the bedroom door slams. A minute later the front door slams and everything's quiet.

Dad was gone. We went back to bed and I laid there thinking about what I just heard 'til the sun come up. I don't know what to do except to keep on tracking things in this journal. I figure that if a person could just learn everything that ever happened in history, he would see all the mistakes people made, and maybe he could fix them or at least not make them in his own life when he grows up.

So I'm sitting here thinking, what was the first thing I can remember. This may sound like a lie, but I can remember before I could talk right. I could understand people talking, but I couldn't make the sounds right myself. My words came out all garbled, like my lips and tongue were talking in different languages.

Anyhow I was thinking about those things when the wind picked up and I see it had clouded over. That can happen pretty fast up here in the hills – One minute it is a perfect sunny day, and a minute later these little hollers have channeled up a storm, clouds boiling straight up the ridges. I could see something nasty was coming so just after I made myself comfortable and started up the thinking process with the aid of a chocolate-chip cookie, the wind puffed up, shivering the tree with some cool wet air.

One bad thing about a tree fort – it ain't cozy. So I shinnied back down and made myself comfortable underneath it, on the side away from the wind. Dad calls that the lee-side. Actually, this is a good place to sit and write or read.

On this side of the tree under the boards we use for the fort floor, the tree sort of curves in like the back of a chair. The roots spread out to the sides, leaving a small sheltered cove-like spot with our fort for the roof. The ground is soft with thick oak leaves and forest debris and smells all spicy. The floor-boards above wouldn't give much protection from the rain if it wasn't for Mooky's old tent canvas. The sloped, canvas-covered floor runs the rain all down to one end away from the tree, so here I sit, dry and comfy as can be, listening to the drops tattoo the forest floor all around.

I had just settled down to write again when I heard some rustling through the leaves that wasn't rain. Suddenly, hurrying up through the trees bounces old Reeko, my dog, tail wagging, glad to see me. I'm not surprised I didn't see her 'til she was almost there because she is a small yellow dog – Dad calls her his mutt, and she blends in real well. Also, she's quiet. She hardly ever barks and never howls at night like some of our pesky neighbor hounds. As she curls up by my knees in our nest, glad to be out of the rain, which has settled into a light drizzle, I start thinking about her and remembering her, and sure enough, there goes all the other memories I was trying to organize, and she takes over.

Old Reeko was Dad's pup before I was born, so she's an old dog now and not nearly as lively as she used to be. Still, she's smart enough to avoid most trouble, and hangs around with me so much, I think of her as my dog. If a dog belongs to whoever feeds her, then she surely is mine because I have been feeding her for as long as I can remember. The middle finger on my left hand doesn't straighten out at the end and is all scarred up because of her appetite. One evening after supper dishes had been scraped – this was before I even started school – Mom told me to carry the scraps to Reeko and handed me the plate full, telling me to be careful.

I watched that plate so carefully that I lost track of my feet and stumbled forward, crashing to the floor. The scraps flew and the dish shattered. The piece of plate I held onto ripped that finger into a bloody mess. Mom plopped me on the counter to clean up the cut, but when she saw the last joint of the finger just sagging there, she yelled for Dad, who had stepped out on the front porch, "Stu, call the hospital, get Doc Hatfield, and start the car."

I could not ever remember going to the hospital before, except if it was to bring Mom home with another baby, and never with me being the center of attention. It was night and it had been raining, so the streets and driveway into the hospital were all rainbowy from the different lights. The hospital driveway was long, curvy, tree lined and lit by lights like I had never seen before, big round almost yellow balls balanced on top of poles. It was so gorgeous I could almost ignore the throb in my finger, and I remember being very quiet in the car. It was so different from when I would be brought there after the rusty nail accident.

We were taken straight in to the doctor in a clean, bright white room that smelled like rubbing alcohol. It was so late, long past my bed time that it was very hard to stay awake. The doctor was wearing a white apron thing, and when he unwound Mom's bandage and looked at my finger all he said was, "My goodness. I believe we can save this, but we'll need to clean it up and get right to work."

He seemed like a nice man with gentle hands and a peaceful voice, and the last thing I remember that night is being undressed and tucked into my bed at home. The great things about it all are these: one, I got a real scarred up finger that barely works but is great to show people; two, everyone treated me nice for a day or two; and three, I didn't get a whipping for breaking the plate and making a mess in the kitchen. And I had old Reeko to thank for all of it.

Although she wasn't a big dog, she acted big but not pushy. Often when Mooky and me were doing whatever, she would just show up and keep us company like she wanted to play with us, or nip at our shoes and jump back, making us laugh and chase her a while. She's great with us kids and friendly with most everybody.

Once she outgrew puppy stage, she was not allowed in the house. We fed her table scraps, and she slept under the house. We don't have a proper basement, though Dad did dig out a crawl space so that at least towards the front of the house, under the front room, a person could walk down under it. But the kitchen and my new room rest pretty much on the ground, as it slopes up slightly toward the ridge out back. And so, although she was technically our dog, Reeko became very familiar with the entire neighborhood along the ridge, and everybody liked her because she was such a friendly dog.

Except that somebody must of minded, probably Mr. McElroy, because one summer day, several years ago, when us kids were playing Cowboys and Indians, and Mooky had just died dramatically, moaning, groaning, and rolling on the hillside by the steps, I saw an official-looking white van drive up to the bottom of the hill, and a man got out carrying a pole-like tool with a grabber on the end. When he started up the steps to our house, Mooky came back alive and sat up to see the new visitor. We both realized at the same time that he was the dogcatcher, and he could only have come for Reeko. Somebody must have snitched on her.

Dad was at work, and Mom was in the house, so me and Mooky went running to find Reeko before the dogcatcher did. There she was, laying under the tree by the swing set, napping away. We went charging at her, waking her up in a rush just as the dogcatcher reached the top steps. "Run, Reeko, run girl! Move! Run for the woods! Go!" We desperately screamed as she danced in a circle. She thought we were playing with her, and we were sure she was a goner. But then she saw the dogcatcher, and did something totally out of her character.

Always so friendly, she would walk up to total strangers to be petted. But as soon as she saw him she hunched down low and slunk under the house. Never had she done this before. She not only hid under the house, but she crawled on her belly right up under the tightest spot of the crawl-space beneath the kitchen. There was no way on God's green earth that dogcatcher could coax her out, nor crawl in after her. He knelt there and after he tried to order her out by yelling, switched tack and poured on the sweet-talk, while Mooky and I stood behind him and yelled at her to stay there and not come out, and told her how good she was to hide.

The dogcatcher told us to go away and shut up, that he had a job to do because a complaint had been filed. We heard the kitchen screen door slam and here came Mom, wondering what all the ruckus was about. She sized it up in a second and stood with her hands on her hips and, like she was scolding a kid said to that man, "This is our property, and these boys live and belong here, not like some others who were not invited onto it. And you are not taking that boy's dog if I have anything to say about it." Then she commenced to join Mooky and me in yelling at Reeko too.

Well, after a couple minutes of this, the dogcatcher gave up poking under the house and stood up, facing Mom. "Lady, I just do what I am paid to do. I don't want to take your kid's dog, so don't let it wander or I'll have to come back. Now good day to you." With that he dusted himself off, took up his equipment, backtracked down the steps, and drove away. Only a few minutes later Reeko slunk out from under the house, scoped out the area for safety, wagged her tail, and I swear she gave us a big grin while we all petted her and told her what a smart dog she was. But then she already knew that.

A thousand times Mooky and me would head off to the woods to explore, and five hundred of those times she would tag along, chasing up a rabbit or squirrel. She never caught much that I ever saw, but that didn't stop her from trying. And I've always been sure that if there would ever be any real trouble, she would warn us.

As the rain settles into a misty drizzle I reach over and scratch behind her ear just where she likes it. She licks my toes and grunts, then dozes off again. I sure am happy she's my dog.

Chapter 10

Why do grown-ups always have to go and tell kids what not to do? Don't they realize that just up and puts a thought in a kid's head that wasn't anywhere in the neighborhood before? It's a sure-fire way to get a kid into trouble. I know 'cause it happened often enough to me.

Today Mom told me – as I was leaving the house headed for my tree, to not go wandering off too far into the woods. There was copperheads out. Of course, that meant I had to go exploring farther than I ever had – so I dropped my pack with my papers off at the tree fort and struck out east down the ridge, across a small holler with no near houses on a dirt road and up the next ridge, just as woodsy and steep but not as high. It was so steep I had to grab hold of the young trees to climb it and worry about copperheads all the time. When I got to the top I couldn't see much so I headed back, hot and sweaty. This reminded me of earlier times.

When I was a lot younger, probably only about six, I was given a scooter for Christmas. Now these two-wheeled scooters are fine toys if you live in a city where there are sidewalks and driveways and such to play on with them. Out here in the country they are as useless as teats on a gander. This is so cool: I can just talk here in my book. If I said "teats" anywhere near here to anyone, I'd probably get my mouth washed out with a bar of Ivory soap again. That has happened to me once or twice, usually when I get mad at someone, and I swear it will never happen again. Lesson learned – no cussing allowed, except for Dad.

Anyhow, I tried pushing it around the house a few times but Mom chased me outside. I fought it around the yard a time or two, but it don't go well through dirt or grass. I took it down the hill to the road, but that red brick road is so bumpy that even if Mom and Dad would let me ride it there, which they don't, I wouldn't want to. So my scooter usually just leans up against the house wall.

On a Saturday morning, Mom was washing and hanging out the clothes on the line, and I had been ambushed before I could escape, so I had to help by handing her clothes pins and such. The wash machine was chugging away in the back room, and she was rolling up the clothes in tight wads and piling them in the bushel basket to be dealt with later. I was sure-enough looking for a chance to escape this drudgery when, out of the clear blue, Mom asked me to run to the store to get a gallon of bleach.

The store is a small country store about a half-mile up the road and around a bend. If it didn't have one broken Esso gas pump bubble-head out front and a rusty Nehi sign nailed to the front wall, a person could take it for an old house such as you see enough of around here. The store has a little of everything in it but not a lot of anything. It is operated by a young cross-eyed woman who mostly stands behind the counter making change and small talk.

I really like the smell of licorice, oranges, old wood, and a hundred years that ooze from every crack in it. They even got a special cooler for soda pop where you look in from the top, choose your soda from the rows, slide your choice into a compartment, slip your nickel into the slot, grab the bottle by the neck and yank it up and out. But, except for Bireley's grape soda, I really don't like it all that much. Too fizzy. They make bubbles up my nose and make me burp. And Coca Cola is the worst. I hate that stuff.

Sometimes if I have a nickel I'll buy a pack of Black Jack gum or a Three Musketeer candy bar. I do like Necco candy wafers, especially the chocolate ones, but they cost a nickel too. I usually don't have any money so I like to just stand by the candy counter and look at all the sweet penny candies – the wands of black licorice or root beer logs and candy corn.

Mom gave me enough money. She knows how much everything costs, and then gave me two cents extra just for me and sent me on my way. But then she had to go and ruin it by a final instruction: "Now you make sure you don't go and take your scooter out on that road. It's too dangerous."

Well, I hadn't even thought of it 'til she up and said that. Then it became a matter of pride: I had to take it, even if it made a whole lot more work than it was worth. So when she went back into the wash room, I dashed around the house and grabbed the scooter, dragged it carefully down the hill and started up the bumpy red road. It was hard work but felt worth it; that is, until I got to the store to make my purchase.

The girl behind the counter chatted with me a moment while I picked out two wands of black licorice. It is unsettling to talk to someone when you don't know which eye to look at and when she seems to be looking at things all over the room but not at you. So I told her thanks and took the bottle of bleach and headed out the door. Right away I knew I was in big trouble – for a couple reasons: One, the copper tinted gallon glass jug was awful heavy for me to carry home, least of all holding onto that little handle which I could only grab onto with one finger. To be safe I had to cradle it in my other arm. But the second reason was the kicker: That stupid scooter. I'd need one hand for sure to hold onto it. But I was game and started home, pushing off on the scooter and hanging onto that bleach jug.

About a hundred yards down the road my finger tired, and when the scooter hit one brick too many I lost that jug. It hit those bricks – a bleach bomb shattered and splattered everywhere including me. There I stood in the middle of the road with the forbidden scooter and no bleach. What could I do? I did what any kid in similar situations would do. I dragged the scooter home and stashed it at the bottom of the hill behind the garage shed and then worked myself up into a good cry as I climbed the forty-eight steps up the hill to the house. Mom came running out at the noise. "For heaven's sake. What happened? What's the matter?"

"That stupid bleach jug was too heavy. I dropped it and it splashed all over me," I sobbed.

"Oh, I'm sorry, Junior. I should have figured on that. Quick, you just run in and change those clothes and I'll see if I can save them."

No scolding, and I didn't lie. I just didn't tell her about the scooter. I figure it was at least half her fault because, I know to this day, that if she had not told me specifically not to take it, I wouldn't have.

I remember another time that will really prove my point. Friday afternoon Mom was doing some baking for the weekend, and the kitchen smelled so good that I just hung around hoping something would come my way. After kneading and baking bread, she asked if I would like to help her make some peanut-butter cookies. Well, any kid will tell you that fresh peanut-butter cookies and a glass of cold milk is better than manna from heaven, so I jumped at the opportunity. I dragged a chair over to the counter where Mom was mixing all the ingredients up – lard, fresh butter, peanut butter, brown sugar, eggs and the rest – into the best tasting cookie dough you could imagine. I got to test it to see if it was good. Mom let me try to stir it up, but I could hardly push the dough around in the big bowl so I gave it back to her. "I can't do it. Here you do it." I sure did admire the way she would mix it all together with that big wooden spatula 'til everything was all smooth and creamy. "Mom, you sure do have strong arms."

She seemed a little embarrassed. "Someday, yours will be even bigger and stronger." I just shook my head in doubt. She saw me and added, "And I guarantee that, Junior."

Now some kids prefer ginger snap cookies, and I must admit that their clovey aroma is one of the finest smells in the world, but peanut butter dough is my favorite before they're cooked. After she got the dough all set and chilled, she called me back in to shape them. That means she would spoon out a lump of dough into my hands and I would roll it into a ball and then carefully place it on the cookie sheet. Usually by the time I got two done, she had filled up the sheet. Then she would take a fork and give me one too after they had been dipped in flour, and we would flatten the balls with the forks in a crisscross pattern. Then these beauties would be slipped into the oven for about ten minutes. I figured that since I did so much work on them, some were rightly mine, so when the first batch was taken out I could hardly wait for them to cool. Man, warm peanut butter cookies you made yourself and cold milk on a sunny day in May. That's mighty fine.

Anyhow, you needed to know what had happened on Friday to understand why I did what I did on Saturday. I think I already told you that Saturday was cleaning day, and so that's when I tried to make myself scarce, as I was not a great fan of beating rugs on the line, mopping floors, or helping with the wash. Mom was collecting a bushel basket of washed clothes to hang on the line out back, and I was about to casually disappear out the front door when she noticed me and stopped for a moment to utter one of those terrible parent commands that virtually demand a kid to disobey: "Junior, you run out and play 'til I call for you to help. And you stay out of those cookies. You can have some later."

Well, that done it for me. I sure hadn't been planning on sticking around, cookies or no, but now it was a matter of pride and I couldn't get those cookies out of my mind. I sat out on the top step, scratching the dirt to the side with a stick, and started thinking about how hard I had worked on those just yesterday, and how I had a right to them if I wanted, and how unfair it was for Mom to forbid them. The problem was that with Mom going out and coming in with wash all the time, there was no way I could be sure I would have time to grab some goodies and get out without getting caught with my hand in the cookie jar.

Slowly I developed a plan. It was daring and would require speed and nerves of steel, but it could be done. The cookie jar sat on the kitchen counter next to the sink, under the hanging cupboards that ran right to the back door. Mom would go right past it every time she went out or came in. Only the screen door blocked her view. Timing was everything, and I had to close the door, if only for a minute to shield me from view. After examining my plan and detecting no flaws, I put it into action.

First, I snuck back up onto the front porch and waited by the door 'til I heard the back screen door slam and saw Mom headed up to the clothes line toting her bushel basket. Then I dashed in through the front door through the front room and dining room and into the kitchen.

Time was flying and so was I. Quietly, I closed the back door and hoped she wouldn't see; and that's where my plan started falling apart. Our back door doesn't stay closed; it has no latch. We lock it by jamming an old kitchen knife into the door jamb after it is closed.

I lost time dragging the chair over to the door and working that knife as deeply as I could into the jamb, knowing I would have to remove it after I got my cookies and open the door or Mom would be all over it – more time spent. Then quickly I pushed the chair along the counter a couple feet to stop at the treasure chest of cookies. Now that I was so close, my mind was in a fever; up on the chair, off with the lid, in with my hand. I could almost taste the reward of my efforts.

Right then, standing on the chair with one knee on the counter, my fist full of heavenly peanut butter cookies, my plan collapsed upon me. There was a banging on the back door, barely five feet from where I was standing. Mom had finished hanging her load, it must have been a small one, and had returned.

Now she was baffled at the closed back door. "Junior, are you in there? Why is this door closed? Open it up this very minute!" Well, that was the one thing I did not dare to do. And if I ran out the front door she might meet me coming around the house, and even if she didn't catch me, the evidence of my pilfering was everywhere. I froze, and Mom was getting mad, shaking the door, trying to wiggle it open.

"Junior, I said, open this door right now! What are you up to?" With that she smashed into the door with her shoulder, and no old knife could have withstood that pressure. It snapped, and as the door flew inward, the broken knife blade flashed toward me. All I could do was raise my right arm. The left was full of cookies, to ward it and her off.

I felt the impact as the blade stabbed into my arm directly above my wrist. I saw it and Mom and did not know which I was more afraid of. For a second it didn't hurt, but then came a flood of blood and a wave of pain. I shook my arm and the broken bloody blade rattled to the floor. Petrified with fear, one hand still clutching the pilfered cookies, the other dripping blood off my fingers from the wrist wound, I stood and howled.

Mom dropped her empty bushel basket, surveyed the scene a second and grabbed me. "My God, what happened? What did you do? Oh, Jesus, Mary and Joseph, what a mess!" And then she went to work, staunching the flow of blood, salving it up, and tightly winding up a bandage around my arm. We had no car, and Dad was at work, so after doctoring me up, she carried me, still sobbing, to my room and told me to wait there and not use the arm until Dad got home. Then we would see if we needed to go to the hospital.

Luckily, the slashed arm was the right one, which was pretty useless to me to begin with, me being a lefty and all, so except for the pain and restriction to my room, it turned out not so bad. I even got some cookies out of it. Mom came in to change the bandage because it had bled through, and when she took it off, the wrist started to hurt again though the bleeding was slowed. She wrapped it up fresh, wiped my tears and brought me some "honestly gotten" cookies and milk and explained to me how God will always punish the wrongdoers.

When Dad got home and Mom explained to him what had happened, he took a look at my arm and said he figured as how it would heal up ok and didn't need the hospital. He also owned as how I didn't need any more punishment for stealing cookies and asked if I had learned my lesson. I nodded my head for all I was worth.

Some people talk about God as though He is far off in space somewhere, or up in the clouds. But I know about how God operates on a personal level, how He watches and knows everything we do. Still, even though we said grace at meals and prayers at bedtime, I never really met Him up close and personal until He really got my attention one sunny noontime when I was riding my tricycle around the yard. Mom stepped out the back door and called, "Junior, come in for lunch."

"No. I don't want to. I'm playing," I answered.

"Now, Junior. Don't be a bad boy. You get your little self in here right now!" she said with her hands on her hips.

My response was just to turn my head and stick my tongue out at her and peddle away furiously. "Why you little brat. God will get you for that!" And she wagged her finger at me.

Just as I circled around the corner of the front of the house, pedaling for all I was worth and wondering what I should do next, she came barging out the front door on the porch and so frightened me, I suddenly jerked the trike to the left, which launched me directly over the side of the hill and down that long flight of cement steps toward the shed and parking area far below.

The trike hit the top step and catapulted me off to the side, while it continued ricocheting on down. I had enough sense left to dig into the sod and cling there while I watched my trike cartwheel and tumble on down. The only thing I could think of was to say, "God, you didn't have to be SO quick." With my trike wrecked and me near scared to death, I guess Mom figured I had been punished enough. Since then I have tried to stay at least on speaking terms with God because I figure He means business. The cookies and trike incidents just prove the point.

Chapter 11

There are two things I am positive of: One – God is very serious about people doing the right things. So when He really cares to, He tends to bring down the hammer quick and hard, which I actually prefer to the long, drawn out punishments. And secondly, everyone I know is pretty serious about Him, but because He is invisible and sometimes doesn't seem to be paying attention, they mess up anyway, even the grown-ups, trying to cut corners.

Mom taught us kids all about God and Jesus and the Virgin Mary when we were little ones; and how God knows everything we even think before we think it. He even knows when a sparrow falls, so He surely has His eye on each of us even if we ignore Him. Sometimes, when kids are mean and get away with it, or Dad is mean, I think maybe God doesn't really care that much. Then I see that crumpled, rusty trike down in the garbage pile and I figure it's like speeding. Dad drives really fast all the time but has only got stopped a couple times. God must be like that. Most the time you can race along on your merry way. But you never know when He is going to turn on the lights and sirens and pull you over.

Holy Jesus school works hard to teach us about religion, ever since first grade. That's Sister Theophila's class along with second grade. Some kids call her Sister The Elephant behind her back, but not many because she is not really very big and is quiet voiced. One of her jobs was to get us ready for First Confession and First Communion.

You can't go to communion without you first go confess your sins to a priest so you don't die and go to hell. And you can't go to confession unless you know all about sins and the proper way to tell them to the priest so he can forgive you and give you your penance.

Actually, he doesn't forgive you. God does. But only the priest knows what God thinks. I don't know how he finds out. The pope is the head of all the priests and nuns, and he is the closest to God. He talks to Him direct and then tells the priests and nuns, I guess. But the pope doesn't live around here but over in Italy. Anyhow, you probably know all these things so I'll get to the main point.

Sin is a very tricky thing. There are two kinds – venial and mortal. Both are bad but venial sins just put you in purgatory. They are like telling white lies or stealing a cookie, or smoking a cigarette if you are a kid. If you can stand the fire for a few years, you will make it to heaven.

But if you commit a mortal sin, even one, and die before confessing it, you will burn in hell forever. Mortal sins are like murders and eating meat on Friday, or snitching food after midnight before communion and such. They are the things you most want to keep away from anyone else knowing. A mortal sin is also lying in the confessional. So you got to get confession just right and count up each sin you do.

One good thing for kids is they can't commit a sin until they are six years old. That's the age of reason. I knew all us kids needed to confess, but I was surprised to learn from Sister Theophila that all adults need to confess too. Every single one, even the pope. But I didn't really see how nuns or priests could sin and need confession, until one day in religion class we were learning about how to take communion.

I raised my hand and asked, "Sister, is it a mortal sin to chew up Jesus with your teeth if He sticks to the roof of your mouth? And how about if you use your finger to pry Him loose?" I asked those questions because Sissy would sometimes talk about how hard it would be sometimes to swallow the wafer. We had been told to pry it off with our tongues, but I was worried. What if that didn't work? I didn't want to accidentally go to hell.

But the nun didn't answer right away. She paused and stared at the ceiling like it was written there. I'd seen my mom do the same thing. Right then I realized she didn't know the answer and that whatever she was going to tell me was just a guess. "Yes, I'm sure it is indeed a mortal sin. The wafer may not feel like Jesus, but it is Him nonetheless. It would be a terrible sin to chew Him."

Right then I also realized that nun was willing to send me and all the other kids suffering from dry mouth to eternal hellfire on a guess or a lie. Since that moment, I've always tried to be very cautious about believing what other people tell me is a sin – unless it is the pope talking 'cause he can't make a mistake.

Now I got to tell you about something that will probably totally disgust you about me; but I got to tell the truth or this book don't mean nothing. I thought I invented a new mortal sin. Some time when I was a little kid, before I started school even, one night I found out that by rubbing my peter a bit, I would get an explosion that felt better than anything else that ever happened. Sissy must have noticed and called Mom (we were still sharing a room at the time) and Mom got mad as a hornet and yelled at me and told me to never do that again.

Later on, sometimes after prayers and tucking in she would barge in and rip off the covers to see if I was touching myself there and scold me and warn me not to or I'd go straight to hell and burn forever. I'd lay there stiff as an ironing board with my hands straight down at my sides. Then she would turn and huff out. Well, it's just the way it is that even if I hadn't been touching myself, after she left I would – just because she'd reminded me about it.

I didn't know this sin had a name at the time, but it does, "the sin of self-abuse," so I guess at least a couple other people must have done it. But because I didn't know its name, and I didn't know how to confess it, every confession where I didn't tell on myself heaped the coals of hell on my head, and when I started Holy Communion, because I took it without confessing my sin, I added to my eternal punishment. So by sixth grade, after piling it on for years, I figured I had a reservation in the deepest pit of hell. And I couldn't confess it to Father Doughty. He would recognize me and hate me forever.

And then God sent me a chance to get eternally clean. Last month a missionary from Central America came to Holy Jesus to talk to us about priestly vocations and the needs of the savages. He was dressed differently from any priests around here. His robe was black and white and brown, not just black. And he had a cool cowl that he could have covered his head with if it rained. He talked to us and during a Sunday sermon announced he would hear confessions next Saturday before he left for Costa Rica. This, I realized, would be my chance to come clean. Incredibly, when I told Mom I needed to go to confession, she said for me to walk on in to church on Saturday – no questions asked.

I could hardly sleep Friday night, I was so excited at the prospect of getting right with God on Saturday for the first time since I could remember. The morning came and I hiked on in to Holy Jesus, knelt in a back pew and prepared myself for confession by searching my conscience for any venial sins I could think of to wrap my big sin in.

When I felt all braced, I went up and knelt along with the crowd waiting for their turns at the confessional. It seemed a lot of people wanted to have this outsider hear their sins. Maybe they had secret sins too.

When it was my turn I gathered myself up, plucked up my courage and entered the dark booth. In a moment the window panel slid open and I began, "Bless me Father for I have sinned. My last confession was two weeks ago." The introduction done, I launched into the list of my evil-doing. "I have lied twice (a fair guess), been mean to my sisters four times (probably an undercount), and committed the sin of self-abuse about a thousand times" (a wild estimate of the total number. Who really counted?)

There, at last, it was out. Maybe it was a thousand, maybe five hundred. I never counted, but I figured God knew and He would just be glad I finally confessed.

But that missionary didn't seem as glad. He was really upset, and he scared me to death when he announced, in a voice loud enough, I was sure, to be heard by the dwindling crowd outside, "Two weeks - a thousand times? Son, you need to stop that at once. I'm telling you it will scramble your brain and make you crazy. Now for your penance say three rosaries and make a good act of contrition." If the priest thought I did all that in only two weeks, did that mean I was forgiven only for two weeks worth? Man, I really botched that confession.

I bolted from the booth and didn't stick around to say the rosaries. I figured I would say them on the way home and couldn't stand to make eye contact with anyone in the church, figuring they heard what was said and also were disgusted with me. Still, I felt excited by my courage and clean for the first time since I could remember.

Once out of the church, I closed my eyes as I crossed the street and prayed that a car would hit me and kill me as I figured that was certainly the only time that if I died I would go to heaven. "Self-abuse" just felt too good to not risk hell over. Besides, I could always confess it again if I didn't die first.

I took about six steps into the street and then opened my eyes. It was empty for blocks, completely empty. No car would run me down, so I figured God must want me to live a little while longer. But on the way home while saying the rosaries I wondered what made the priest think doing such a thing would make me crazy and would scramble my brain. It sounded like the dumb warning parents give you sometimes when they want you not to do something and can't think of a good reason.

If I was crazy, how did he know I was telling him the truth? I know I am one of the smartest kids in the class and fastest runner in the school, so how is my brain scrambled after all these years? I came to the reluctant conclusion that he knew no more about it than the good sister knew about chewing the communion wafer. And I arrived home spiritually clean but no longer so sure that anybody else could tell me what was the real truth about sin.

Chapter 12

Man, this is it – the last day before vacation. I woke up at the crack of dawn because I don't want to miss a minute of it. The Bob White is calling up on the ridge in the deep grass below the tree line, and it seems like it's calling straight to me. The sun still isn't over the top, but it is lighting up the other side of the valley.

We got our grades yesterday so that is over and done with. Father Doughty came to each room and called us out individually to give us our report cards. The only B I got was in arithmetic, but Sissy beat me; she got all A's. Anyhow we don't have to worry about any more grades until September. All I can say is HOO-RAY!

I pushed my window sash up all the way to let the morning in. I feel like bursting and don't want to write about anything that makes me feel black. At Holy Jesus the last day is the best day because as soon as they take attendance, all the 5th to 8th graders will pile into the cars out front that folks have carpooled, and they haul us down to the docks to board a genuine Ohio River paddle wheeler, and we'll take a cruise down and up the river. Grades one to four will go on a school picnic to a park on the edge of town. That's nice too, but nothing beats being on the O-HI-O.

The first thing we do after we board is to run wild for a while, exploring every corner of the boat we are allowed to see. Then we break into our natural groups and talk and figure games to play. The seventh and eighth graders flirt a lot with each other. Some even sneak off to a corner of the boat and talk quietly and hold hands – until one of the good sisters sees them and breaks it up.

The Ohio pulls me like a magnet. I can stand for hours and watch the paddle wheel dig into the chocolate colored water and listen to the throb of the motors. The water falls away from the paddles like a hissing waterfall back to the river and bubbles off behind the boat. Once in awhile a big log or a whole tree drifts by. I expect the captain has to keep a sharp lookout for such floating trash 'cause we have never hit a single one. Creeks and sloughs spill into the river, and I like to imagine the most interesting-looking one may be Harvey's Creek.

Once we get rolling the breeze picks up, and it can get a mite cool so I learned to bring a windbreaker or sweater, even if it looks like the day is going to heat up. If it does get too cool for you, there is always the lounge, where you can warm up with some hot cocoa for a nickel. We are supposed to save our lunches for later, but most of us dig into them in pretty short order. We don't want to lug them about all morning. A jelly and peanut butter sandwich and an apple never tasted so good as by the railing of a riverboat. And when you throw the core away over the side, you watch it arc back to the stern before it plops into the water.

This is the second year I have taken this boat ride, and my dream is to one day save up enough money to buy a real ticket and go all the way down to St. Louis or maybe even New Orleans. I've traced the route on the map and done it in my mind a million times. I wouldn't come back until I was rich. Then I'd buy the whole mountain and my family would all live there forever. No one could kick us off.

Once in a while we pass under a bridge and I look up to watch for overhead cars or trains. I wonder if the folks driving up there envy us our boat ride. They can't know it is only for the day and we will be back to school by 2 p.m. to be dismissed for the summer. I bet they think we are going to St. Louis.

Mooky walks over and we chat a bit about summer and our plans and look for fish – a real waste of time in that water. This is his first riverboat ride and is really excited about it. It is hard to tell him how bad it is at home, so I pretend it is just like normal. There is no way I can even think about leaving the mountain. I've almost made up my mind that if they go, I'll run away and live up in the woods like an Indian.

But I'm still hoping that it won't come to that. Mom and Dad always fight but then make up. I've been praying steady every night as hard as I can and if God hears prayers, he must have a mountain high batch of them just from me. I figure that sooner or later He'll have to answer, just to get me off his back. Even so, with Him a person just never knows. He just might not care all that much.

That thought and the river air combine to chill me just a bit, so I put on my jacket but don't zip it up. Mook and me are both just leaning on the rail, not saying nothing. I don't want him to walk away 'cause he's bored, so I ask what he likes most about summer.

"Everything, Junior. Every blessed thing. But especially baseball and TV. My dad bought me a glove and he's been showing me how to throw and hit a baseball. I may sign up for a summer league to learn how to play better. They got them for kids like us. You wanna join?"

"Nah, I don't have a ball or glove and don't know how to play. I don't like that game much." The only time I had ever handled a baseball was at last summer's recreation program. I gave it up after wearing myself out throwing the stupid ball up into the air and swinging away at it trying to hit it to some other kids and my bat never touching the ball's leather hide. It was downright embarrassing. The grown-up in charge then tried to toss it to me underhanded, and I couldn't hit that either. So he called another kid in to hit and sent me to the outfield where I stood in a pack of kids, most of whom had gloves, and tried to avoid the ball when it was hit my way. "I guess we'll go to Wisconsin to visit relatives, and I'll probably go swimming a lot. And there's always the woods to explore."

"I guess that all sounds like fun too." But I could see he was thinking about baseball, and that left me out. So I switched the subject.

"Do you remember McElroy's grapes?"

"Man, that was the most fun!"

Mr. McElroy is a grouchy old man who lives at the foot of our hill, just to the north along the road, across from Harvey's Creek. Mooky lives on the ridge to our south, just past his grandpa's house. The McElroys live in a big solid two story brick house. They have six kids, the youngest of which is a son one year older than me. His name is Danny, and he is one of Sissy's best friends. He will come up to play with her; she will have him dress up in her dresses and wear lipstick and big hats, and he don't seem to mind as long as he's around her. But if Dad should come home while Danny is here, the kid will quietly sneak off home all scared. He's friendly with me and Mooky, but we don't really run together too much. When Sissy told Granny about their playing dress-up once, she called him a candy-ankle, whatever that is.

Anyhow, their two oldest boys have finished high school. Sam's the oldest – he's okay; he'll recognize me and call to me when he sees me, but Johnny's a little weird. He's about a year younger than Sam and walks around with his head cocked over to one side a bit, like he can't keep it up right, and he wears long flannel shirts even in the summer – with the sleeves rolled down. I asked Dad about him once 'cause he don't seem quite right sometimes, and Dad said, "Long sleeves hide needle tracks," and wouldn't say no more when I asked him what he meant.

Their family seems to be doing all right now, the house is in good shape and all. Mr. McElroy works for the county. But it didn't used to be that way. I remember when there was always hollering and fighting down there and my folks told us kids to stay away from them. One time when I complained about having to eat peas for supper, Dad told me to be thankful I get to sit at the table and eat regular-like. He knew old man McElroy would come home drunk, beat up his wife, then he would sit on a chair and cut off chunks of baloney and throw it on the floor and laugh watching the kids fight for scraps.

I didn't know if he really did that, but his reputation was mighty bad in our house, so I didn't put it past him. I quit complaining about the peas, but used Dad's story time to brush them into my hand under the table, where I would hide them on the board running beneath the table top. Later on I would remove them, if I could remember.

Nowadays I can't imagine Mr. McElroy behaving that way. So I asked Mom how come he stopped beating his wife and such. She laid down her fork, looked at me and said, "Well, once he came home like that and laid into her, and the two oldest boys jumped him and beat him up. They told him if he ever hit their mom again they'd kill him. So you see, Mr. McElroy got religion, so to speak."

I sat there stunned, as if I had been hit. There was my own mom as much as telling me that when I got big it would be my job to beat up Dad, and me without even a brother to help out. I don't think either one of them noticed what it meant to me because Dad added, "That's the way it is up here. I had to straighten out pop once too." And we went on eating and talking of other things. But the idea still grips me. I figure I would either have to ambush him with a baseball bat, but I don't think I could hit him hard enough, or find a gun and shoot him. Otherwise, he'd kill me.

But back to old man McElroy: Me and Mooky loved to torment him. We figure, with his past, he's got it coming. As long as I can remember, he has planted grape vines on the hillside sloping down from our place to his. Mom always told me to stay out of his grapes. He had seen us boys there a while back. So now me and Mooky crawl on our bellies like snakes down the hillside through the deep grass beneath his fenced and wired up vines. When they are ripe, fat and purple, there is nothing like them Concord grapes.

We lay there, half-way between my house and McElroy's, in the shady shadows, devouring those wonderful juicy grapes, spitting seeds, feeling like outlaws, making our plans for future raids when the rest would ripen. And we always leave plenty behind so he doesn't catch on to us.

One night we took our war against McElroy a step further. I had the bright idea of putting big rocks in his driveway, just to irritate and confuse him when he left for work in the mornings. So when we were sure he was in for the evening, and no one was paying attention, we rolled and lugged stones up from the creek and into his driveway. It was mighty hard work for two small boys, but thinking about him hitting those stones or standing and scratching his head made us laugh.

We worked 'til we had to go home to clean up for bed, and we could hardly wait for tomorrow to see the effect of our prank. Unfortunately for us, by the time Mooky came running over to get me and we raced over to the hillside to see, Mr. McElroy had already carried the stones away and gone to work; and we dared not tell anyone what we had done, so there we stood. We looked at one another and had the same thought at the same time – all that hard work for nothing.

"Yeah, and it was the dumbest prank we ever pulled. From now on if we play a joke on someone we make sure we stick around to see their reaction."

"For sure, and let's not do pranks we got to work so hard at either."

Mooky and I both laughed at the memory we could never tell another person, except in the confessional, and gazed at the bluffs on the far side of the Ohio as they drifted upstream past us.

Chapter 13

June, 1958

"Mooky!"

"Junior!"

"Moo – key!" with the upward twist on the second syllable of his name. "Come and get it!"

"June – yore," just two powerful sounds. "Supper!"

"I hate to admit it, but you're right, Junior. Your ma sure can holler. She beat mine flat."

We had been arguing about whose mom had the loudest voice for near as long as I could remember, and so we finally decided that since it was officially summer vacation now, we would devise a final test to determine the undisputed champion. At suppertime, which was the same over most the ridge for everybody, we would take up positions down on the bank of the creek across the road and midway between our two houses. Our backs were against the east bank so we couldn't look up and see our moms. It would be a decision based solely on what we heard. And there was no doubt about it – my mom had better lungs and more staying power. I sure felt smug.

"It's because of her 'Lucky Strikes.' Your ma smokes 'Camels.' They fog you up more," I said.

"Na'ah," Mooky said with a poke at my shoulder. "I'm telling you, old son, she's just had more practice yelling at your dad."

I responded with the only thing I could think of – the all-purpose, "Oh yeah; well your mom wears combat boots," to his retreating back as he ran to his home. I liked being called in for supper. It makes a body feel appreciated somehow. So I stubbed out the Lucky Strike I had pilfered from her purse, flicked it into the creek, and headed up the hill.

And a grand supper it was. While Sunday suppers are often things like fried chicken and mashed potatoes, and don't get me wrong, they're mighty fine in their own right, it's Saturday suppers that I looked forward to the most. They come after a day of running and playing, games and pranks, scrapes and trying to avoid Mom's early morning housecleaning, rug beating and such.

So Saturday suppers tend to be just a bit less dressed-up. My most favorite of all is pinto beans that have soaked all night, and then cooked up maybe with a big ham bone in for flavor and peppered up so that you can hardly come into the house without your mouth starting to water. I have actually, on occasion, had a hard time speaking because it smelled so good my mouth flooded.

Maybe Mom would dig some uneaten mashed potatoes out of the fridge from earlier in the week and fry them up into mashed potato patties, and dished out some fresh-picked and cooked collard greens from Mooky's grampa's garden. That's one thing we have never had, a house garden. Mom says that with all she has to do, she just doesn't have time. And the finishing touch, made only after we kids had been called in to eat, was cornbread hot out of the cast iron skillet, cut into wedges and served out on the plates first before you lather it all up with those delicious pinto beans.

I mean to tell you, Sunday supper may take more time, and we may have to use napkins and be more polite, and that fried chicken is mighty fine too, but there ain't nothing in the world can top Saturday.

One of the funniest things I can remember happened of a Saturday evening just recently. Me and Mooky were out back playing knights—me Galahad and him Lancelot—each of us had a garbage can lid for a shield and a broke off broomstick for a sword, and we were flailing away having a grand old time, clanging our shields, leaping about, jousting and such.

Mom was in the kitchen cooking pinto beans for supper. Since she hadn't soaked them the night before, she was pressure-cooking them on the stove to soften them up. Dad was home for a change. We hadn't seen him for a couple days. He was sober and in the kitchen talking to Mom while she cooked. The back door was open and we could hear most of what they were saying. He had lost his job- he said it was because of the recession; Mom said it was because he was fired, but he had found a new one selling shoes.

Mom didn't care because he had drunk up so much money and chased around so much that he hadn't made the house payments, and we were going to have to move for sure. Plus, Mom was getting bigger again, and that meant she would be bringing home another baby this fall. Whenever she got big, she would go to the hospital and bring home another baby girl. It was useless to ask otherwise. Where was the money to come from? She wanted to know. She had to get a job, find a house, and he had to leave – a "separation," she called it.

He talked about how he wanted to stay and that somehow he'd make it better, and I was hoping she would listen because as mean as he can be, that's usually only when he's drunk. I feel all knotted up and panicky if I think of him gone or us moved out. Anyway, they were working it all, jawing back and forth when "WHAM!" it seemed like the whole kitchen exploded. Mooky and me dropped our "swords" where we stood and stared at the kitchen. Suddenly the screen door slammed open and here came Dad and Mom, piling out the door like they were shot out of a cannon. I honestly did not know my dad could run that fast, and Mom was almost pushing him out the door.

About a half-dozen steps into the yard they stopped and we came running over.

Dad was breathing hard. "My God, Maggie, what happened? You okay?"

"A lot you care. I see you beat me out the door."

"I was just closer to it. The pressure-cooker exploded, but I think it's safe now to go back in. Let's see." And we all edged nervously up to peek through the screen door. "Jesus H. Christ! Will you look at that!" and he laughed. He stood there with his hands on his hips and started laughing and laughed 'til his shoulders shook.

We all sidled by him and what I saw I have never seen before and don't reckon I ever will again. The whole kitchen – ceiling, walls, floor, windows, cabinets, the whole thing was covered with dripping, plopping, steaming pinto beans. The pressure cooker jiggly-thing that let's off steam must have got stopped-up, and then our evening supper had turned into a pinto bean bomb.

"Maggie, I may have said it once or twice, but I never really meant it until today that your cooking would kill somebody," and he cracked up all over again. I giggled and even Mom softened a bit, and after Mooky ran off to his house to tell his folks and to have a more normal meal, Dad, Mom, Sissy and me had a laughing good time cleaning up that kitchen mess. We only had fried baloney sandwiches for supper that night – but it almost felt like old times again.

Chapter 14

Old times sure seem far off. Bathing now is so easy with running hot water and a regular tub and all. I remember when I was so little that Mom would have to bathe me by standing me up in the big tin tub after she had poured in a teakettle of boiling water heated on the range into the cold water she ran into the tub 'cause we only had cold running water. It wasn't very deep, sometimes the water wasn't very warm, and she could scrub pretty rough. But I only had to go through this production once a week, on Saturday night. Other nights we cleaned up at the sink, face and hands and anything else Mom thought needed attention.

I remember about the last time I had to endure this misery of her scrubbing: and it was aggravated by Mom's ignorance of how a boy's body worked. I must have been about three or four years old, before Dad built on the addition to the house, and I was standing there in the lukewarm water, shivering while Mom scrubbed me down. My peter was as stiff as a twig, and once in a while she would push hard on it to try to force it down.

Any boy knows that only makes it hurt like it is going to break off, and it don't make it go down. The first time I just said "Ow," and tried to squirm away, nearly tumbling out of the tub backwards. But a minute later she tried to lever it down again, saying, "Put that thing down," like I had some say-so in the matter.

Her pushing down on it hurt so bad I almost got a little mad and snapped, "No, it's supposed to be like that. Leave it alone. You're hurting me."

Well, she looked a little ashamed, like she hadn't thought of that and said, "Oh, I'm sorry." And she never touched me there again. I figured that even though she married Dad, and he had a peter, maybe his didn't get so stiff. Maybe mine was inferior somehow.

Next Saturday, after the water was ready in the tub, Mom plopped me in and told me to clean myself and she would check me over and dry me off when I hollered for her. That was nice because I could play in the water for a while and not get scrubbed so hard. But it must have worked just as well at getting clean because when I was ready to get out, she wrapped me in a towel and scooped me off to my room to get my pjs on. And the only area of my body that drew her special attention was behind my ears.

Baths in the tin tub may have been uncomfortable, but they were a piece of cake compared to when we had to go out to the outhouse at night. In the first place, it wasn't really near the house, so if you didn't stop to put on shoes, you could step in or on almost anything. And when the weather was bad, rainy or cold, you'd hold it in and lay awake until you felt you would bust a gut. And then you'd still have to make that awful run sooner or later.

Even though Dad would move the outhouse every so often, it always seemed to stink when you got inside, and I did not like to dangle my backsides over that drafty hole where bees or flies or spiders or something even worse would have me at its mercy. It certainly was not my most favorite place to go. But at least it was quiet and the Sears-Roebuck catalogue gave me something to look at while I would wait for nature to take her course.

When I started school at Holy Jesus, on the first day of first grade Sister "The Elephant" showed us all around, and of course she showed us where the bathroom was. The boys' room was a big tiled room with three stalls which were kind of like the seater holes in our outhouse only cleaner and with soft tissue paper rolls instead of catalogues. But when the nun showed me the toilet and flushed it, I knew I was in huge trouble. In the first place the seat did not stay down: When I held it down it was ok, but as soon as I released it, it sprang up and banged off the wall. How on earth could I ever climb up on that thing?

And secondly, when the nun flushed it to show us how it worked, the water gushed and roared and raced down in a terrifying whirlpool. If I were to somehow mount that thing and it would go off on its own or something, it would suck me down for sure. So right off the bat I knew that going to that bathroom, at least for "number two," was out of the question.

So every day before school I started a new routine. I would be sure to empty myself out as completely as possible at home, hold it all day if I had to, and then run to the outhouse as soon as I got home. There were a couple painful afternoons, but my will never wavered, and my body did not betray me – at least not for a couple weeks. But then it happened.

One afternoon after lunch I really had to go. The pressure built and built but I held on, staring at the second hand on the clock at the front of the room, trying to force it to move faster, knowing I would never make it to the end of the day before my bowels burst. But then, magically, the bell ending the school day rang, and the kids raced out the door, squealing and laughing. Many were being picked up by parents, or walking off with their big brothers and sisters. I could scarcely waddle to the school door and saw Sissy standing outside smiling and waiting.

"Hurry up, Junior. School's out. Let's go. Mr. Yost said he'll give us a ride."

Right then I lost it all. I had fought so hard, and now when victory was so close, I filled my BVDs with a solid load. My heart and self-respect were shot, but my pride helped me cover enough to say, "No, I want to walk. I know the way home."

With a shrug of her shoulders, Sissy turned and skipped away to the car at the curb. Mr. Yost waved me to the car, but that was the last place I wanted to be, so I just waved back. Sissy said something to him, and the car full of kids pulled away from the curb. Slowly and unsteadily, crying softly to myself, I walked down the street. I didn't know what was going to happen when I got home – there was no way to hide my disgrace. What would

I say? Would I be scolded, laughed at? I didn't know. I was too ashamed of myself to care.

There was only one person in the whole world that for sure would not make fun of me or scold me – Grandma Carter. And she lived just a couple blocks off the route home. Instead of turning south at the Kroger grocery store, if I was to go straight ahead two blocks and turn right I could come in to her house from the alley and probably not meet anyone else. So that's what I did.

But when I came up the dirt alley behind her house, all my courage almost fled me. I stopped and shivered there with one hand on the back gate. Surely she would be disgusted with me too. Still, she was the one person I knew who had never hurt me in my whole life. Before I could turn away, my hand lifted the latch and pushed open the squeaky gate almost by itself. And I went in.

A couple steps and I could see her through the screen door, bustling around her kitchen, humming a song, probably a church hymn. Dad said she was the best pew-jumper he'd ever seen, that when she really got going in church, she could up and leap a pew without even catching a heel. That didn't sound like grandma, but then there's a lot I don't know about grown-ups. I listened just inside the gate to her singing, and I couldn't go no farther. I just stood there, heavy seated, smelling my stink, and crying. There could not possibly have been a more miserable first-grader in the world. I couldn't go in and I couldn't turn away. Then there she was at the door removing her apron and stepping out to me.

"Land a' Goshen, Junior. What on earth are you doing here? And what's the matter, honey?" And with that she wrapped me up in her soft hug so close that I knew, even as I buried my head in her bosom and sobbed, that she knew everything. "Oh my goodness. You had an accident. Just you come with me this very minute." And she took my hand and led me in through the kitchen and into the bathroom. "Now you just take those dirty old things off," and she carefully helped me out of my jeans, and then, even more carefully stepped me out of the soiled BVDs and cleaned me up, never once making a face or asking me to explain.

"Wait here, Junior. I'll be right back." And she disappeared out the bathroom door only to reappear a minute later with a baggy but serviceable pair of underwear and a pair of jeans that were longer than me, but after rolling up the legs a few times and tightening up my belt – they worked. At least they were clean. It felt like I was born all over again, clean and new.

And then Grandma did the most wonderful thing of all. She called home and I could hear her talk to Mom. "Maggie, yes honey, it's good to hear you too. I just called to tell you that Junior dropped by after school today for a visit. No, I'm sure you didn't tell him to; he just did on his own, such a sweet boy. And we're having such a nice visit, I thought I'd call and ask you if he could stay for supper. No. No trouble at all. Colonel's not coming in 'til later, and we'll drop him off. Would that be okay? No. Buster doesn't have to come in. Oh, all right. We'll probably be done about seven. Fine. We'll see him then. Bye, honey."

She hung up, turned and smiled at me in the doorway. Grandma never lied. But she came as close as she could or ever would in this life that one time; and she smiled at me, that warm, gentle, almost sad smile of hers that seemed to say, "I know what you are going through, and I'm here with you." She dug up some picture books for me to look at. I liked to read the pictures and try to figure out some of the words, and sat me on the front room sofa while she continued her house chores and supper making.

Grandpa showed up in a bit. Colonel, that's what she called him, had been drinking and was in a foul mood. He looked surprised when he saw me on the sofa reading and asked what was I doing there, leaning in to me so I could smell his sour rotten breath, and glaring at me with small, watery black eyes behind his thin, greasy black hair combed straight back.

Grandma told him to leave me alone, that I had stopped in after school and was staying for supper, and he was to go clean up. Grandpa digested her news and instructions, shrugged and walked away. And in just a bit we sat down, said grace, and commenced to eat. Before we could finish a piece of apple pie desert though, a horn honked out front. "Colonel, would you just bend your head out the window and see who that is."

Grandpa got up and leaned to see. "It's Buster. I'll be right back. C'mon Junior." Sure enough, it was Dad in the big green truck.

I looked at Grandma and before I could jump down and run to the front door, she said, "Junior, before you go, you better go to the bathroom and clean that pie smear off your shirt." I really didn't see any pie on my shirt, but if Grandma wanted me to go, I would. When I closed the bathroom door, there was my jeans and clean BVDs, still just damp to the touch, draped over the side of the tub with the little electric fan blowing on them. I did a quick switch of clothes, and when I stepped out of the bathroom I couldn't help singing. Grandma had pulled it off. She had protected me, had covered for me, and I would have died for her.

From the front door, I saw Grandpa with one foot on the running board of the truck, leaning in the passenger side window, talking with Dad. Grandma was standing on the porch. Bending down to me she said, "Now, it was mighty nice of you to drop in, young man. You stop by anytime you want. I'm always glad to see you." Grandma was one of the few people I ever knew that would smile only with her eyes. The corners of her mouth may have been pointing down, but her grey-green eyes were laughing and dancing. She hugged me again, and I tried to hug her back. Feeling as light then as I was heavy before, I skipped down the walk.

"Bye, Grandpa," I said as he swung open the truck door and I hopped in.

"Did you have a nice visit?" Dad asked as he shifted into gear and the truck lurched away.

"The best." And that's the way I will always remember my grandma.

Chapter 15

Summer's only a few weeks old and already I can feel things are off kilter, not the way they should be. I started out writing this thing hoping I could track down what went wrong so I could fix it. I don't think that is possible anymore. Mom told us she is filing for a legal separation from Dad, not a divorce, just to see if they can work things out. But now I just can't stop writing.

Mooky is in summer league baseball, Sissy is off with her friends, Dad ain't around much, and Mom is sad-like and edgy. Sometimes she'll cuss or swing out and hit us kids for small things she used to ignore. I was sitting on the front porch steps feeling all empty and recalled when all us kids used to play like crazy in the summer, my sisters and their friends jumping rope and turning cartwheels and the like, while me and Mooky would be playing cowboys and Injuns, taking turns dying. When I think about those old times now, they seem so far away, like maybe they were in a dream or something not real. Or maybe I was somebody else.

I just got back from wandering up into the woods. It was so deathly still I kept looking over my shoulder to see if somebody was staring at me. That feeling of being spied on got to me and kind of drove me out. I feel like I want to be nearer to real people. So I got out my notebook and here I sit up in the big tree in the back yard.

The woods are wonderful but sometimes they feel haunted, not exactly unfriendly, just occupied. The first time I ever felt it was years ago; I was exploring by myself and when I stepped into a grassy area that looked like it had once been someone's field but was now abandoned, I had a strange sensation. When

I stepped out of the shadows into the sun, I heard a strong voice say, "Stuart." Just that, nothing else. I looked around, but there was no one there, and that voice was so clear that I answered, "What do you want?" Maybe it was God. I don't know. What really scared me though was that the voice called me by my real name, not "Junior" like everyone calls me. Needless to say, I did not stick around there and hustled home pretty quick. I'm still waiting for that voice to call me again.

I think the voice could have been God, but it could have been a spirit. They are there in the woods. You can feel them often enough. Maybe some of them are Indians. Maybe it was Chief Harvey. That's who the creek was named after. I once asked Dad who Harvey was and why they call the area we live in Harveytown. He told me Harvey was a local Indian chief who sold the land off to the whites so they named it after him.

I bet he felt sorry after he sold the hills, and I wouldn't be surprised if his spirit still prowled his land. If I'd been him I would have fought for it. Others may be the spirits of pioneers. I know that when you die you go to judgment, but sometimes I think there must be a line-up or something so a spirit don't get in right away. Or maybe the spirits just love the woods and get permission to stay in them for a while.

The first time the woods spooked me out was one summer day years ago when I was exploring on my own. I'd never been in these woods before. Dad warned me there were 'old boys' in there, brewing up moonshine, and they wouldn't take kindly to snooping kids. Him saying that made me mad. I'm no snooping kid. I live here. These woods are as much mine as anybody else's. Besides, I'm the fastest runner in the whole school. Even Dad can't catch me when I mean for him not to. Still, maybe there is something to what folks say because every time I've neared this stretch of the woods I get a hackily feeling that sort of wards me off. So that day I brought Sissy along for company.

She's smart and don't scare easy. True, sometimes she's overbossy, but I still generally like her company, leastways when my blood-brother Mooky ain't available. But, just like her, it wasn't till late afternoon, when the air was hot as steam off a kettle so's that even the little critters that normally haunt the woods were quiet and laying low under some leaf or rock, that we set off.

Reeko, my little yellow mutt with short legs and a curled up tail, whined and panted in the heat, and slunk under the house when I tried to roust her up to come with us. So it was just Sissy and me as the kitchen screen-door squeaked open and slammed behind us. I picked up my favorite walking stick where I left it at the edge of our legal property. Dad says I should always take a stout walking stick when I go exploring the woods. It's a handy thing for climbing up and going down steep hills, and great for tapping those copperheads out of the way.

I told Sissy I had something to show her and led the way, across one ridge and up another. I wanted to get there and back before dark. She chatted some, but the heat put the nix on that soon enough. We reached the edge of the woods and plunged in, hoping it would be cooler, but we were mistaken. It was just as hot, and the air felt heavy and gloomy, and I wondered if maybe I should've picked a different day or got an earlier start. We stopped for a minute. She plopped down on a fallen tree and said, "This better be good, Junior, because I am not enjoying this one bit. And my legs are getting all scratched up." And that was true as turnips. Angry red welts scraped her legs.

I wanted to tell her it was her own darn fault for wearing such a flimsy sun-dress to go exploring in, but I was afraid that if I did, she would turn around and stomp off in a huff. So instead I said, "It ain't far now, and it sure is worth it. I never seen anything like it in all my born days." And that part was true too. I never seen it, only spotted something deep in the woods once from a distance, and I needed her company to bolster me up.

I must've said the right thing. She gathered herself up, brushed herself off, and stood. "Well, let's get on with it, brother. Day's getting long."

I pointed my walking stick like a sword and said, "Onward and upward," like a knight in a book. Sissy grinned and off we went. Leastways, in the thick woods there was a lot less underbrush, so it was easier walking. But man, it sure was quiet. I struggled to find the way, and after a bit I started recognizing the area, a small gap in the woods, now all growed up with volunteer scrub-oaks and such. Then followed some broke-down wormy apple trees that had been planted ages ago, and straight past them a ways was a broken down house all growed over with vines and ivies.

"Damn," Sissy said low. She didn't swear much so when she did, she meant it. I could tell by her squinty eyes and the way she hunched her shoulders, she was shook. "I never knew this was here." Slowly, we snuck up on the place like there might be someone home. Of course there wasn't. "This ain't no old log cabin," she said. "This's got a second floor. Least it had one before that tree crushed it." It must have been the heat that made the air so wavy. We stepped nearer. "Stop," she ordered. "Junior, don't you see the gate?"

Our path came around the side, but out front was sure enough a rusty old metal gate, nearly buried under green stuff that grew up and over it. To either side of the gate was a stretch of some staggered and broken pickets, just as dilapidated and grey as the house itself. Still, I didn't see why the gate mattered so much.

"Why would anybody build such a place way out here, miles from anyone else?" she asked. "And what ever happened to them?" She stopped walking. I could sense her brain working overtime. "Let's go through the gate," she said and pointed. "It's the right thing to do. There may be ghosts or haunts around and they need respect."

Her saying that surely made sense, but it also made the hair on the back of my neck rise. I let her lead the way. She put her hand on the top of the old gate and tugged. The gate and the fence attached to it waggled. Sissy said, "I'm sorry. I didn't mean to do that." I realized she wasn't talking to me. She pushed on it. It squeaked uncommon loud, like it was complaining about being disturbed, but it opened, and we stepped onto the house's property. If it was possible things quieted more, like my ears were plugged, or like everything was holding its breath. I felt like I was in a picture, but a picture with eyes looking at us. I glanced about to try to catch the spy, but everything stayed dead.

Two slow steps closer to the porch. Wavy old glass panes

reflected us back on ourselves. I stopped and pointed over to the right side of the walk at a pile of rocks. "What's that?" I asked. I didn't really care. I was just stalling. Inside that old house was the last place on earth I wanted to be.

"Go check it out," Sissy whispered, and I stepped towards it.

"It's an old well, Sissy," I said as I carefully leaned over the weed-covered rubble. "I read that sometimes folks would throw valuable things down them for safe-keeping if they had to leave in a rush."

She joined me and we both peered into the shadowy depths. We saw nothing – at first. Then our eyes adjusted to the murk. "What's that?" she asked. "Something moved."

Then I saw movement at the bottom of the well. Not just something – somethings. Snakes, copperheads by the dozens slithered and slunk across the floor of the dry old well. Their movement made a papery, scraping sound, like mean whispers as they shifted around. We both stood up, took a step backward, and froze.

We both felt it. This whole place, and whoever still lived here, was telling us we were not welcome. Then the gate clicked shut behind us.

Maybe it was just out of balance and closed on its own. Or maybe the haunt what hung around here done it. I don't know and I didn't care. The sound of that gate slowly creaking shut was like a bullet fired at us. We jumped and completely forgot about the house. I was too scared to touch the danged gate, so I lifted myself like a deer in flight right over a low stretch of fence. That gave me a head start over Sissy, who did the respectable thing and stopped a moment to open and leave through the gate.

Like I said, I'm a fast runner, the fastest I know. But Sissy caught up to me within a hundred yards, and with cheeks puffing and elbows pumping, passed me by, her flimsy sun-dress and legs clawed by briars and brambles.

The weird gloom of the haunted forest gave way to the normal gloom of the woods as evening settled in, and we stopped to catch our breaths. "Junior," she gasped, "that was so strange." And then she did something strange herself. She laughed. "Do you think we can ever come back?"

I noticed then that in my panic I had dropped my walking stick by the snake well. "Sissy," I said, "I don't think that place likes us, and I don't figure to make it angry at me. It got my best walking stick," I added as we started walking again, "and that's all of me it's getting."

When we told Mom what happened, she said as how she didn't recollect the place we described but that we most likely just spooked and drove ourselves into a panic, and maybe she's right. But since then I have tried any number of times to find that old place again, with no luck. I'm beginning to think that places can be ghosts just as well as people.

Folks hereabouts know all about that kind of stuff. Two summers ago all us kids were playing in the yard just as I described at the start of this chapter. A man called Crazy John lived all alone with his old hound just past the Evers' place, back up on the ridge. Mom used to scare us when we were out playing too late evenings by saying, "Come right in or Crazy John will get you."

When I would go visit the our friends the Nortons, just past Crazy John, I would always look up on the ridge to see if he was out on his porch with his dog at his feet. Sometimes he would wave or wave something that could have been a gun at us. If I saw him, I would put my head down and speed up 'til safely past his place.

The story was he had killed his wife and when the sheriff with his deputies came out to get him he fired at them and they shot at him so they were sure they had perforated his hide good, but he just laughed at them until they left. Probably it wasn't true, but us kids couldn't be sure. Anyhow, you get the picture. We all figured he was not a person to be trifled with.

So we were all playing, like I said, when out of the deep grass shuffles his old mangy hound. It had never been to our yard before so its sudden appearance like that startled me. I figured I had to tell Mom. And she said, "Crazy John is dying, Junior. The old lady from up the holler is sitting with him, but no one is taking care of his dog, so he drifted over here for food."

That sad old dog with floppy ears moped around for a couple days until we all just came to accept it in the background. We fed it dinner scraps along with Reeko, who did not seem to mind sharing her food with such a droopy neighbor. Other than for mealtime, that old dog didn't stir from its spot in the front yard.

Then, just when we thought that hound was gonna be a piece of our yard furniture forever, the weirdest thing happened. It was of a sunny afternoon, and us kids were goofing off out front as usual, working on cartwheels, when suddenly that old dog sat bolt upright and his ears lifted like he was listening for something. Then he howled like only an old hound can – long and mournful. Suddenly, he spun and lurched for the woods, straight as a string, howling and running as fast as his old stubby legs could carry him. It spooked me good. I dashed into the house. "Mom, you'll never guess what just happened. Crazy John's old dog just sat up and howled like a banshee. Then he took off for the woods. Should I go fetch him back?"

She kept on slicing potatoes into a pan without even looking up. "No, Junior, just let him go. He won't ever come back. Crazy John must have just died, and that old dog's following the spirit trail." She said it so mater-of-fact like, I felt that I should've known that, even though I had never heard of a spirit trail before. I went back out and sat on the porch step and thought about the dog and the "Spirit trail" while the other kids played. Mom was right. We never did see that dog again.

Mom seems to have a knack for tuning into such things. She says it is because of her "Bohemian heritage," whatever that means. Sometimes when she is in a jolly mood, she will call us her little Bohunks. I remember one fall night, the same year Crazy John died. We were all sound asleep.

Grandma Carter had been real sick and losing weight 'til it made me almost cry to see her. Mom said she had a stomach cancer, and it was eating her up from the inside. We prayed every night for her, and I never meant my prayers so much. But still she weakened. That night Mom came and softly shook us awake and quietly told us to get dressed. Grandma had just died and we had to go pay our respects. I felt like I did when Dad would hit me in the gut with his fist. Sissy was crying. Talulah and Wendy were too sleepy to know what was happening.

We piled into Dad's new green Packard, and he drove us to Grandma's house. I was surprised to see how many people were there. A lot of people from the Baptist church she attended had come by. I felt like I was drowning; they kept saying how sorry they were. Grandpa looked so terribly sad with his puffy red eyes that I felt sorry for him. Granny was crying out loud, "Why her, God, why her? My Gertrude was so good. She was my only child. Why not take me. O God!" And some women almost had to carry her away from the bed where Grandma was laying.

All us kids just huddled around Mom. Dad's face was twisted up. His hair needed combing and his face was all bristly, and it sounded like every word he said had to be squeezed out of his throat. Then Mom pushed me from behind and said, "Go say goodbye to your Grandma." So I went over and stood by her bed. I had never seen her in a nightgown before. But her face looked all waxy white and her mouth wasn't right. It looked like an imitation of my Grandma. And she looked so skinny. Then Mom leaned over and said, "Kiss her goodbye."

"I don't want to, Mom." Grandma always kissed me on the top of my head. I had never kissed her unless she picked me up. This way wasn't right.

"Do it now, son." And she nudged my back. Reluctantly, I leaned in and placed my lips lightly to her forehead. The coldness of her skin made me jump back. And then I knew what had happened. It was like a light came on in me.

"She's not there, Mom. That's not her. I'm sure of it. That's just a shell or something. Grandma's gone." It was a relief knowing my Grandma was not trapped there in that skinny, icy corpse. But where had she gone? Was she following some spirit trail? Was she in judgment, or heaven, or nowhere – had she just gone cold and died like a fish? I wondered about these things for a long time.

Then one Sunday evening while we were sitting and eating and talking about Grandma, Sissy up and says, "Mom, how did you know Grandma died? Ever since that big tree fell on the line during the storm, we had no phone. So how did you know? Who told you?" Sissy was right, I suddenly realized, and held my breath waiting for Mom to solve the mystery.

She put her fork down carefully, looked at Sissy and said, "Your dad and I were sound asleep that night. I can't even remember what I was dreaming of, when suddenly, clear as a bell, there was Gertrude's face, full and smiling like she used to be, before the cancer. 'I'm leaving now, Maggie,' she said. 'Goodbye.' And then she disappeared. Well, you can bet your socks that woke me right up. I turned over and shook your dad. 'Wake up, Stu. Your mom just died,' I said.

He was as grumpy as a badger at being woke up like that and groused at me, 'Now what put that in your mind, Maggie?'

I said, 'I just know, that's all. I saw her and heard her clearer than I see and hear you now.'

Mom dropped her voice to sound more like Dad's again. Us kids were riveted to our seats. 'You better not be puttin' me on, woman.' That's what your father said. 'Because I got to work in the morning.'"

Dad just sat in his chair and looked at Mom, not saying nothing. So I know she was telling the gospel truth.

No one knew what to say after that, so we talked of other things. But later on when it was time for night prayers, I thanked God for taking my Grandma home, for making her hurting stop, but most of all for letting my mom know so she could tell us goodbye. There was no doubt now that my Grandma was in heaven and that the thing they put in the ground on the hillside by her church was just the worn out husk she left behind, like the June bugs shells left on the trees when they die.

Chapter 16

Usually when I go exploring, I go alone or with Mooky. But he's busy a lot this summer. And once in a while a body can use some company. So today, just while I was at the kitchen table making me a lunch to pack, up walks Talulah and asks what I am doing. Now Talulah ain't very big. As a matter of fact, she is shorter than me. But she is two years younger than me and a girl. So what can you expect? Sometimes I like her and we have good laughs. Other times she makes me madder than anyone in the family. She has a hair-trigger temper, black curly hair done up usually Shirley Temple style, and runs faster than any girl I know.

She makes me mad because she so likes to argue and sometimes is as mean as a snake. But I do admire her toughness and lately have come to feel some sympathy for her. Though she is Dad's favorite, she has taken her lumps from him too. That, plus she doesn't have a lot of friends nearby caused me to make an offer to her I never have before. "I'm going up to the woods to explore. You want to come with?"

"Sure, Junior. Just let me make my lunch." We threw together a few things from the fridge, a couple cabbage leaves and some crackers and then headed to the door, stopping only to put on our shoes. One great thing about summer is, except for church and a few other times, you don't need to wear any shoes. At first the stones and gravel and hot pavement make it miserable. But if you just see it through the first week or two, your feet toughen up like leather – or almost. It would probably be okay to go exploring barefoot, but then there's snakes you might step on. I don't want to risk it, so I made sure we both put them on before we headed out.

Really, the one main reason I don't like to go exploring with a girl is they talk too much and most times it is the stupidest stuff they talk about – like their friends, or what happened to them, or who likes whomever. It bores me to tears. I prefer to go quietly, to look for animal tracks, paths or spoor, and to listen to what the woods say. When I find a snake sunning on a rock, I can poke it with a stick to make it slither away.

When Sissy saw me do that a few years ago, she nearly had a hissy-fit. I didn't think Talulah would react that way. Sometimes, if I make too much noise, I will hear a sudden rustling in the underbrush as something big hustles away. At the edge of the woods I found my new walking stick right where I stashed it, against a young maple, and using my Barlow knife, trimmed a small one from a branch that had broken off in the wind for Talulah. She grinned and challenged me to a sword fight – "On guard." We swished them back and forth a few times, rapping our sticks together, and then we set off.

One summer, a long time ago, Dad told me that Mom liked flowers and she would especially like it if I would bring her some for a bouquet. "Only don't pick her own," he warned me. "Bring wild ones," and he pointed out the different ones to me. By now the mountain laurel that can cover a mountain so dense and the rhododendron are all done. But there are oxeye daisies and touch-me-nots, and flowers I don't know the names of that love the heat of summer or the shady woods. I would never pick from her morning- glories growing on the trellis Dad strung for her beside the back door. And she would be hurt, not happy if I picked from her flaming orange spotted tiger lilies.

We hiked right up over the ridge top and down the other side. I was still uncomfortable with taking her to the tree fort, so when we got close I veered us off to the right, to the south. What if she told her friends about it and they came up and ruined it. But there was another place, almost as secret, that I figured she would like. We hiked through undergrowth just a bit denser than before 'til the woods opened up to a wide, shallow, rocky gully, now mostly dry but which in spring time would carry off considerable water. We stopped just short of it.

"I want to show you a place, Talulah, but you have to promise not to tell anyone or to lead anyone else here. This is a secret place and I'm trusting you. Cross your heart and hope to die."

"Okay, cross my heart and hope to die." She loved a mystery.

"Not even Mooky knows about it yet."

"Wow!" that impressed her 'cause Mooky usually knew everything I knew. But the truth was I had just found out this place by accident myself last week, and it was so beautiful that I had already been back three times. The first time I plucked off just one blossomed stem and brought it home in my pack to ask Dad about. Funny thing is you'd expect a Mom to know more about flowers, but that ain't the way it is with us. I guess it's because she's from Wisconsin and they got different flowers there. And rare is the day I can stump Dad about a plant I pack in.

"Now where on earth did you find this?" he asked, turning it over in his hands. I haven't seen any around these parts, though they are common enough elsewhere." And he handed it back to me.

"Oh up in the woods a ways," says I vaguely.

He chuckled as I casually tucked it back in my pack. "That's good" says he. "Some things need protection from people, or they'll love it to death. You keep it quiet about what you found. The flowers will be happier."

So now me and Talulah took a half dozen steps more, and she gasped and froze. I felt as proud as if I had just given her a million dollars without it costing me a cent. There, sprawled all over the banks of the gully in the freckled shadows of midmorning was a colony of cardinal flowers, clumps of them spreading out their rich scarlet finery, showing off only for themselves and God and now for us.

"Oh, can I please pick just one?"

"No, you mustn't and you promised not to tell. How can you do that if you bring one home and everybody asks you about it?"

"But they're so beautiful. It looks like heaven." She crossed her arms across her chest.

"Could be but it ain't, so just look. You can walk through them if you want, but don't hurt them."

She cocked her head and looked at me funny for a second, then carefully made her way down the slope and using her walking stick, brushed the bunches of flowers aside until she stood about half-way up the other side of the gully. Then she turned and shouted, "Look at me. I feel like Dorothy in Oz. Only it's all red instead of green." She held her arms out to either side and spun around in a slow circle and looked back at me. It was all so pretty, red everywhere and right in the middle of it a spinning black haired girl in blue jeans.

She slowly worked her way back to my side, and there we sat and ate our lunches, talking about little things and her school days, her poking at things with her stick, just feeling the warm breeze slide up the gully and watching the yellow and orange butterflies dance around our scarlet flowers.

"Junior," she asked during a lull, "do you think Mom and Dad are going to get a divorce?"

It surprised me to realize that she was worried about it too, and old enough to know about divorce. I said, as honestly as I could, "I don't know. Dad ain't hardly around anymore and Mom has got her spirit dead set against him. I hope not. But I don't know." I didn't know, but I had my blackest suspicions. Once things start going bad it's my experience that they usually just keep on going 'til they can't get any worse.

We didn't say any more for a long time. After we were done with our lunches we just laid back with our hands behind our heads and listened to the crows taunting each other and a few cicadas chirping to each other. Then, almost as if it was there was some kind of a signal, we both got up and dusted off our rumps. I left the crust of bread from my sandwich for neighborhood critters, like Granny said a person should always do, and we worked our way home back and over the ridge, taking our time, stopping to pick flowers for Mom's bouquet – daisies, some Jacob's ladder, even a few late bluebells.

I knew Mom would take them with a smile, smell them and place them in a pint jar of water on the kitchen sink window 'til they wilted. As we broke into the sun from the woods above our house, Talulah said, "I never seen anything so gorgeous red in

my life. And don't worry. I won't tell anybody. Thanks, Junior."
And so far Talulah has been as good as her word. Maybe she ain't
so bad after all.

Chapter 17

Talulah is a natural Tomboy. She's the fastest girl I know, will try to climb trees like a boy and will cuss like a boy. She has even had her mouth washed out with soap. She's wiry, tough, mean as any kid at school, and won't back down from a fight. The difference between Talulah and a boy in a fight is this. If two boys fight, it usually starts with a challenge and a chance to back down. There's often pushing and shoving while they try to get brave, and then some punches get thrown. A bloody nose or a fat lip, a black eye, may be the worst that happens and then it's over. The two guys may even walk away together if it was a good fight, and later you could see them on the same sides in a baseball game or something. Tempers fly and then they cool down.

Talulah ain't constructed that way. If someone gets in her face, boy or girl, it don't matter. She'll get right amongst them. She's just as good at badmouthing and telling someone off as anybody I ever seen. And does she get worked up. When she reaches her breaking point, Katy-bar-the-door, she goes right to work. She'll hit, punch, claw, bite, pull hair, and kick until the other kid gives up or runs away.

I've seen guys back off from her. Even Sissy, though she's older than me will steer clear of Talulah's dander. I got a licking from Dad a while back after her and I got into it. She took my cap pistol and wouldn't tell me where she hid it. One thing led to another and before I knew it she was flying at me like a crazy hawk. I surely did hit her a couple times, but by the time Sissy broke it up, my shirt's buttons were ripped off and I had red claw marks across my face. She had caught my lip and nearly ripped it off. I mean to tell you, I was very glad that fight was over. But she stayed mad and went to Mom who told Dad.

At supper when Dad heard about it, he told me to go to my room as soon as I was done. He'd be by shortly. And he was. Usually for minor fights he might whack my bottom a couple times and tell me to behave better the next time. But this time he took off his belt.

"Dad, this ain't fair. I didn't start it. She stole my pistol and hid it. When I tried to make her give it up, she got mad and attacked me. I had to fight back."

"That don't matter, J.R. You could have walked away. You don't hit your sister. Now drop your trousers."

"That still ain't fair." This was serious. "She started it and I know you ain't gonna whip her for it. Why do I get it?"

He folded his belt in half and snapped it once to make the leather pop. "You're a smart boy, but you haven't learned boys don't hit girls – not twice, not once, not ever. You're not so big yet, but one day you'll be a man. Most all women will be smaller than you. Punching a girl twice then could really hurt her. So you learn now."

I panicked as he approached me. Reaching for straws, I grasped the wrong one – the one, you might say that broke the camel's back. "But you fight with Mom. I seen you hit and punch her even." Well that was the end of the discussion. He bent me over the bed and with my dungarees down around my knees, he laid that strap heavy on my backside.

"It ain't the same. You just do what I tell you. Do you understand?

"Yes. I do. I'm sorry. I'll never do it again. I promise. Please stop."

Four strokes with the belt was the normal licking. He gave me six and left me crying over the edge of the bed when he walked out. I guess I had it coming, but I still think I was right. After that I did not get into any more fights with Talulah, mainly because I just shied away from her. But that's not to say she still can't cause me considerable grief.

One summer day right after lunch, Mooky and me were
playing soldiers and marbles. How it's played is like this. He
brings over his bag of green plastic soldiers, and I bring out mine.
We both bring our bags of marbles. Out back under the big tree
where the roots wriggle out of the red ground, it is worn and
sandy. We hauled some sand back to our battle site from under
the swing set Dad had set up. And we spent hours, it seemed,
building forts for our armies.

There were bazooka men, officers with pistols, soldiers lying
down, kneeling, and standing. When we were both satisfied they
were as secure as we could fairly make them while still exposing
them to enemy fire, we would sit behind our forts and fire our
marbles at each other's troops. We made up elaborate rules to
make it fair. You could only fire two marbles for each soldier, and
then we would stop and count casualties.

Soldiers were counted wounded if they were knocked face
down, killed and out of the game if they were belly up. The prone
soldiers could not be wounded, only killed. Wounded had to be
taken back from the lines to the hospital for one round and then
they could resume combat. We would play this game until one or
the other ran out of men who could fire back. A winner would
be declared, and then we would pack up our troops and marbles
for another day. It was great fun.

Anyway, on this day, right in the middle of the battle, I see
Talulah waltzing over from the swings. She sure couldn't play
army with us. So she had to go.

"What do you want? Can't you see we're busy?" I asked,
showing my annoyance. Mooky didn't even look up from his
troops.

"I just want to see."

"Well see somewhere else. We don't want you here."

"I don't want to talk to you, Junior. I just want to talk to
Mooky." And then she smiled at Mooky and confused me
completely. "Mooky, do you love me?"

"No way, Talulah," and he picked up his casualties.

"Talulah, go away and don't be stupid. He doesn't love you."

"I'll make you love me, Mooky. I got a stone. Now do you love
me?" and she hoisted it over her head.

Mooky sensed danger, and I could not believe what I was seeing. He stopped playing with the soldiers and brushed some blond curls out of his eyes.

"No, Talulah. I'll never love you, and you can't make me."

Instantly, she crashed that stone down right above Mooky's forehead. I heard a thunk like a melon being tapped, and the blood starting pouring down into his eyes. I thought she had cracked his head open. Mooky leaped to his feet, screaming in pain, and dashed out of our yard to his home, leaving his army behind.

"Now look what you've done. You've killed him. Mom!" And I scooped up all the troops and marbles in our bags and ran for the house, leaving Talulah standing there with her bloody stone.

Mooky hadn't been killed, thankfully. But he did have to go to the hospital and have stitches put in his head. He was not allowed by his folks to come over to our house for three weeks. I could go over there, but Talulah couldn't.

But a month later the stitches were out and our armies were once again at war in the yard. Marbles were flying. Soldiers were flipping. I looked up and there she was again. Mooky noticed her this time and we were on our guard. Her hands were empty. So we were more sure of our safety. But still she seemed dangerous.

"Do you love me now, Mooky?"

"Talulah, can't you get it through your thick head that I do not l…..." He never finished that sentence. Talulah had hid a piece of broken brick in the back of her shorts. When she heard how his answer was going, she pulled it out, and before he could duck or raise a hand in defense, she smashed him on the head again, in the same place as the first time. I was in shock. This was impossible. Mooky got to his feet, blood running down to his eyebrows already, took the brick piece from Talulah and threw it away. Then, without saying a word, he ran home.

There was nothing I could say or do. This insane five year old girl had twice busted open the head of my best friend. I sat and sobbed in frustration. For sure, his parents would never let him come over to play again.

Back to the hospital he went for more stitches. Talulah was scolded, threatened, and then spanked. But I did not think her punishment nearly severe enough. Mom said it was because she had not yet reached that magical time – "the age of reason." But I knew two things: One, if I had done that I would have gotten thrashed within an inch of my life. And two, Talulah knew perfectly well what was right or wrong and planned it out. The way she was going, I seriously doubted she would ever live to reach the age of reason.

It wasn't until after school started that fall that Mooky was allowed by his folks to come back over. And that was only after Mom had taken Talulah by the hand and led her over to the Campbell's house and made her apologize to their whole family in person and promise never to hit Mooky again.

I just wonder why she couldn't have fallen in love with his little brother Andy instead. Or maybe one of the jerks at school, like Mike Alder – she could bust his head clean open for all I cared.

Chapter 18

One thing I am sure of is that everybody changes over time, but it can be either for the good or bad. There's no telling which way a person's gonna go. And if you was to not see them for a while and then meet them again, you might just find yourself wondering what happened to that person, and why, that made them such and such. For example, Sissy and me used to play together all the time. But not so much any more. And then there's Talulah. I used to positively hate her and avoided her when I could, but now she is easier to take, for some reason. I think about her different now than when I started writing this back in April. Either she's changed or I've changed in the last three months. The fact is, she's undoubtedly the reason I started this book in the first place.

One thing about her has never changed. If a body needs someone to take a risk with, to do something for the first time, she's the one to ask. If it strikes her fancy, she'll do it and do it up right. Let me give you an example.

I surely do not remember when my first hair cut was. When I was little, Mom would just trim it off as it grew, until Dad and her figured it was time for me to go into town to a regular barber shop. Then he took me in to Brinke's Barbershop: That's where we always go. Dad says he was worried I might put up a fight about it so old man Brinke was real careful and even gave me a sucker, probably cherry – my favorite – to keep me quiet. Dad says that by the time I was done there was more hair on my sucker, he called it a hair magnet, then there was on the floor. But that didn't faze me. I would just lick it and pull the hairs out of my mouth.

He says Mr. Brinke was really sweating though because of my double cow-lick, one in the front and one in the back, that makes my blond hair grow out different from most folks and makes it hard to comb and keep down. I always wished my hair was like Dad's, jet black and wavy with a widow's peak. I thought it made him look like Superman.

Anyhow, to get back to the subject, I do remember the next time we went in. Dad asked me what kind of hair cut I would like. That was a novel thought for me. No one ever asked before. Hardly anybody ever asked my opinion about anything. One of my favorite people I had heard about was Davy Crockett so I said, "I want one like Davy Crockett."

Dad and Mr. Brinke just looked at each other, and then Dad said, "You heard him, Mr. Brinke. Give the boy what he wants."

Mr. Brinke turned to my head and asked, "What does Davy Crockett's head look like?"

I thought he was being silly 'cause everyone knows about Davy Crockett. So I said, "You know. He wears a coonskin cap."

"So you want a coon skin cap hair-cut?"

"Yup." And so it was decided. Dad never said a word. And bald old Mr. Brinke went to work with a grim smile.

All the way home, sitting by the open truck window, I sang "Davy, Davy Crockett, king of the wild frontier." And when I strutted into the house you coulda heard Mom yell from Mooky's.

"What have you done to the boy? What is that? His head looks like a fuzzy bowl with a pony tail. My God, Stu, how could you let this happen?"

"Maggie, don't worry. It's what he wanted. It's Davy Crockett's coonskin cap, only blond with a cow-lick." Dad chuckled and shook his shoulders like he does when he thinks something is really funny. "It'll grow out in time."

And it did – too fast for my liking. After a while, when I looked in the mirror, it just looked odd and shaggy, not much at all like a coon skin cap. So when we went back to the barber shop with specific instructions from Mom about no more Davy Crockett, and I climbed up into the big chair onto the booster seat, and Dad asked what I wanted, I really had to think for a moment. Cowboys and Indians was the main game Mooky and me played. We took turns being the one and the other because although the Indian always died in the end, he was always brave and warlike. It occurred to me that an Indian haircut would be just fine. So I says, "I want my hair to be cut like an Indian."

"You mean a Mohawk, where it's left just down the middle and the rest is shaved off?" Mr. Brinke asked.

"Yes, that's it. Is that okay, Daddy? Will Mommy get mad?"

"Don't you worry, J.R. If you want a Mohawk, that's what you'll get. Your mom will just have to get used to it."

Mr. Brinke looked at me with a little smirk while I gave it a final thought. "Yup, that's what I want."

"Okay. Here we go." And the hair flew. When he was done and turned me so I could see in the mirror and asked, "Finished. How do you like the cut?" it was the head of a stranger that looked back at me. I had to stick my tongue out at the mirror, to be sure it was me – totally bald except for a blond topknot about 2 inches tall that ran from front to back. I loved it.

In the truck on the way home, I did get a bit worried when Dad said, "When we get home let me go in first to soften her up. Then you come in."

But that plan didn't last long. Dad went in the front door while I listened on the porch. As soon as Mom saw Dad she asked, "Where is Junior and what have you done with him this time?"

"Now just cool down, Maggie. He got the haircut he asked for and it is not a coon skin cap." He paused. I could hear him smiling. "It's a Mohawk."

"A what? Dammit, Stu. How can he go to church looking like a wild Indian? Bring the boy in so I can see."

Dad pushed open the screen door and said with, I swear, a little laugh in his voice, "Come on in, J.R., and show your mom your new haircut."

So in I stepped, head up, proud of my topknot.

"Oh, God. And I can't fix it without shaving him bald. Stu, you paid a whole quarter for that?" She walked around me in a circle, wringing her hands.

"Mom, I don't want it fixed. I like it this way!"

Then she looked over at Dad, who was laughing to himself, shaking his shoulders, sitting up against the kitchen sink. "Stu, you know I can never trust you to get that boy a decent haircut again."

"I'm sorry, honey. It just seemed like that he should have a say-so about it all. It's his hair."

She glanced my way and I could see she was trying not to smile just a little bit. And that relieved me considerable. "Can you imagine what Sally and Grandad will say?" And then her mouth just broke into a tight smile. She whacked me once on the seat to send me on my way with a, "Go on outside and play Indian then, you little savage." And I let the screen door slam as I raced off to show Mooky.

I needed to explain all that to you so you could understand what happened later. Mom was true to her word, and the next couple haircut times, she came along too. After a while she figured she had watched the barber enough so that she could start trimming up my hair herself, so I did not need so many trips in to town.

One Saturday morning, after 'Howdy Doody' and the cartoons were done on TV, and Sissy had run off to play at the McElroys, Mom was hanging the wash out on the clothesline while Talulah and me were playing on the swings. Suddenly, I had a bright idea.

"Talulah, would you like to help me with something I'm thinking of? I need a haircut, but I can't do it myself. I can't see the back of my head or reach there. I need someone else to help with the scissors." She dragged her feet to stop her swing and looked down at them a second before fixing me with sideways look. I knew the chance to play with Mom's forbidden scissors would appeal to her.

"Maybe. On one condition." Oh, great, I wondered. Now what? "I'll cut your hair if you cut mine." Now this was new ground. No one had ever cut Talulah's hair. It was jet black, just like Dad's, and Mom always did it up in long spring-like curls that hung down all around the sides and back of her head. She called them Shirley Temples. Dad said it was her crowning glory and it was never to be cut. "I'm tired of Mom always fussing with it," Talulah said. "Will you cut mine, Junior? Will you, please? That's the only way I'll cut yours."

She was begging me, and so I figured that if we got in trouble over this she would share at least part of the blame. Besides, it would be fun to cut her hair. She would look different. So I agreed and we headed to Mom's sewing area to find scissors and went to work.

I cut Talulah's hair first. I didn't know how to cut a girl's hair so I just took hold of each of those long black curls and snipped them off at their top. When I was done with that, her head looked uneven somehow so I tried to smooth it off. Then I added, just as Mr.Brinke had said to me, "There, all finished. Now how do you like that cut?" and had her stand up to look in Mom's vanity mirror.

She shook her head back and forth, looking at both sides, at the little bunches of hairs that stood at the roots of her former curls, and said, "Great, that's much better. Now it's my turn. Sit down."

I was glad she liked it. If she had not, she could have hurt me with those scissors. I sat still and she stood to the side trying to get the hang of those big black-handled tools. She snapped them a few times and giggled. "Take it all off, please," I said, like I was talking to Mr. Brinke. I figured that would be the safest bet, rather than having her try to create something and mess it up. She set her jaw, cocked her head, and went to work with determination. I felt the scissors gliding across my skull in paths like a farmer mowing a field. Hair fell like straw.

She worked hard and it didn't take long before I heard, "There, all done."

"Are you sure you got all the hair? I don't want some hairs left and looking weird."

"Well, most of them."

"I want them all gone, Talulah. That's what I said."

"Okay then. Just lean back then a bit and close your eyes."

I did what she said and felt the scissors once again, this time snipping across my forehead, picking off those stray hairs, no doubt.

"Now I'm done. Let's go show Mom." She set the big scissors down and flexed her tired fingers.

I stood and peered into Mom's mirror. Talulah had been as good as her word. She had clipped off every hair on my head – including my eyebrows. When I felt where they should have been and looked at her, she said, "I wasn't going to cut them off, but you said to cut off everything." She shrugged and grinned and tossed her spiky head.

I wasn't sure how Mom would take it and felt better that we were in it together than if I were the sole guilty party. I was still worried, but Talulah didn't seem to have a care in the world and skipped out the back door. I followed, making sure the screen door didn't slam.

"Look, Mom," she shouted as we stopped and stood side-by-side next to the trellis of Mom's blue morning-glories. "Junior and me gave each other haircuts." She grabbed my hand and smiled. I wasn't sure what to expect; maybe Mom to explode and get mad or scream and cry or something. But what she did next totally surprised me. She just froze there with a clothespin in her hand and stared at us with her mouth open. Maybe it was sun glare, or maybe we were in the shadow and she couldn't see us real well. Anyhow, she just stared, not making a sound. I don't think she even breathed. Then Talulah said, "See, I don't have those dumb curls anymore," and shook her head. That broke the spell.

Mom's voice actually dropped 'til it was just above a whisper. "Wait 'til your father sees what you've done. He will completely blow a gasket." I hadn't thought of that. "Don't either of you move from that spot 'til I get back." And she left her wash and rushed past us into the house. Probably she was going to call Dad and tell on us. Or worse yet, maybe she was so upset that she was going to get a belt and whip us herself.

I turned to Talulah, who was not smiling anymore. "Talulah, I think we're really going to get it now. I'm sorry I cut your hair."

"That's okay. They can spank me, but they can't put the hair back on." And she stood by me grimly. That's when I realized my little sister was braver than me. Of course, she had never got a real belt licking, only the open hand on her bare bottom. Still she was showing real courage, and at that moment I was proud to be her brother.

In a moment we heard the screen door close behind us and knew Mom was back. Would she whip us herself, or did she have some other new punishment cooked up? She walked past us a lot calmer than when she went in, then turned and faced us, holding up a little brown box in front of her face. "No one will ever believe this," she said. "I've got to get a picture of it. Junior, you look like a cue ball. Talulah, you look like nothing I ever saw before. Your dad will shit bricks. Say cheese." And she brought the camera up to her eyes.

Mom hardly ever swore like that in front of us kids. Talulah and me stared at her open-mouthed. Then we realized we were not in trouble at all and grinned for all we were worth. The camera clicked, and Mom laughed.

Dad was stunned, mad, and cussed a blue streak when he got home. But Mom said, "What's done is done." He cussed some more. She said, "Stu, will you please watch your language in front of the kids. The hair will grow out in a while." He settled down a bit, still mad, and she added with a shrug, "They wanted it that way."

Since then, I've always had to get regular haircuts. I have never seen the picture she took, but I know Mom has it hidden away somewhere.

Chapter 19

I really owe a lot to Talulah. Like I said, it is because of her that I started this writing job. About three months ago now, Dad came home one evening three sheets to the wind. Usually, like I said, he favors Talulah. But when he hits the bottle hard he don't seem to recognize how he hurts people. He even likes it. I've seen him pinch Mom 'til she's bruised and almost crying, begging him to stop, and he thinks it's funny.

Mooky says his dad calls acting like that 'a mean drunk,' and some people are just like that, and there ain't nothing you can do about it. Even if he don't pound up somebody, he can still say or do awful hurtful things that he won't remember later. Like he did in April to Talulah.

It was all the way around a bad day for Talulah. It started off like a normal Saturday morning. After cartoons and Cheerios and playing in our rooms, we all ran outside to play. It was gorgeous. The new clover blossoms were just opening up, pink and white, and purple violets were blooming over by the rill. The air was cool but the sun was warm on the face. We weren't even wearing sweaters.

On a lark, to "get ready for summer," I suggested we all take off our shoes and run barefoot in the yard. We were laughing and carrying on having a great time racing around in the cool heavy dew, seeing the wet tracks we left behind. But after a bit I decided to put my shoes on. Our feet were still tender, not nearly as tough as they get after running barefoot all summer. I was sitting on the back step, next to the morning glories, slipping my shoes on when Talulah suddenly yelped and grabbed one foot and started dancing around in the dewy grass. "I stepped on a bee and it stung me on the foot." I ran over to see, and sure enough, the groggy bumblebee was still trying to crawl away.

"Well, come on to the house, Talulah, and Mom'll fix it up."

She whimpered, and still clutching her injured foot, started hopping to the back door. All of a sudden she yelled again and dropped right down on the wet ground, sitting there, crying like a baby and holding both feet. "I stepped on another one. Oh, they're killing me." I couldn't believe it, but she was telling the gospel truth. Here she had up and stepped on probably the only two bees in the yard dumb enough and slow enough not to be able to get out of her way. So there she sat, crying while I ran in to get Mom. That incident just set the tone for the whole day for her. It put her in a bad mood, so I just steered clear of her.

She got scolded, got her butt whacked, and was even sent to her room several times for sassing back to Mom and causing trouble, but she always came back out looking just as ornery as when she went in. Finally, Mom just pretty much left her to her own devices, and I ran off to play at Mooky's.

When I came home for lunch, Talulah was nowhere to be seen. Mom said she was to stay in her room and not have lunch because of her misbehaving. I felt a little sorry for Talulah but not too much and asked what she had done. "That little scamp sat down and broke most my clothes pins before I caught her, and then she lied about it. Her father will have to deal with it when he gets home tonight. I've got the mending to take care of." I had heard Dad up early rustling around going to work. He had an out-of-town plumbing job he planned to finish by noon.

But he didn't come home after noon. In fact, he didn't pull in 'til nearly dark, and when he did, we could tell by the sound of the truck skidding on gravel as he parked, by the squeal of the brakes as he hammered them, and by the slam of the truck door, that he had stopped off at the bar for a few beers on the way home. When he climbed the steps up the hill to the porch, he even put his hands down on the steps in front of him so's not to fall backwards. The scowl on his face let us kids know to stay out of his way, which I did. One thing I cannot understand is why Mom didn't.

"Where you been, Stu?" (As if it wasn't obvious) "We all ate already and supper's cold. We didn't know when you'd be getting in so there it is. Some cold roast beef and potatoes are in the fridge. Help yourself. I've got to start cleaning up the kids for church tomorrow. I sure could use some help around here, but I don't figure you're in any shape to give it."

"Maggie, get off my back. I work like a slave all day and what do I get? Filthy tired and told that the shop's laying off, and I won't have a job. A stinking paycheck that wouldn't feed a bird, and your constant whining. So shut up and let me be. The least you can do is take care of the kids and have some supper ready when I get home."

Mom turned and took a step towards him. "What'd you say, you stinking drunk? You get fired? Is that what you said?"

He yanked open the fridge, looked at the roast beef dish and took out a beer instead. "I didn't get fired, just laid off, and not yet. But I gotta start looking for a new job by this summer. Damn recession's cut business so bad Roberts is laying off some men and trying to give us some lead time."

"So you did get fired. If you didn't drink it up and got yourself home, we could make do with the pay you get. But I don't figure there's much left now, is there? Look at me, Stu. Is there?" But he just took a swig from the bottle and flopped down on the sofa, stared at the ceiling and drained the beer. Even though Dad ignored her, she really lit into him. And the more Mom yakked, the more upset she became 'til she was nearly yelling.

"And as for the kids, I do the best I can. But I need your help. For example, you can't just leave all your stuff out where they can get into it." And before she could stop herself she spilled the beans. "Like today, Talulah was a holy terror. She broke my clothespins this morning and this afternoon, when she was supposed to stay in her room, she got into your records and busted up some and colored on others."

That got Dad's attention sudden-like. He loved his records and kept the record player in his bedroom. Sometimes of an evening he used to play them – maybe Hank Williams, but usually some big band stuff like Tommy Dorsey or Glen Miller, and us kids would dance around while he and Mom would watch and laugh.

But when Mom told what Talulah had done, he didn't laugh. He swayed to his feet, dropping his beer bottle on the floor and not caring. "What did you say?" His voice sounded sober even if he didn't look it. He made a bee-line for his room without waiting to hear anything more and sure enough, there on the floor by the record player were his albums. Each album had about eight records in sleeves and they were lined up next to each other. He sat on the floor and opened one up. He looked all confused, like he didn't believe what he was seeing. "Where are they?" He flipped the empty brown paper sleeves back and forth like maybe the missing records would magically appear. "Where did they go?"

Mom walked to the kitchen, reached into the broom closet and brought out a brown paper grocery bag and sat it on the table. "Right here. I was doing the sewing this afternoon. Talulah was in her room, but she must have sneaked into ours and got into your precious records. I cleaned up the ones she colored on the best I could."

Dad stood and slowly walked to the kitchen table, staring at that bag. Then, leaning his hands on the table, he stared down into the bag at the brittle black broken shards of records and almost looked like he was going to cry. Then he swore quietly and I knew Talulah was really going to get a licking. She was still in her room where she had been sent after supper. "Talulah, get out here this minute. I'm going to tan your hide!"

Talulah appeared at the door. She wasn't used to getting a licking from Dad and though she knew she had committed a terrible crime, she wasn't sure of how to tread the new ground. So she did what she knew how to do best – fight back. "No. I don't want you to." And she stood her ground.

"You're going to get it, so don't make me come for you." And he started removing his belt. She saw it, but instead of making her humble, it made her mad.

"No, I said. And I hate your rotten old music. And I'm glad I busted them old records up."

Dad's face went real ugly. Before she could even take a step back, he reached into the open doorway, grabbed her by her hair and with a roar tossed her so she rolled clear across the kitchen floor. "You goddam little bitch! You're really gonna get it now."

She had tumbled into a corner and before he could grab her again and yank her out, she scrambled behind the washing machine. As he reached down for her, she started kicking out at his hand. I stood paralyzed to my spot. Sissy gathered Wendy and Tootsie and hurried them into their bedroom. Mom still stood by the bag of broken records on the table, with a hand in front of her mouth.

Talulah's foot must have connected with Dad's hand once because he let out another roar and heaved the wash machine out of the way, ripping the piece of black rubber drain hose off its back. Before Talulah could make her escape, he started laying it on her thick.

Mom suddenly yelled, "Curl up, Talulah. Curl up." But my little sister wasn't listening, leastways not at first. She just screamed and kicked. After he connected once or twice and stood over her like a shaggy bear over a little dog, Mom's message must've got through 'cause Talulah brought her knees up and covered her face with her arms. But still she screamed each time the hose whistled and fell with a thunk across her back or legs or arms. Dad kept hitting and hitting.

I couldn't stand it a second more, feeling more and more like throwing up, so I ran out back in the dark and fell by the big tree next to the swing set. I didn't want to listen, but I couldn't help but hear that hose hitting and her screaming and begging. I prayed like I never have before. "Please, please, God. If you ain't gonna stop this please don't never let me forget this. I got to grow up and never forget this. I can't never let this happen to my kids, if I have them. Please God." And I threw up. A few seconds later the hitting stopped, and the screaming turned to crying, both Talulah and Mom.

That's when I knew I had to write everything down to make a record of it, and to try to go back and fix what broke. I can see and hear that night today just as plain as my hand in front of my face, and I know now God ain't never going to let me forget.

Chapter 20

July, 1958

The only two good things that came from her whipping was that Talulah got out of school for a week while the bloody welts on her back and legs healed up, and Dad seemed to have a lot of his meanness drained out of him, at least for a while, and he cut back on the beer too. It was about that time that Dad stopped coming home every night, and that actually made it a little easier on us kids. We had to walk in to school, or hitch a ride in part way with a neighbor sometimes, but that was okay. Most of the time Dad was there of a morning and gave us a ride in while he was still working and then while he was looking for a new job.

Now that it's July, those April days when I started this seem like years ago. Back then I wished it would warm up a bit, but now we are all melting in the heat. Mom says this is the hottest she has ever seen it this early. Today the thermometer by the kitchen screen-door reads 101 degrees in the shade. The woods are sweltering and airless and quiet as even the critters and haunts must be too hot to make any noise.

The little rill that seems so merry in the spring is all dried up now, and Harvey's Creek has slowed to barely a trickle. In a few spots, shallow pools of over-warm water have been cut off as the water level dropped, trapping little fish who splash and die.

Walking to the Huntington swimming pool is a struggle because of the dead heat in the holler. If it wasn't for the honeysuckle growing in spots along the way, that a person can pluck and suck the sweetness out of, I don't believe there would be any pleasantness at all to the hike. In the mornings it is cool for only a short time before the sun blasts up from behind the ridge and shrivels the grass in the yard to brown brittle little shards that crinkle under foot.

On days like this, if I can't get cool in the woods, I spend more time inside because Mom turns the big box window fan on which pulls the air through the house, whether it wants to go or not. If I come running in from outside, she'll cool me down by putting a wet face rag on my head. It helps for a bit. Another way to keep cool is to just go somewhere really hot, so that when I come out everywhere else feels cooler.

I'm sitting here in my room writing, having tried to do just that. The door to the attic is from my room. None of us kids are supposed to go up there, ever since Dad built this part of the house. There is no proper floor up there, just some left over boards Dad spread around so he could get up there to store things. He and Mom stuck boxes of old clothes, pictures, furniture he needs to fix someday, and other odds and ends around the space.

When the new addition was first built, before my room was even painted, and Dad was showing me the new bathroom right next to my room, suddenly the bathroom ceiling sprung one leg, then two as pieces of plasterboard rained down. A high-pitched call for help followed a squeal of fright. Sissy had been snooping around and must have stepped off a board upstairs and plunged her foot directly through to the bathroom. As soon as her first leg poked through, Dad had turned and was racing up the stairs. If he hadn't got there just when he did, Sissy would surely have brought down more of the ceiling along with herself and crashed into the toilet.

I stood there and watched her legs disappear back out the hole they had made as Dad yanked her back up. That left quite a repair job, and Dad was none too happy about having to do it. Since that day, he had placed a flip latch high on the door on the stairwell door, but never found a lock for it. Anyhow, us kids were strictly forbidden to ever set foot in there again.

The problem with that rule was it was impossible to enforce. Having the door to the attic from inside my room meant all I had to do was close my door to the kitchen and move a chair over to stand on and flip the latch back. Dad was usually gone, and Mom was busy doing house work. All I had to do was creep up those stairs silently, and watch my step when I got to the top.

There was one window facing the woods at the east end of the attic and none where it tied onto the rest of the old house. Very often the air was awful close up there. When the sun shone, the black shingles would heat up and the temperature would soar. On the other hand, on cool but sunny spring or autumn days, the attic was really pleasant, and I liked to sit on a box by the open window and look out back toward the ridge, or smoke a filched cigarette and read. It was kind of like being up a tree only not so breezy. And one of the most beautiful things I ever saw was from that window.

In October, a couple years ago, I was sitting just so when I heard a familiar baying. It was the Evers' hounds trying to run some poor critter to earth. Mr. Evers had about a half-dozen of them, and once in a while he would let them out. They would pick up the scent of a coon or other animal, and you could hear them hounds for hours in the woods, now afar, now closer. They'd start up, shut down, then start up baying again. That day they started up, faded a bit, then came on strong and stronger. I realized they were getting close, and that meant whatever they were running down would be here ahead of them.

As I was straining to look toward the noise, there was a rustling in the corn field above McElroy's house to my left. Out of that tan corn stepped a doe of the same coloring. She high-stepped out into our yard, ears flicking nervously, but her black eyes big and calm. Part of me wanted to yell to her to make her run from those idiot dogs, but the rest of me overruled it and I watched her silently from the window.

This was the first deer I had ever seen, and I was dumbstruck. She wasn't nearly as big as I thought she should be. She looked almost fragile, probably not four feet high at the shoulder. But her shiny coat and graceful motion were hypnotizing. It looked like she wanted to run but was considering something else. The baying drew close and I expected any second to see a flurry of black, brown and white explode from the same place in the corn field she had just exited. She kind of hop-walked across the yard and crossed beneath the big tree, in the speckled shadows under the attic window.

Mr. Weis, Mooky's grandpa, loved to garden and cultivated nearly an acre up behind his house. Dad said it was the old country German in him. He always had great veggies and gave us a lot in the fall. He said his motto was to plant three times more than you need. That way you can lose one-third to the weather, one third to friends, and then you'd have just what you need left over. But he didn't figure on giving any to the critters and waged constant war to keep them out. He had even fenced it in with a five foot high metal mesh fence that Dad said must have cost him more than the garden was worth.

I watched that doe pick up and place down her tiny black front hooves as dainty as a princess as she approached that fence. I was sure those dogs would be on her in a second and was about to yell at her when she just lifted herself up into the air and floated over that fence and silently disappeared in Mr. Weis's sweet corn. It was like magic, and just as she flew off, a mob of crazy hounds burst into our yard. They charged the fence; they bayed up and down it, looking for some way in and making a terrible racket until Mr. Weis came out of his house with a shotgun and let go a blast of buckshot.

He hated Mr. Evers and his dogs and allowed as to how he would be consigned to perdition before he would let them dig through his fence. The blast, and his yelling chased them off, and in a while I heard them called home, so I know the deer escaped – by choosing to jump into a fenced off area instead of going around it. How could she have known? Since that day I would often look out that window and hope to see another such beautiful sight. But something like that probably only happens once in a lifetime.

Anyhow, I knew that today, if it was 90 degrees in the house, it would be 120 degrees up in the attic. So if I was to go up there for a while and then come back down, the house would feel cooler. That was my theory. What happened was I got up there and it was hotter than I could ever remember it being. The window was closed, so not even that was useful.

I rummaged through a box of old baby toys to pass a few minutes but got too hot to stand it, so I started over to open the window. Before I got there though, I heard a buzz and felt something feathery light settle on my upper lip. It was a hornet. Someone once told me that if you stand perfectly still, a bee won't sting you. You can bet I stood like a statue, nearly crossing my eyes trying to watch it and not to breathe. It walked around like it was surveying the place, and just as I was starting to hope I would escape, it plunked down and nailed me good before flying up to its nest glued beneath the house center ridge.

I may not like bees very much under the best of circumstances and have made war on them in my own way, but today I had actually been polite to one and my reward was this – to be viciously attacked in one of the most sensitive parts of the human body. My pain was aggravated by my sense of the unfairness of it all. I stormed down the attic stairs, not caring if Mom heard me and knew where I come from. When I blurted out what happened and showed her my lip, already swelling she quelled her scolding look and went to work. She made a baking soda poultice of some kind to put on it and "there-there'd" me a bit before sending me off to my room to calm down and rest.

So here I sit, hot and miserable and probably looking as stupid as a penguin, with a tender lip swollen to what feels like the size of a coffee cup, writing about our good-for-nothing neighbors and their dumb dogs.

I quit!

Chapter 21

Mom just brought me some peanut butter cookies and a glass of cold milk and checked her poultice. I told her I guessed I could eat the cookies and drink the milk in spite of the size of my upper lip. When she saw I was writing she asked what it was about, and I told her I was writing about our neighbors so I would remember them if we had to move. It was only half a lie, and I was hoping she would say that she and Dad were working things out and we wouldn't have to move off the mountain. But all she said was, "That's real nice because a person needs to remember the good," and left the room.

Like I said, the Evers family live just past the McElroys, up on the ridge but a little lower than us. There's a whole pack of them, eight kids left, and those hounds. I don't see the oldest daughter much since she got married and moved off the ridge down into town. Then there is another daughter, Marla, about Sissy's age. Douglas is one year older than me, and Sam is my age. But we've never hung around much.

When I was just a little boy and pointed out their house to Dad, he said I was not to go over there and to stay out of the woods behind their place. Mom said they were "a bad influence," and I was forbidden to play with them. Since they lived kind of far off, and Mooky was much closer, we never did become much of friends.

After Sam, they had four girls in a row before the last was born, a little boy baby who is just learning to crawl. Only four of the girls survive. One, when she was about four, got too close to the space-heater they were using to heat their house, and her hair caught fire and she burned to death.

They are the poorest people I know of and all ten of them living in a house no bigger than our house was before Dad added on. I couldn't see how they did it. The house itself is of faded grey clapboards that I don't think has seen paint in a hundred years, if ever. They only have a pump-handle well and a two-seater outhouse. Sam says they are planning to get in real plumbing this year, if his pa can afford it.

The only car they have is an old black Ford rust-bucket that has sat up on blocks ever since I can remember. They got to walk everywhere, even in to the grocery store. When I asked Mom what she meant when she said their kids would be a bad influence on me, she said, "They don't even go to church, any church, and they let their kids run wild. Half the time they don't even send them to school." Honestly, the way she described it, their lives didn't sound all that bad to me. But our paths seldom crossed. Their house seemed aimed in a different direction, and when they did go to school, it was the nearby public school. What did connect us was their hounds.

Like I said, Mr. Evers ran his hounds and hunted up in the woods. Every so often you could hear a gun shot, hunting season or no. And it was said that the Evers ate as much 'coon as beef. But that changed last summer. We were just in the middle of a dry spell, not like this summer but bad enough. I had been kind of hanging around over there ever since Mooky and I were playing down by the creek and Douglas and Sam showed up one day. They looked dirty and ragged but smiled real friendly and asked what we were doing. "Looking for crawdads," Mooky said. "You want to help?"

"Sure," Sam said, and they joined right in. "I'm Sam, and this is Douglas."

"Right, Douglas Evers with the news," and his brother laughed. It sounded like an old joke between them. I don't get it.

Mooky and me introduced ourselves and before long we were playing like we knew each other for years, splashing around and turning over stones. After a while Douglas asked, "You guys want to come up to the house? We can get out the .22s and shoot crows."

"Now why you want to go and do a thing like that?" I asked.

"It's fun, and besides they're good eating. Ain't that right, Sam?" Sam nodded vigorously.

"I don't know. I only hunted with my granddad. I don't think my folks would like it."

Mooky just said, "No thanks, we gotta get going now. So long, you guys. Come on, Junior."

"Well, come on over anytime. Don't need no invite. There's always something to do."

I thought about their dogs. "Thanks, See ya." And off we ran.

Meeting Sam and Douglas opened my eyes to a lot of things last summer. I told Mom and Dad I met them and they didn't seem like a bad sort to me. After working my folks a bit, they gave in and said it would be okay for me to play with them as I wasn't a little kid anymore. But I was to behave myself and not get in any mischief with them, and never be shooting their guns. That was just fine with me, and it wasn't long before I found myself wandering into their yard.

One of their little sisters was digging a shallow hole in the dirt while her younger sister, who looked to be about three, sat nearby clutching a naked, dirty, hairless rubber doll with one eye. "Whatcha doing?" I asked.

"Diggin' a grave for Emma Jane. She's dead," the older one said. I wanted to ask how they could tell, but thought better of it and instead asked if Sam or Douglas was in. The three year old just sat there with her nose running, but her bigger sister said, "Sure. Go on in."

I would've knocked on the kitchen door, but it was wide open, and I could hear plenty of noise coming from inside. Their mom, a big lady in a faded dress that looked like it was the only one she owned, was cooking something in a skillet that smelled like bacon but not quite, when she saw me standing there. "Now who the blazes are you?"

"'Scuse me, ma-am, can Douglas and Sam come out to play?"

She laughed a great big missing-tooth laugh. "My lands, ain't you nice and polite. You're that Carter boy from over yonder, ain't you?" and she nodded towards our house and turned down the stove burner.

"Yes, ma-am, and I met Sam and Douglas the other day. They said to come on down. Is that okay?"

She wiped her hands on the sides of her dress, an old calico print, looked at me directly, and said, "You come right on in, young man. I'll call 'em." She turned her head and in a whole 'nother voice nearly rocked the boards loose from the walls, "Sam, Douglas, you got company."

In a split second the two came ripping through the house. They saw me and welcomed me like I was kin. "Come on, Junior. Let's go." And we all turned to head out the same door I had just come in.

"Now wait a minute, boys. Douglas, why don't you show yer comp'ny around?"

"Ma, there ain't nothing to show." She made a threatening face. "Oh, all right." He turned around. "Come on Junior. See. This is our house. And this is the kitchen." Dad had called their house a shotgun shack. When I asked what that meant, he told me it was because it was such a wreck that if you fired a shotgun inside, the pellets wouldn't hit anything. There are so many cracks in the walls, they'd sail right through. I had laughed at his joke, but now, standing in the kitchen, I could actually see light between the boards of the siding. There was no plaster on the inside.

Sam led me into the front room, where I had the surprise of my life. There was a hole in the wall to the north that was about two feet high and nearly big enough for me to crawl through. All four girls and the baby slept in one small room in two beds. When I asked Sam where he slept he waved at the front room, furnished with two dilapidated sofas, where two other sisters were watching a TV show, and said, "Right here. We get to stay up as late as we want, 'til the TV stations shut down."

There was a rifle leaning against the doorframe. "What's that for?" I asked. "Expecting company?"

They both laughed at my joke and Sam said, "Actually, pa mainly uses it to shoot rats that try to come up through the floor." And he pointed to a few splintered holes in the wood that looked like something had been chewing through. I never heard of anything like this before.

146

Over by the hole in the wall was an old coffee can that smelled bad. "Whatcha keep that thing around for?" I asked.

"That's the pee can for when we got to go during the night. We just dump it out in the morning," Douglas said, and I backed away from it.

The Evers may be poor, but they got some things that I thought were really grand. Their oldest sister had gone and moved away, but she left behind the hugest stack of funny-books I ever saw. Sam said she was a funny-book nut, but when she got married, her husband said he would keep her so busy she wouldn't have time to read no funnies. And then Sam added with a wink, "You know what I mean?" I didn't.

Over the course of the summer, Sam and me got to be pretty good friends, and if there was trouble to get into, Douglas led the way. They would steal cigarettes from their mom and share with me. We would sit out back behind the dog kennels and smoke and talk. I learned to inhale so as not to cough and to let the fag hang just so out of the corner of my mouth and the proper way to flick the ashes.

When we got thirsty, we could go into the house, but I preferred to drink straight from the well. If you hadn't used it in a bit, you had to dump some water down it, prime the pump is what we call it, and then pump the steel handle 'til you could feel the water rising. Then one more good pump and the coldest clearest water I ever saw would come splashing out, and I quick would catch some in the big tin cup that always hung there on a metal hook and gulp it down or pour it over my head.

One day we were sitting in the shade, just talking, and Marjean, their ten year old sister, wandered over. She struck me as a dumb girl whose eyes were too far apart and who liked to grin at me like she thought she was cute - which she wasn't. We were talking about what we were going to do when we grew up. Douglas was planning on being a big-league pitcher, maybe for the Pirates. Sam shrugged and said he'd like his life to stay the same as it is now. I confessed as to how I always wanted to be a railway engineer and drive a huge locomotive and make all the cars on the road stop or get out of my way.

Then, to be polite, I asked Marjean what she wanted to be when she grew up. She thought hard on it a second and said, "Well, ma's been sleeping with that sailor man Jonesy when pa ain't around. And so has Perla. So I'm figuring on sleeping with him too, soon's I'm old enough." That's honestly what she said. I never heard anything so dumb in my life. I looked at Douglas and Sam, but they didn't say nothing, pretending like they hadn't heard.

It felt mighty awkward 'til I changed the subject and asked if they ever played with the dogs, and I got a quick lesson. "Hell no!" Douglas said. "They ain't no pets. If Dad found out we'd done such a thing as to let them out to play with them, he'd tan our hides. No sir. Them are working dogs."

And except for one time when we all went into the kennels so I could be introduced properly, I never did see much of those dogs. They were kept in a big pen, fenced in with tall wide boards. Inside the pen were the kennels proper, roomy wooden structures that they would lounge around on and in or under in holes they scratched out of the red earth. I thought they looked hot, but the boys just shrugged their shoulders and said as how the dogs liked it that way. Douglas would pull their ears, said they liked it, to make them howl. I thought to myself the hounds did not seem partial to having their ears yanked, no matter what Douglas said. He also could throw a rock harder and hit a can or bottle he was aiming at better than anyone I ever saw.

Interesting and disappointing to me was the fact that the boys really didn't like to explore the woods. Maybe that's because their dad spends so much time there. They would rather hang around the house or walk into town to see what was happening. That was off limits for me, so after a while I kind of stopped going over there.

And then Mom put the kibosh on the whole thing on account of what happened one day over at the Evers place. I was sitting on their front porch in the shade reading through the stack of funny books. Doug and Sam got antsy and decided to have a BB gun battle. They only had two air rifles and I knew Mom would be mad if I got involved, so I said I just wanted to read the funny books.

Actually, some of them weren't funny at all. In the pile their sister had left behind was about a dozen Classics Illustrated comic books, with stories about King Arthur, Treasure Island, and others. My favorite was "20,000 Leagues Under The Sea." Captain Nemo is cool. Like I said, I was sitting on the front porch reading while they organized their war. They only had two rules – no shooting up close in the face, and the first one to get hit loses.

They each grabbed a rifle and took off to hide and stalk each other. Before long I could hear the plunk and ping of BBs, along with laughs and charges of cheating. Then it grew quiet. I thought maybe they had got tired and quit or gone somewhere else.

As I looked up from King Arthur, wondering what they were up to, here comes Sam, quiet as a mouse, sneaking around the corner of the house. If he saw me he didn't show it. He was clearly on the prowl. He was so silent that I thought Douglas would be in big trouble when, just as Sam passed me, not ten feet behind him skulked Douglas around that very same corner. He was stalking Sam and grinning. Slowly he leveled his gun and, pop, nailed Sam right in the behind. Sam jumped and howled and spun around. "You're dead, Sam. I nailed you good."

"You asshole. That was no fair." And he fired back.

It didn't take but a minute for those two to empty their guns at each other, and standing as close as they were, there were a lot of hits. At first they ducked and 'ouched' but after they got mad they just stood there, the both of them with tears streaking their cheeks, pumping BBs for all they were worth. Then they threw their empty guns down and went for each other full throttle. This was not my fight, so I stayed out of it. They rolled and fought until they were both bloody-faced and exhausted. Then they quit. At least they neither one of them screamed for their mom. She was big enough that she probably could have busted both their skulls with one swipe.

Douglas, being the older and a little bigger, seemed to have had the advantage of it, but Sam got in his licks too. They both swore at each other as to how they'd never play BB gun war with such a cheat again. I thought they were both about as dumb as a stack of toes in that anyone could have guessed what was going to happen when you play such a game.

When I was describing the shenanigans at supper that night, Mom put her fork down and looked at Dad. He looked at me and said, "That's it, son. We don't want you going back over there. Those are dangerous people. You could get hurt." My protests were useless. "That's my final word on the subject. Those boys are idiots, and Douglas, for sure is going to end up in jail. He was caught stealing candy from the gas station down the road yesterday."

Well, that was news to me. If he had stolen something how come his folks didn't punish him or he get arrested? They hadn't even mentioned it to me, but Dad's logic was ironclad. "Those boys together don't have the brain God gave a piss-ant, and their pa is a no-good moonshiner who's slower than molasses in January. You mess with those boys anymore, I'll mess with you." I could see there was no getting around it so I stopped playing with the Evers. But at least I had read all their comic books, some of them more than once.

I was mighty thankful a few weeks later, that I had stopped going over there. The biggest disaster I could imagine happened. Like I said, it was dry last summer, and Sam and Douglas one day set things on fire. I was in the back yard playing when I heard a howling. It was Evers' hounds again, but the baying was different. For one thing, it was coming from only one place, their yard. When I looked up I saw smoke rising over there and although I couldn't see their house from our place, I knew where it was. I ran in and told Mom to come quick. She ran out back and took one short look before she dashed back to the telephone. While she was calling the fire department, I was listening to that awful sound of hounds burning up.

What little wind there was that day was blowing our way. If the fire was to get to the woods, there would be nothing to stop it. The whole ridge would go. Right then Mooky and his grandpa, Mr. Weis came by on the lope with rakes. "Grab a rake and get your shoes on, Junior, and hurry up." I did and off we flew.

I had never been involved in something so important before. Then we heard the bells of the fire truck coming up Harvey's Road from town. The only problem was that truck was useless down on the road. And it couldn't get up the face of the ridge. We were really getting afraid. The kennels had gone up like a bon fire, and the hounds were silent now.

Douglas and Sam were out stomping what they could while their mom was furiously working the pump and flinging buckets of water out back of the house to keep the fire away. Mr. Weis brought us nearly up to where the fire line was eating through the grass northeast of the Evers place and said, "You ain't much of a crew but you're all I got. I'll be first and shovel up dirt over the flame. You two walk behind me and rake out any grass you see. Smother the fire but be careful it don't get you. If it gets to that corn field behind McElroy or up to the trees, we lose."

I never knew that old man could work so hard. And he must be near sixty. In just a couple minutes I was gasping and my feet were hot from stomping out little blazes, but I figured if he could do it so could I. We fought the fire without talking. All I heard was the scrape of the shovel and the crackle of fire. My arms felt like fifty pounds, but I could see we had slowed it down some. Still, we had to keep backing up, working south toward the corn field and our place, and if the firemen couldn't get up here we would eventually lose this battle for sure.

Then we heard an engine gunning and here came the fire truck, bouncing right up McElroy's hill. It didn't care about his grape vines or the corn, just drove right over and through them. They had found the only slope that truck could climb. I cheered when I saw it and the men riding it.

The shiny red and chrome truck bounced to a more level area and then the firemen went to work with the hoses, shovels, and rakes and sprayers. They didn't waste a second and their voices were crisp and businesslike. When a second truck hauled itself up the same slope I didn't think life could get much better. I plopped down right where I was and watched.

Poor Mr. McElroy. He'd never grow grapes on that hillside again. Those trucks completely rode them down. But that was a small price, and I'm sure he was more than willing to pay it.

151

Within fifteen minutes those men had that fire stopped dead in its tracks, and a half-hour later there wasn't even steam as the trucks emptied their tanks on the burnt earth. The chief went over to talk to Mrs. Evers while the two trucks slowly made their way back down hill and headed into town.

Mooky, his grandpa, and I walked back home carrying our tools. Mom stepped out and called to us, and handed us each a glass of ice cold lemonade, it was the best I ever tasted. It felt like we had stopped the whole fire ourselves. The sweat just poured off us in ashy grey streaks. I supposed I looked as filthy as Mooky. "That was a close thing, boys," Mr. Weis said. "We nearly lost the ridge today." Then he shook his head.

"All their dogs are dead. They burned up," I said.

"And that's too bad too," he added. "Those boys, sure as shooting, started that fire out back, making some mischief. And it's a crying shame. Still, what can you expect from white trash like that? Thanks, Maggie, for the call and the lemonade. And you boys did men's work too." He gave Mooky a hug around his shoulder and patted my head.

His words gave me a lot of food for thought. They made me feel all full and proud. Still, I felt it was just dumb luck that I wasn't over at the Evers. It hadn't been that long a time since I had sat out behind that same kennel smoking with those two. Feeling like that made me think about the timing of things. It easy could have been me that flicked the ash of the cigarette that started that fire. But it wasn't. So instead of being the goat, I was a hero.

After Mooky and his grandpa left, I took off my shoes and looked at them. During the battle with the blaze, it must have been closer than it seemed. The soles of my sneakers were all melted. "Well, Junior. It looks like we're going to have to take you to town and buy you some new shoes. These are ruined." Mom took my empty glass and started in.

"I guess you were right, Mom."

"About what, Junior?"

"That bunch," nodding toward our distant neighbors, "is bad news, and I'm done with 'em." And I never went back.

Chapter 22

This past Independence Day we had company-come-to-visit. Uncle Everest and Aunt Reno dropped by in the afternoon. I haven't seen them since last year, and when they drove in I don't think any of us kids but Sissy recognized them. Not that you'd forget them if you ever met them. Uncle Everest drives a big black Buick, so shiny you can see stars in the hood. He's Dad's oldest brother, but you'd never know they were kin by looking at them. Where Dad has a full head of thick black hair, Uncle Everest wears thin brownish hair around the sides of his bald head, almost like a wreath. And he dresses real fancy, all in a white suit and straw hat and shiny red alligator shoes.

I was up in the old apple tree on our front hillside with Mooky. We were pretending we were repelling a pirate ship and were using the wormy, hard, little green apples for ammunition. The pirates had cleverly disguised their ship to look like our garage, just within the limits of our throwing range. When Uncle Everest stepped out of the Buick, a contrast in white on black, Mooky and me were so into the battle that it took a moment for us to heed his "Cease-fire" order. Uncle Everest smiled at us and in good military tradition, saluted and shouted, "Requesting permission to come aboard, Captain," before he bent and opened the passenger door for Aunt Reno. In return, we gave him a rousing "hip, hip, hooray," and climbed out of the tree.

Aunt Reno then emerged from the Buick on Uncle Everest's arm and they started toward the steps up to the house. Where he was thin and crisp white, she was a pudgy woman with a pug nose, dressed in a tan skirt, matching blouse, red vest, and wearing a flat-topped hat that looked like it was decorated around the sides with red roses. We never saw such a sight, and kids came a scurrying from every corner of the yard to see.

Mooky begged off and headed home as was only proper when company comes a-calling. When they finished their climb to the front porch, there was Mom at the screen door, wiping her hands on her apron and smiling for all she was worth. We didn't usually get such grand company, and Mom was glad for it so she could pick up any juicy gossip and family news.

Uncle Everest took off his white straw hat nice and polite when he got up to Mom and mopped his forehead and top of his head with a clean white hankie he had in his lapel pocket. "Hello, Maggie," he said. "We were in the neighborhood and it being the holiday and all, thought we'd stop by for a family visit. May we come in?"

"Everest. You're just as polite as you ever were. Of course you can come on in. Please get out of the heat. Reno, it is so good to see you again."

If the climb up all those steps had tired her out, she didn't show it. Aunt Reno stepped up onto the porch and gave Mom a hug. When she tried to kiss Mom though, she missed and kissed the air by her cheek. I got to hand it to Aunt Reno though. She covered up well and didn't let on she'd flubbed up the kiss. "Maggie, you doll-baby. Least ways I know how you keep yourself so trim, climbing up this mountain just to go in a house every day. And how many kids are there now? Seems like a dozen."

"Oh, Reno," Mom blushed, "There's five now and another one on the way. Can't you tell?" And they disappeared into the front room. I couldn't hear what Mom was saying but it must have been funny because Aunt Reno let out a belly laugh and Uncle Everest chuckled. I followed them in. "Can I interest you two in a glass of iced tea or lemonade? Please sit down." She directed them to the sofa.

Uncle Everest did a quick survey of the room and said, "Thank you very much. That would be greatly appreciated. Lemonade would be just fine." He sat, carefully hitching up the legs of his trousers at the knee so they didn't get the "knee-bubble." "By-the-way, is Stuart in? I've got some news for him."

"I'll be back with the lemonade directly. Junior, go down to the basement and get your father." Mom called the dug out area below the front part of the house the basement, though it wasn't nothing like a regular basement. Dad was down there working on the furnace, trying to repair some ductwork before we had to move. Normally, I would have just yelled and stomped to get his attention, but that wouldn't be polite with company, so around the house I went. By the time Dad had washed up and joined us in the front room, holding onto the neck of a Black Label, everybody was chatting away, with Mom doing most of the pumping for news from Aunt Reno with Uncle Everest chiming in once in a while.

Dad dropped himself into his favorite chair by the TV and smiled at his older brother. "Everest, you old con artist. What are you up to these days? Still running that crew of cripples out of that basement office? And Reno, you're sure looking fine, as usual, and even more red-headed than ever." And the palaver started all over again with teasing and laughs.

In a bit Mom refilled the lemonades and Dad lit up a King Edward cigar. I never did find out what it was Uncle Everest did out of that basement office with his crew of cripples, but I did learn that he had resigned from some city job to run a school for wayward boys, quit that and now was back working for the city. After a while he shifted toward the front of the sofa and set his glass down.

"You know, Stuart, I heard about your job situation and as a returning veteran, you could get a job on the Huntington police force tomorrow if you wanted. Just give me the word."

"Now why on earth would I do that? You and I both know they're all a bunch of crooks."

"Not all of them."

"Yes they are. Every one. Damn, Everest, I know them all. And no way would I work with that lot. Besides I don't know a thing about being a cop. So thanks, but no thanks. Now what really brought you out here? You got to admit, it's been awhile since you've climbed that hill."

"Actually, little brother, seeing how you were doing and making that job offer was one reason we came by. We're not getting any younger. Look at me. I'm near forty and got no kids but I got a good income. You're 33 and got no job but have a house full of kids. Time's passing."

"Now why on earth are you talking like that? Remember what pop used to say? 'I'm just as young as I ever was – and then some.' And he slapped his knee for emphasis, the way grandpa does sometimes.

"And that's the second reason why we dropped in," Everest said. He shifted to get more comfortable, pulling up on the crease in the knee of his pants again. He stopped smiling and looked directly at Dad. "Pop's dead."

Dad stood up and then sat right back down. "When did it happen? How? Where is the body?" The room went quiet, as the news sunk in. My grandpa was dead. Maybe I hadn't liked him particularly, or he hadn't liked me much, but still, he was kin, and now he was gone. I hoped he was with grandma and not in the other place.

Uncle Everest fiddled with the brim of his hat. "I don't know exactly when, a couple weeks ago, I guess. Somehow the morgue in San Francisco traced him back here and notified me – just two days ago. He was almost unidentifiable. They found him dead in some alley – looked like he had been drinking, got in a fight, was beat up and left to die."

He looked around the room, catching Mom's eye. "You know he was simply lost ever since Ma passed away. She was about the only one in the world that cared whether he lived or died. Without her, I don't believe he wanted to go on. Don't ask me why he went to California. I haven't a clue."

Sissy got up suddenly and left the room. I could hear her crying in her room. I know she always liked grandpa. He talked nice to her, and she remembers how when she was littler he would rock her. "The body's still out there. They want to know if we'll pay to ship it back here so we can give him a proper burial."

"So that's your game this time." Dad leaned forward, talking through his teeth. "So much for family togetherness. You want me to spring the bucks to bring the rotten corpse of that old drunk back here. Well, that's money I don't have, and if I did I wouldn't spend a penny on him – alive or dead. If you want to give Pop a 'proper burial' you'll have to do it yourself. Even if you do haul his carcass back here, I wouldn't go to his funeral." He rose and Uncle Everest did as well. "Everest, you and Reno are welcome to stay for supper, if you want. But you know how I feel about Pop."

"I'm mighty sorry to hear you say that, Stu. You shouldn't carry that much bitterness around in you against any man, much less your own father. It'll eat you up from the inside. He wagged a bony finger at Dad. "And you're a lot more like him than you realize, a lot more."

"Save your breath, Everest. It won't work on me. Pop yanked me out of school in eighth grade and worked me like a dog 'til I joined the navy. You finished high school, so you got a good education. He paid me pennies on the dollars that I earned and chiseled me worse than he ever did anybody else. And he drank up every cent he ever made and Ma ever saved. I'll see him in hell. I don't need to see his corpse."

Uncle Everest turned his hat over and looked inside like there was something there he needed to see. Then he looked up and said, "Well, I guess that's that then. But, little brother, I was sincere about the job offer. Please reconsider, for your family's sake."

"I'll take care of my family, Everest. I don't need your help."

"Whatever you say, Stu." He sighed. "Reno, I guess we should be going." She rose, fetched her hat, and screwed it onto her head. "Maggie, thanks for the lemonade." She held both Mom's hands for a moment, opened her mouth like she had something to say, thought better of it, and dropped them.

Dad held open the screen door and led the way to the porch. He stood there with his fists stuffed in his pockets and his shoulders hunched. As Uncle Everest passed him, Dad said, kind of low, but I caught it. "Don't think I don't appreciate what you tried to do for me today, Everest. But this is one thing you can't ask. I can't do it." With that, my uncle and aunt descended the steps to the Buick and left.

Even though Uncle Everest had brought us bad news, Dad didn't seem to take it hard. He allowed as how since he had cleaned up and all, and it was so hot, there was no need for him to go back to work on that filthy furnace. And besides, since it was July the Fourth he had a surprise for us, watermelon and firecrackers.

He brought out a whole string of firecrackers from a small brown paper bag, and us kids all wanted to light them off right away. Even Sissy came out to join in the mayhem. But he wouldn't let us, without he first gave us the rules for their proper use. Every year, he said, some careless fools would blow their hands off because they didn't handle them right. You have to light them and toss them right away.

As he talked to us, he separated each cracker from the rest of the string so that they wouldn't go up all at once – so they would last longer. Then, while he was still talking, he lit one, and Wendy jumped back while Talulah covered her ears. Tootsie stared and sucked her thumb. I leaned in to see the fuse hiss and sparkle. Sissy just stood and watched, with her eyes squinted up, expecting an explosion.

Suddenly Dad realized he still had the cracker in his hand, and it popped just as he dropped it. "Sonofabitchingbastard!" he sang out, hopping about, flapping his hand in the air. "Let that be a lesson to you. Here, Sissy and Junior. Take these and for God's sake be careful." He gave each of us a handful of crackers and Sissy the book of matches. Then he forced his lips into a smile and, still shaking his hand, disappeared through the kitchen door. "Maggie, come here a second. I burned my hand."

"I was watching out the kitchen window and saw the whole thing, you crazy fool. Come here. Let me see it."

And we were off. Like a bunch of wild Indians, we ran around the yard. Every minute or so, Sissy or I would light a cracker and toss it up in the air. The girls would run and scream. But then they'd be right back, jumping up and down, hollering for more.

Dad came back out in a bit carrying a watermelon and wearing a white gauze bandage around one hand, and stood watching us and laughing too. That was the most fun we'd had in ages. In no time, it seemed, we had fired them all up and ran over to him begging for more.

"Sorry, that's all the crackers I had." Our disappointment was obvious. "But I got something else I'll show you. Only you have to stay way back from this one. It's a cherry bomb, and it really will blow off your hand if you're not careful, so stand back now." With that, he sat the melon down on the picnic table by some newspapers and reached in his pocket to extract and light a large cherry sized firecracker. He tossed it and to our delight, it made a terrific bang.

"I only have two more. Let me show you what they can do." Dad went to the garbage bag behind the kitchen door and pulled out a large tin can that used to hold beans. "Now you kids lay down over here while I launch this rocket can." We hit the dirt while he lit the fuse and then quickly plopped the can over the cherry bomb. Then he backed up quickly. BANG! That can blasted off and sailed ten feet into the air. We all clapped like it was Sputnik or something. Dad was so pleased with how that one had worked, he did it again, much to our delight.

"What else you got in the bag, daddy?" hollered Wendy. "Any more fireycrackers?"

"'Fraid not, Doll Baby. But I do have something even you can handle, Blondie." He reached in and brought out a handful of small boxes with pictures of black snakes on them. "Let me show you how these work. They're called black snakes." He held out a small black pellet about twice as big as an aspirin. "These don't pop, but watch what happens when I light one."

He sat it down on the ground and put a match to it. In a second the pellet started to change. It looked like a big black worm was busting out of it, twisting every which way, hissing as it grew. Tootsie squealed and hid behind Sissy. Then it was done. He passed them out and we burned them off for a while more. I decided to save a couple to show Mooky when he came back over.

"Stu, I hate to tear you away from your playing with the kids." It was Mom from the kitchen window. "But if we're going to make hamburgers, I need buns and some ketchup. Would you mind running up to the country store to get some, please?"

"You kids stay out of trouble now. I'll be back in a bit, and we'll do sparklers, cut the watermelon, and see who can spit seeds the farthest." With that, Dad walked away.

Right then, as hot and sweaty as we were, Mooky came running over, yelling, "You guys, come on over to Grandpa Weis's. He's making iced cream again." That's all he had to say. We all cheered and ran to Mom to beg permission. At first she said that it would spoil our supper. But when we really put the pressure on her, she gave in and said okay, we could go, but we were only to have a small dish and then hurry back, as Dad would be home soon.

Mr. Weis cranked and the ice cream maker spun. When he stopped and removed the handle and lid, he scooped out chocolate ice cream that tasted the way I figure the person who invented it intended. No ice cream I ever ate anywhere else even came close. And later there would be watermelon, and when it gets darker - sparklers. There may have been hard news today, but it turned out about as wonderful as we could hope for. I wished we could have a Fourth of July every day.

Chapter 23

This summer is so dry it's hard to make spit. Still, no matter how miserable it gets, it seems a body can get used to anything. When I used to think on Dad leaving, it would make me crazy sick, but this summer he's gone a lot of nights and we're still here making do. When he is around, he is sober and on good behavior. Mom says if he gets mean one more time, she is calling the cops. I don't think she would, but I'm not sure.

It appears to me Dad's big mistake was not knowing how stubborn Mom really is. If she makes up her mind, she sets off and don't look back. Once she decided to separate from Dad, that was it. Earl's given her a lift into town a couple times to see a lawyer, and she don't tell us kids much so we'll have to wait and see. There ain't no sense in fearing what you don't know, because what you don't know can be wrong. That may sound crazy, but here's what I mean.

It's like when I was about eight years old and was exploring the neighborhood beyond our homes with Mooky. One day we might explore in the woods behind our houses, the next day across Harvey's Creek and up the west ridge. Another day we hiked almost into town. I mean to say, the two of us covered ground. But we shied away from exploring the area along the ridge to the south of our houses, up towards the country store.

The reason why was there is a farm there that is run by two old bachelor brothers, the Sather boys, they're called. What little contact I have had with them was pleasant enough. Every Friday morning these pencil-thin silver haired old men in bib overalls, who looked so much alike I never could tell them apart, would deliver a dozen eggs for 25 cents, which according to Mom is very dear, and occasionally buttermilk and fresh churned butter which were used for waffles and pancakes. Dad pointed out their farm to me when he took me up to the general store. But then he warned me to stay off their property because they had an unruly bull that had attacked and gored some people. I did not need more convincing so had never set foot on their land.

One morning Mooky and me pooled our money and discovered that between us we had 57 cents, hoarded from lost teeth and piggy banks. We decided to spend it at the country store and build up a stash of goodies that we kept in two coffee tins for 'emergencies' up at the tree fort.

We were so eager to get to the store that we decided to take a short-cut across the Sather's farm and then cut down to the store. We both knew about his bull, but figured we would avoid it somehow. So off we went, our money jingling in my pocket, safe in the marble bag I had emptied just for this purpose right before we left. We felt rich, smart, and just a bit cocky.

From Mooky's we crossed behind the Chamber's place before we hit Sather's farm. We looked every which way for that bull before we scrambled over a wood rail fence into a tobacco field. It was still early in the year and easy going. The barn, chicken coop and house were set in a cluster of trees back up against the ridge, near the woods.

We didn't reckon the Sather boys would see us from there and if they did, so what. We would just wave and go on our way. Laughing and singing, we marched down the rows of tobacco and started climbing the fence to cut kitty-corner across the pasture that lined the road to the store. The store itself was just out of sight. We figured this short cut had saved us half the time it would otherwise have taken and were planning to use it every time we went to the store as we dropped into the pasture on the other side of the fence.

Only a couple steps into the field, Mooky froze and pointed. "Look." And there it was. Up by the gate to the barn but definitely in this pasture stood a big black bull, its tail swishing slowly back and forth. I prayed it didn't see us. We took a few more steps, cautiously. It turned its head and looked our way, undoubtedly wondering who the intruders were. But still it didn't move toward us. We walked a little faster until we were nearly halfway across the pasture. The huge black beast turned toward us and took a step, sizing up its quarry. The fence looked a hundred miles away.

"Quick. Drop to the ground. We'll crawl. If it can't see us, maybe it will forget about us," I ordered Mooky. We both hit the ground and started crawling in the prone position, the way we did when we played army. Only this time it felt for real. I looked over and the bull had stopped after taking a few steps in our direction, and we crawled on, terror coursing through our veins. If it charged us, I knew we'd never make it to the fence.

Thistles, rocks and dirt – that's what I remember most about that crawl. What may look like a pleasant little stroll through a green pasture when you walk by can be a most miserable thing to crawl through. And then as I thrust my left elbow forward, it met something soft, a cow-pie. I couldn't stop to clean it off, just had to keep crawling forward, Mooky grunting by my side. Ever so slowly the fence approached and our hopes rose. Maybe we wouldn't be trampled or gored to death by Sathers' mad bull after all.

By then the bull had gotten his curiosity or defensive nature up and started deliberately walking our way. Mooky saw this first and jumped to his feet in panic, breaking the mounting tension. "Run, Junior, run. The bull's after us." Before he even finished speaking I was on my feet and we were racing toward that fence while the bull broke into a thundering gallop after us. We didn't look back, but we could hear it closing as we attacked that fence. Only when we fell to the other side, safe but by the skin of our teeth, did we look back at the death we had so narrowly avoided. "Mooky," I asked, studying the bull, "do bulls have teats?"

"No. I don't reckon they do. Why?"

"This bull does." It was a fact. Our mad bull was a little old slouch-backed cow that was lame in one hoof. She slowly jogged over to the fence and stopped about five feet away, eyeballing us with her soft, big brown eyes. The low slung udder bag left no doubt that the nightmare object we had imagined really was a harmless old milk cow.

Mooky and me looked at each other. We were an embarrassed mess. We spent a few minutes picking the burrs and field lice off our clothes and dusting off. I swiped a handful of grass at the cow manure on my elbow, and Mooky did the same on a sneaker coated in the brown goo he had accidentally kicked into.

"But it wasn't our fault. It could've been the bull. How could we tell?" Mooky asked.

"There really ain't no way but to check it out. And we hadn't dared do that. We could've been killed. Shoo, cow." And I raised my arms to her. She jumped back a couple steps and then continued chewing her cud and staring at us. "She's more afraid of us than we are of her. And our plan would've worked even if it had been the bull. Right?"

"I guess so. But man, was I scared!" Mooky said. Then his thoughts turned to more immediate concerns, "You still got the money?"

"Sure do. Hear it jingling?" and we strode off down to the store and to sweeter things. Still, I can't help but think that a lot of times if I could just stand and face my fears, they wouldn't be half as bad as I am afraid they are.

Chapter 24

From April 28 to yesterday, July 29, we barely had a quarter inch of rain, according to the weatherman. It was one of the worst dry spells anyone can remember – and hot to boot. And today started off more of the same, white hazy sky and a burned out land. The grown-ups complain a lot but us kids just get used to it and make do.

Sometimes we will play fort or house down in the cellar that Dad dug out under the house. It may smell musty but it is quite a bit cooler than outdoors. Even with the big box window fan set on "high" the house ain't any cooler than outside, and when I went in to get a drink of water there was Mom, who usually is bustling about getting sewing or washing or cleaning or something else done, just sprawled on the sofa in the front room with the fan churning away. "It's almost too hot to breathe," she said. So you get the picture.

Right about 1:30, when Mom was trying to sell Wendy and Tootsie on naps, and them not buying, the haze turned grey and thickened. Then the breeze picked up a bit. Next thing you know the grey turned to bubbly green looking clouds, and the wind started gusting, dancing the tree branches about and kicking dust up stinging my eyes.

Without even a rumble of thunder or a flash of lightning, great big drops started plopping down hard in the dust, popping and making circles like moon craters. Just when we thought it was about to come down good, it all stopped and got real quiet. I was afraid it was just another false start and would blow over, but it seemed a few degrees cooler so I sat on the swing while Talulah lay on the bottom of the slide, and we watched those clouds boil along.

When we heard a far rustling we looked west across the valley, past Harvey's Creek and saw the trees disappearing like they were behind a veil. Several seconds later the creek disappeared and we felt the first sheet of rain. Before we could get up and into the house we were soaked, and the wind nearly bowled us over. Man did that feel good.

Mom was dashing through the house, closing all the windows on the windy side and shutting off all electric appliances as she went, including the fan. Its big blades slowly spun on their own as the wind pulled the old air out of the house through the kitchen door, which stood wide open.

It was like we had all forgotten what a rain storm was like. Standing at the back screen door, we watched the woods on the ridge appear and disappear behind sheets of driven rain and I thought how all the critters would be so thankful, and how the firemen could relax this afternoon down at the firehouse and maybe play some checkers.

"Mom, can we go outside and play, please?" asked Talulah.

"Yeah, Mom. It's not thundering or lightning," I added.

"Please, mommy," Wendy was jumping up and down in excitement. The nap was long forgotten. Sissy just smiled.

"Well, I guess. But if you so much as even hear a rumble, you all come running. Got that? Now get your bathing suits on." Thirty seconds later, amid squeals, laughter, and more energy than that house had seen in days, we were all piling out onto the front porch only to be pelted and instantly drenched.

We made mud pies and threw them at each other, dammed up runoff streams along the side of the house for makeshift ponds, and splashed in puddles down by the road where the holler runoff all met. When we got too cold from the windy rain, we would huddle with our teeth chattering in a little lean-to Sissy and me had built with cinder blocks left over from Dad's construction projects. A piece of plywood held down with two more blocks formed the roof.

Wendy's lips were turning blue and she was shivering, so Sissy took her in. Talulah and me splashed around for a while 'til we got bored and cold, then went in too. We'd had enough. The whole world had changed. Where the air before had been stifling and dusty, it was now cool and clean.

Wendy was sleeping on her bed, and Sissy and Mom were sitting together by the slowly turning window fan. It rained steady all afternoon and evening and then let up. The evening was foggy and still, except for the frogs down by the creek that had suddenly found their voices. Once the rain stopped, the temperature crept right back up again, so we did what we have done many times before on such nights to keep cool.

We dragged a couple mattresses down to the floor of the front room and Mom put the fan right in front of us and turned it on high. For a few minutes, we would get right up close to it and talk into it. It's fun to hear how the spinning blades chop up your voice. It makes you want to clear your throat when you don't have to. Then we would pull the sheet up to our necks, and in a bit would all fall asleep. Somewhere in the night, Mom must of always turned the fan down to "low" 'cause that's how it always was when we woke up.

This morning it was different, though, because the rains returned, and it rained steady for hours. So I've been spending most of the day here in my room reading and writing while Mom and the girls find other things to do. Right now I can't think of a better place to be than in this room. The floor's nearly smooth enough to write on. Dad put down a piece of creamy white with some kind of red flowery vine linoleum.

I got everything I need in here – my bed with a comfortable pillow and a home-made quilt Granny gave us, and a pine chest with four drawers for my clothes. It's got eight knobs on the drawers that I like to spin and pretend are dials on a space ship control panel, like for Flash Gordon or Commander Cody – Sky Marshall of the Universe. There is a small table I use for my desk with a lamp, and a window to the woods.

There's no curtains on my window, just a pull down blind. In my closet is a cardboard box in the corner filled with comic books, and on the shelf over the hanging clothes is a big package wrapped in brown paper. Inside it are two pairs of cowboy chaps Granddad made for me before he died. Except he never called them chaps. He called them hair-pants. I sometimes take them out and stroke them, remembering him. When I close my bedroom door, no one can enter unless I say so, except for Mom or Dad. This is my place, and I will never give it up.

So it took me off-guard when the door opened and Sissy led the girls into my room. Before I could say anything she said, "Mom said we could go play in the attic if we are careful." Like I said before, playing in the attic was usually forbidden, but I guess a lot of rules that used to be so in the past are changing now.

Talulah and Wendy pranced right through like a couple baby ducks following their mother. Sissy unlatched the door to the attic stairwell, and up they went. I heard them stomping around for a moment and then heard the window slide open. It pulled the air right up through my room and made it even more comfortable. I thought I'd have to remember about that if I needed it on another hot day.

Dad had nailed down a couple floorboards so they stayed put and nobody would step through the ceiling again. I could hear the girls playing up there, pushing boxes, talking quietly, and once in a while laughing. Sissy gave most of the orders but Talulah would order her right back.

Once I heard an odd rumbling noise up there but couldn't figure it out. Curiosity got the better of me, so I snuck up the stairs to take a look. Wendy and Talulah had crawled into an unused roll of linoleum and Sissy would roll it across the attic while they crawled through. As they crawled and flipped over inside, it looked and sounded like more fun than a carnival ride. I guess that's what Mom means when she says that on rainy days you have to make your own fun.

And that's one thing we are good at, making our own fun. When I was a little kid I loved playing tag, hide and seek, crack the whip, kick the can, rock the swing set, and so much more. Some evenings we would even have kids join in and play with us that we didn't know, just because it was fun, like catching lightning bugs. Even now, on this rainy day we made our own games. I watched for a minute from the top of the stairs and then walked over to Sissy and helped her roll the linoleum back and forth while the girls inside squealed and laughed.

Chapter 25

August, 1958

Today the morning mail brought the official papers saying we have to leave our home within thirty days. Mom showed them to us and explained it all. Talulah says she will not move and went to her room and slammed the door. I'm thinking that if only whoever wrote up those eviction papers would come out here, they would see that we are rooted here, like trees, and that tearing us out could destroy us.

I said that to Mom and she told me that was silly, that people move all the time, that she had moved down here from Wisconsin, and that besides, it wasn't the bank's fault that Dad had not paid anything on the mortgage for months.

She also said that when we move off the ridge, Dad would not be living with us, that he would help us find a place in town and that he would have to find a place for himself while Mom and him either work things out or "part company." I can't believe she said that. This is all so strange, I can't hardly think about it. Things have changed so fast on the outside around here, but on the inside I can't seem to catch up, and don't even want to.

Funny thing is I guess we all knew this was coming, one way or another. In religion class the other day we were asked how we would live our lives if we knew the world was about to end. Everybody had lots of ideas. I didn't know how I would behave, but guess now I'm about to find out. Mom says at least we'll have time to say goodbye to our friends. Sissy says the move is okay with her because Dad's not her real Dad anyway and besides, she is starting high school and would like to have friends in town nearby. But then she wiped her eyes. I think it's hard for her too.

She may not be Dad's kid by blood, but he is the only Dad she ever knew.

I remember how happy she was three years ago when she turned eleven. We had a regular birthday party for her, inviting all her neighbor friends, boys and girls alike and she played games and laughed 'til she cried. She said she felt like a princess. When the party was done, all her guests were picked up by their parents or walked home. Later that evening we had supper with chocolate cake and ice cream again. It surprised her, and she clapped her hands. When she blew out the candles, Dad asked her if she had a good day. She said, "Oh, yes. It was the best ever." Then he excused himself and went down to the truck, telling us to continue with our cake and ice cream. He'd be right back.

We were just finishing up. I couldn't eat another bite, when we heard Dad on the front porch banging around with something. "Come on out here, Sissy. There's something I want you to see." Of course we all jumped up and barreled out front, Sissy first.

There stood Dad next to the finest looking bicycle I ever saw. It was a blue and white girl's model bike with white handlebar grips holding multi-colored tassels and ran on whitewall tires. It had a battery powered push-button horn and front light. It was trimmed in chrome, and the rear fender had a riding bench on top.

Sissy took one look at it and ran to Dad, reaching up and giving him a big hug around his neck and babbling how this was the finest day in her whole life, and she'd love him forever. He seemed almost, but not quite as surprised at her reaction as she had been at seeing the bike. Dad is not much of one for public displays, but he did give her a quick hug back before releasing her.

She straightened herself up a bit and examined her new bike. "This is exactly what I've always wanted but never dreamed of. Oh My God! Sorry. Please, please, please, daddy, can I ride it now?"

"It's getting dark soon, Sissy. Why don't you wait 'til tomorrow?"

"Oh, daddy, I'll never sleep tonight if I can't ride it. Pretty please with sugar on it. I'll just go down the road a short piece and be right back. I've got to try it out. You just got to let me."

Dad looked like he was seriously thinking it over, while she looked and sounded like she was going crazy. Then he smiled and said, "Okay, just a short ride tonight. Be careful on that narrow road. No car will be looking for a girl on a new blue bike. And you must promise me," and here he knelt on one knee in front of her to eyeball her and took her hands to make her eyeball him, "that you will be very careful about giving people rides on the back. Those spokes are dangerous, so no little kids, no Wendy, no bare feet. Those are the rules."

"I promise, daddy. No little kids, no Wendy, no bare feet. Now please help me take it down the hill."

When they got down the steps, Dad walked the bike over to the garage. "You don't have to bring the bike up the hill each day. Just park it in the garage and throw the latch. I don't want to see it left in the yard when I drive in." I really don't know if Sissy heard him. She was grinning so hard and constantly brushing the tassels and such that she seemed in a different world. And then she pushed it forward, hopped on, settled on the seat, and wobbled off, steadying as she picked up speed. I cheered and she circled the bike around us and beeped the horn.

It was a grand sight. She wobbled just a bit when she slowed and then she straightened it out and aimed down the road. When she disappeared around the curve past Crazy John's, I wondered if she would ever come back, and then there she was, headed back to us. She braked it to a smooth stop in front of the garage and reluctantly dismounted, throwing down the kick stand. Then she stepped back to admire it. Dad took it and wheeled it inside to park it for the night. Sissy watched, and when he closed the door said, "Daddy, I still don't think I'll sleep tonight – and maybe not 'til September." He chuckled.

Sissy was as good as her word, and though she let me ride it on occasion, it was a little big and heavy for me then, not as fun to ride as it was to think about riding. And she never carried anyone barefoot on the back – except once.

At that time Wendy had not turned four yet. She was really just getting back on her feet after polio, and we all babied her a lot. No one wanted to make her cry. The doctor said that upsetting her was bad for her health, that she also had a heart murmur, whatever that is. Although she was small, blond and frail, she could be just as stubborn as Talulah when the mood hit her.

One nice September Saturday, when Dad was at work as usual, Sissy was giving short rides on her bike to us and neighborhood kids – all but Wendy. Well, that seemed the height of unfairness to my little sister. She begged and begged and was starting to get herself all worked up 'til Sissy caved in and agreed to give her just a very short ride. "Set her up on to the back, Junior, and let's get this over and done with." Like the rest of us, Wendy was wearing no shoes. "Sissy took a doubtful look over her shoulder and said, "Now, Wendy, listen. You must hold your feet out to the sides. Do not let them get near the spokes. Do you understand?"

"Yes, I understand. Let's go." And she continued to chatter as Sissy slowly pushed off. She didn't go far, just past the McElroy's and then turned around. Suddenly, from around the curve sped a black car and in a moment was nearly on Sissy's rear fender. The driver honked and startled Sissy who swerved to get out of the way. We heard a scream and thought the car had hit the bike because Sissy stopped so suddenly, tipping over the bike and spilling Wendy on the ground. The car disappeared up around the bend, and we raced over to Sissy and Wendy. Both were crying and screaming, but Wendy's hands were covered with blood.

Sissy looked panicked. "Oh no! Wendy's hurt bad. Daddy's going to kill me. He told me not to give her a ride. Oh, what am I gonna do? I'm dead. I told her to keep her feet out of the spokes. Wendy, Wendy, stop crying. Oh, Junior, what am I going to do?"

Talulah had already raced ahead to get Mom, and I carried Wendy up to the house. Blood kept dripping all over from her foot, and she wouldn't stop wailing. By the time we got to the top steps Mom was there and took Wendy from me. "Oh, baby, what happened to you? Shush now. Quiet down. It'll be okay," and hurried her into the house. Mom carefully laid her on the kitchen table. She started right in to clean up and bandage the

foot as best she could, stopping only to tell me to go next door to
get Mr. Weis.

When I told him what happened, he grabbed his hat and
came right away. Wendy was all red-eyed and blubbering, and
blood was already seeping through the wrap Mom had put on
her foot. Mom's face looked ashy. "Herman, I'm sorry, but I need
to get Wendy to the hospital, and I don't have time to find Stu.
Can you please drive us in? I'll call him from there."

Mr. Weis glanced at Wendy and said to Mom, "Young lady,
don't you worry about a thing. Just splash some water on your
face while I carry this youngster down to the car." With that he
scooped up Wendy and carried her out and down the steps. "And,
Junior, grab another towel to put under this foot."

We hurried down the steps. Mom didn't even slow down as
she stepped around Sissy's bike and climbed into Mr. Weis's car.
"Young lady," Mom ordered, "put that bike away. Then get up
to the house and watch the kids. We'll deal with you when I get
back." And with that Mom and Mr. Weis were gone.

Sissy picked up her bike and pushed it back into the garage
and closed the door. Her face looked so torn up and her eyes were
so afraid that that it was all she could do to climb the steps up to
the house and await her doom. It had only been about two weeks
since she got her dream come true birthday present, and now I
was honestly worried for her. Talulah and me sat on the top step
and waited. "Junior, do you figure Sissy's gonna get whipped?"

"I guess so. She disobeyed Dad twice."

"I just hope he don't hurt her too bad." And she chewed a
fingernail.

"Me either, Talulah. Me either. Wendy shouldn't even have
been down there."

In a while Mr. Weis pulled his car into his garage and got out
alone, so we knew Dad had met Mom at the hospital, and a half-
hour later his green truck pulled in. Dad got out first, walked
around the cab, and took Wendy from Mom's lap. Her whole foot
except for her toes was wrapped up and she was quietly snuggled
into Dad's chest.

When they got to the house, Dad walked right past us and took Wendy to her bed and laid her down. Then he came out and quietly shut the bedroom door. We were standing in the dining room when he said, "Sissy, come with me to the front room." She did. "Now sit down." She was wringing her hands with fear and could barely keep from sobbing. "Wendy had a serious accident. I know you didn't mean to hurt her, but a part of her heel is cut off right down to the tendons. Those spokes sliced her up like baloney. Do you know what I mean? I told you specifically not to ride her on the bike 'cause her legs are so weak, and any riders had to have shoes. Remember?" She started sobbing. "I know you feel terrible but that's just because something bad happened and you got caught, not because you did wrong.

Your Mom and I have talked about your punishment on the way home." Sissy groaned and hid her face in her hands. "I'm taking your bike away for one full month. But I don't want you to forget about it. So I'm going to hang it up on the garage wall so you'll always see it and be reminded of today."

"Daddy, no. I'm so sorry. Wendy begged me to. I didn't want to give her a ride. Please don't take my bike away. I'll take a licking. Please. Please."

"I'm sorry, Sissy. It has to be this way. You come with me now and help me hang it up."

"No, please." But he took her hand and, with her sobbing, climbed down the steps to the garage. I watched as he opened the garage door and sent her in to bring out her bike. She walked it out to him, and he parked it at the side facing the house and then went in for his tool belt and ladder. He had Sissy watch while he climbed the ladder, drilled holes, inserted a chain and attached one end of it to the inside of the garage wall. Then he took the bike with one hand and threaded the chain through its frame, climbed the ladder and pushed the chain end through the other hole back into the garage.

I watched the bike rise off the ground as Dad pulled the chain from inside the garage. It was so high off the ground that none of us kids could reach it even if we jumped. He padlocked the chain inside the garage and walked back up to the house, with Sissy begging and crying the whole way like her heart was broke. That bike hung up there on the garage wall for one full month. We saw it every day. And when he took it down and fixed it up for Sissy again, she never carried another person on it.

Now, whoever would move into this house, how will they know the story of that bike and garage? And how will they ever guess what those two holes were made for, so high up on the garage wall?

Chapter 26

Now that I think on it, I believe it was the fall of that year, when Wendy had her accident and Sissy lost her bike that things started to go really sour between Mom and Dad. I was just starting fourth grade and knew the ropes around here and at Holy Jesus pretty good. Each school day always started out the same. We would all get to school about 7:45 and mill around out front for a couple minutes waiting for the doors to open. Rain or shine, warm or cold, the doors don't open 'til 7:50. Then the nuns would all come out and one, usually Sister Mary Martha, the eighth grade teacher, would ring a bell. Everyone in the yard would gather around the flagpole and we'd all recite the pledge of allegiance. I think that was also the year they added the words "under God" to the pledge. Then we'd all crowd into the school behind the nuns and go to our classrooms.

This was the same routine, like I said, we always followed until one chilly Tuesday in October. We all gathered out front as usual. The nuns came out at the same time and rang the bell, but when we clustered around to say the "Pledge," Sister Mary Martha couldn't talk. She tried but gave it up and stood there crying into a hankie. We had never seen such a thing and pushed in closer for a better view.

Then Sister Mary Catherine stepped forward and told us in the saddest voice I ever heard her speak, "Boys and girls, I have some very sad news to tell you. This morning during Mass Father Gorski had a heart attack. The doctors say he died instantly." Those are the only words I remember directly. There was more, and a priest from St. Joe's came and talked to us all in our classrooms.

I couldn't believe it. Father Gorski - why I had seen him just the day before on the playground. He had come out of the rectory at lunch time and was standing there talking and laughing with the boys by the basketball court, giving them pointers on how to shoot a layup the right way and watching them play. He was a real friendly priest and everybody liked him. Dad and him seemed best friends and would always chat a minute after Sunday Mass.

Dad told me once that Father Gorski had been a chaplain in WWII in the Pacific and all the men who knew him, whether Catholic or not, thought of him as a brave and good man who also had some kind of special protection from getting himself blown up. Mom told me Father James Gorski had helped convert Dad and got him to agree to raise his kids in the church. He also got Dad involved in the school. Dad even became the Boy Scout troop leader at Holy Jesus and said he loved it. And I do believe that is the truth. He even took the boy scouts out camping once during the winter the year before.

It really doesn't snow much here but it did that winter. During Dad's camping trip Mom was worrying out loud about how all those boys and "your father" were doing in their tents out in the cold. What if they can't get the fires started because of the wet wood and such? And the snow kept falling in big fat flakes making the ground wet and slick.

Late in the afternoon, just as the pale light started draining out of the clouds, the black church car that Father Gorski drove pulled into the parking area and he and Dad climbed the steps up to the house, stomped their feet on the front porch, and bounced on in. They were laughing and talking and looked like regular people. It somehow didn't seem right to me to see a priest acting like that. Mom welcomed Father Gorski and asked how the camping went.

"Maggie, your husband is a remarkable man and quite creative when he has to be."

"What do you mean?" she asked.

"Well, I was a bit worried when I saw the nasty weather setting in, so last night I drove out to where the scouts were camping, and what do you suppose was going on? One of the best organized and enthusiastic snowball fights I have ever seen. I have to admit I joined in and delivered a few hits of my own."

"Yeah, and you took a few too, James," Dad added. And they both laughed.

"Then we settled around the fires to warm up and dry out a bit. And since the weather had turned sour, instead of going out and working on wood lore with the scouts, your husband here cut up some line and showed the boys how to tie different knots. I had forgotten he was a navy man. All in all, it was a grand time, and very educational."

"So everything's okay?"

"Everything is fine, Maggie." And Dad kissed her cheek.

"Well folks, I really have to be getting back to put some finishing touches on my Sunday sermon. I'll see you at Mass tomorrow. And, Stu," Father Gorski hesitated, "try to be on time for a change." As he laid his hand on the doorknob, he turned and added, "I really do appreciate what you're doing for the boys, Stu. I wish I had more time for them myself." With that he was out the door and gone.

"Well, wasn't he in fine spirits!" Mom said. "Just don't let all his kind words go to your head now, Stu."

"Maggie, I really had a good time. I never was a scout. You know I didn't finish grade school. But, honey, camping with those scouts was a blast. And James is okay."

And that year, Dad was busy with the scouts a lot of his free time. They went camping again, in better weather, and even took me with them one night on a campout. I liked being with him there, but all those big boys made me feel shy. I felt out of place at the camp fire, and after just a few stories, I turned in to the tent and fought to get to sleep on the bumpy ground under my sleeping bag. Still, I could tell Dad had fun and the boys liked him.

Once he even took me to a "Boy Scout Jamboree," which was held in a big building where all the different troop units had booths and demonstrated scout skills, making fires without matches, setting up fire pits, wood lore, and the like. I really had a good time there and didn't want to leave, and told Dad I wanted to be a scout.

Dad told me that if I wanted to be a boy scout, I first had to be a cub scout. So one fall day, right after school started on the same year Father Gorman would die, he gave me a Cub Scout hat, shirt, tie and belt, and enrolled me in a local den. The only problem was that they met after school at the den mother's house, and I would have to walk home because Dad would still be at work. But that was fine with me, so he drove me over to Mrs. Mitchell's home, just a couple blocks from school, and introduced me. She smiled and chatted and showed me around and explained what it was the cub scouts in her den were doing, and then we drove home.

I went to the first few Cub Scout meetings and had a pretty good time. Everybody seemed to know each other 'cause they were all town kids. My favorite activity was when we made a paper maché map of an area based on a photograph. Our work may have been sloppy but it made that photo come to life in 3-D, and I could just imagine my little green soldiers climbing and fighting on the hills and valley. Mrs. Mitchell told us what we were doing was making the land "to scale."

I probably would have stayed in the scouts longer but there was really just one thing that I could not stomach about being a cub scout. And that was this: Whenever anyone had a birthday, they had to run the gauntlet. That meant all the boys stood in two lines facing each other. Then the birthday boy would have to crawl down the lane between the two lines while they swatted his behind.

I suppose it was all meant in good fun, but I couldn't do it. I couldn't hit a kid, for no reason, that I hardly knew. And I was certain that I would never crawl through the gauntlet, letting other boys hit me.

When one boy had a birthday, Mrs. Mitchell said, "Come on, Junior, take your place in the gauntlet now." I just shook my head and stood back 'til they were done hitting him. He didn't seem to mind, even laughed. But I hated it and would have stopped them if I had the courage. The next meeting there was another birthday boy, and I could see the writing on the wall. No making paper landscapes could make this all right. Scouting just wasn't for me. As they were forming up their gauntlet, I sidled out the kitchen door into the yard, wondering what was I to do now.

A minute later Dusty, her boy, stepped out. I don't know whether his mom sent him or whether he came on his own, but thankfully he didn't try to get me to go back in. "Whatcha doing, Junior?"

"Nothin'. I just don't like the gauntlet. It's dumb."

"Yeah. I guess so. You know what I like to do out here by the woodpile?"

Pleased that he so quickly changed the subject, I asked, "No. What?"

"Look for wood ticks. Do you know the only way you can kill them is to burn them? You can't possibly squeeze them to death. I know right where they are." And he turned over a small log on their wood pile. "There's one right now." And he pinched up a tiny, harmless looking little bug that crawled all over his hand and then onto the other.

I was fascinated 'cause while I had heard of ticks before and how they would sink their heads in you and swell up with sucked blood, I hadn't ever really got up close and personal with one before. "Ain't you afraid it will latch on to you and drink up your blood?"

"Naw. Ticks walk around for the longest time looking for just the right place to sink in. See?" And with that he handed it to me, and the tickly little thing scurried around looking for a soft tasty spot, I supposed. "I swear you can't kill it. Pinch it. Go on. Pinch it hard. See? There it goes." And sure enough, no matter what I did the little tank of a bug just kept looking for supper.

Dusty took it back from me and brushed it off his hands onto the logs where it had come from. "And if you ever get bit by one, don't yank it out 'cause its head will pop off inside and you could get infected. If you got a match you can make it hot. But don't burn it up. Then it will leave on its own to try to find a cooler spot. Say, you coming back in? Gauntlet's done by now."

"Nah, I think I better get goin' on home. I gotta walk, and it's a long way out in the country. Thanks, Dusty. See ya." And with that, I waved and we parted company. I never saw him again. It was on the walk home I decided to quit cub scouts. I figured if my folks asked, I'd tell them why, but I wouldn't tell them if they didn't ask. I just wouldn't go to the meetings anymore.

I knew this meant that I could never be a boy scout and go camping with the big boys and my dad, but the truth is, there's only so much hitting a guy can stomach. And the funny thing was that no one at home ever asked me why I didn't go back to cub scouts. Mom and Dad had been arguing about something or other when I got in, and then a couple weeks later Father Gorski died.

Chapter 27

When a person has a birthday up in the hills, it's usually a big deal and all the kids in the neighborhood are invited. There's lots of food and games, and it can last most of an afternoon. I turned twelve today and got to invite anyone I wanted to my party. Besides my family, there was Danny McElroy, Sissy's friend. Of course Mooky and Andy showed, along with Tommy and Jessie Sue Chambers, who live just past Mooky's, before you get to the Sather farm. And Ellie Norton, who everybody teases me about, calling her my girlfriend. She lives just past Crazy John's old house in the other direction. So our place was full.

One of the coolest things was when Mooky's grandpa brought out his ice cream maker and we got to help crank the handle and make the ice cream, just like back on the Fourth of July. It really didn't take long and he spooned out big scoops of peach ice cream onto our chocolate cake slices. It didn't hardly taste anything like the box ice cream Dad brings home from Kroger once in a while.

Mr. Weis makes it, but his wife, Tootsie puts up the peaches. Yep. That's her real name. She was my baby sister's godmother, so Mom named her after Mrs. Weis. She's a real nice lady but don't get out much but she sure likes to can stuff.

I am sure glad she does. There is nothing as good in the whole world as their peach ice cream. To my mind, it even tops chocolate..

I like Mr. Weis. He is my godfather. Being a godparent means they are supposed to look after my spiritual upbringing. Truth be told, they never seem to pay a lot of attention to us. But still, Mr. Weis seems solid and kind. And he makes great ice cream.

Other than that we played the typical birthday games, like pin the tail on the donkey and blind man's bluff. For a bit we played Bingo and guests won party prizes. Then most of us went out on the front porch and played spin the bottle.

To play that game, you spread everyone around in a circle and try to have an even number of girls and boys. We take a piece of chalk and make an X with it on the floor, then put a Coke bottle in the middle. Then you take turns spinning it. If a boy spins it, he's gotta kiss the girl it nearest points to. If a girl spins, well, she's gotta kiss a boy. We had four boys – me, Mooky, Andy, and Danny. And four girls – Sissy, Talulah, Jessie Sue Chambers, and Ellie. I almost wouldn't play the game because two of the girls were my sisters. And Jessie Sue hardly counts.

She is two years younger than me and don't seem too bright. She is kind of chubby, has a chipped front tooth, and probably wouldn't have been invited except I invited her older brother Tommy, who wouldn't play this game, as he didn't like Talulah or Sissy much and sure as shooting, was not going to kiss his little sister. Jessie didn't want to play either as she is a bit shy, but we talked her into it so we could have enough girls to make the numbers even.

It's a funny thing how it happens sometimes that a bunch of people will do mean things together that none of them would do if they were just by themselves. I've seen it a million times at school. That's what happened when we played spin the bottle today. The game started off okay. I hated it when I had to kiss Talulah or Sissy, but that only happened a time or two and they just got little pecks of the forehead.

I don't know who started it, but nobody wanted to kiss Jessie, and it got so bad that when the bottle would spin and it would point her way, all the kids would hoot and laugh, and Danny would pound the floor, and we'd spin it again until you couldn't even see her face, all hidden down the way it was behind her dish-water colored hair.

It made me feel worse and worse for her. I remembered that pup being thrown in the creek. The only reason she stayed was I think she was too hurt to get up, and she probably figured that if she did leave she would be hooted all the way to her home. So each time it happened she just got glued harder to the spot she was squatting on.

It was only a matter of time before one of my spins pointed her way, and the jeers and laughs broke out. "Yuck." "Sorry 'bout that, Junior." And, "Sooiiee, oink oink." You get the picture. She really did look as miserable as a half-drowned puppy all hunched over like she was, just expecting to get kicked again.

I stood up and the shouts picked up, even from my own sisters. They must have thought I had figured out a new way to humiliate Jessie even worse. And to be honest, when I first stood, I wasn't sure what I was going to do. Maybe I'd even leave the room. If I stayed did I want to risk my family and friends making fun of me over this ugly neighbor kid?

As I walked around the circle and stood by her, things quieted a bit, and then she looked up at me. I'm not sure what she expected, maybe the last straw, maybe the remark that would finally bust her down into tears. I don't know. But in her blue-grey eyes I saw hope flicker, and that decided it for me.

Quickly I stooped down, closed my eyes, and kissed her lips. They were soft, and I did not even notice the chipped tooth. When I stood back up, I was as surprised as anybody and didn't know what to say or do. What if all my friends start making fun of me? "Thanks, Jessie. Thanks for coming to my party," was all I could think to say.

She sat up straight then and pushed a curly strand back off her face, and the dimple on her right cheek appeared and deepened as she almost smiled and then looked back down at her hands. I walked back around to my spot and sat down, half expecting some smart remark from Danny or Sissy. But the weirdest thing happened – nothing – nothing at all. My friends did not make fun of me. And Danny didn't say a word. We just played more spin-the-bottle and nobody made fun of Jessie Sue anymore. The game broke up a few minutes later, but my friends were still my friends, and who cares what your sisters think. You're stuck with them and them with you forever anyway.

And once in a blue moon, on days like this, you just might make a new friend. As we were saying goodbye to our guests, Jessie Sue's big brother Tommy, who's one year older than me, kind of walked me aside a step and said, "I heard how you stood up for Jessie Sue in there, and I want to thank you for being nice to her." He almost turned away, then stopped and said, "Oh, by the way, I think you might have one little problem now. Since you're the first boy who ever kissed her, she thinks you're her boyfriend now. Good luck." And with that and a chuckle, he left.

Really though I don't reckon I'll ever have much trouble with her as our families don't mix much and besides, in a few weeks or so they say we gotta move off Harvey's Creek – but not tonight.

Chapter 28

One of the hard parts about being a boy is that grown-ups all seem to believe you gotta "go through a phase" of hating girls. I cannot remember a time when I did not think girls were mighty fine creatures – except for a few, like Imogene Castro, and Talulah once in a while. But overall, they are easier to get along with than most boys, smile nicer, and don't seem as mean. In other words, they're safer.

That don't mean you want to hang around with them all the time 'cause they really aren't very good at the fun games like playing war, skipping stones, climbing trees and such. Still, there's no denying that there is something about a girl that naturally makes me want to talk nice to her and walk close with her, and maybe show off a bit.

Up here on the ridge there ain't many of 'em my age. Ever since I could remember, folks have teased me about Ellie Norton being my girlfriend. It started when we were little kids. Me and Sissy were invited to her big sister Marla's birthday party. They live way down past the Evers and Crazy John. Her big sister is a year older than Sissy, and the only reason I was invited was so that her little sister Ellie would have company.

At the party everyone thought we were so cute and made a big deal about it. They played a game where two people would hold up a blanket, two kids would go behind it and kiss. Then they would drop the blanket and try to catch the two kids kissing. Mostly, this was a game for the big kids, but they let Ellie and me play.

When Ellie and me kissed and they dropped the blanket, all the kids clapped and cheered like we did something really big so we kissed again. Ellie never said a mean thing to me. If her folks had been Catholic, and we had gone to the same school, we might have become better friends sooner. We're in the same grade, after all.

Still, Ellie Norton is to my mind about as fine a girl as I ever met, and she seems to like me too. But I really think she became my girlfriend the way big kids think about it just last summer. Mooky and me were playing football in the yard between his house and his grandpa's. I would throw it, he would catch it, then I would tackle him before he scored. Then we would switch and he would pass it, I would catch and he would try to tackle me.

I only ran about three-quarter speed so he could catch me once in a while. When he caught it, I could catch him but he is stronger, so sometimes he could break loose before I tackled him. So the game was pretty even.

Mr. Weis stopped and watched us for a few minutes, leaning on his hoe before heading up to his garden, and once when I was chasing Mooky and leaped and caught him from behind, wrapping up his legs, with us tumbling to the ground, Mr. Weis remarked, "You know, Junior, if you had some meat on your bones you could be a good football player," insulting and complimenting me at the same time before going about his business.

To get back to Ellie. That day, for some reason she had come drifting by along the ridge and watched us for a minute. Naturally, we showed off a little bit and tossed her the ball, which she caught. As she flipped it back to us she asked if she could play too. That ain't as strange as it may seem: Up on the ridge kids often seem to sort of slide along the ridge and see who is around to play with. That day we were probably the only ones out and we didn't think nothing of her request except maybe being a little annoyed because at first we couldn't figure out how to work her into the game.

It took us a minute to puzzle it out. We changed the rules to make it three-cornered football. Whoever caught the football got to choose which way to run, and the others had to catch the ball carrier before he or she crossed the goal. Another rule we changed for Ellie was that we couldn't tackle her, just two-hand tag her.

The first time I tossed her the ball, she dropped it, but she caught on quick and didn't drop an easy one after that. Ellie was quick but not fast, if you know what I mean. She could dodge and spin out of the way such that it was admirable, but she couldn't outrun us.

We had a really fun time playing until she stumbled once making a dodge move and didn't jump right back up but sat there holding her right knee, rocking and biting her lower lip like she was trying not to cry. We stopped playing, and taking my hand, she stood and limped over to a glider swing under two trees in Mr. Weis's yard and sat on it. Her knee was really skinned red. I guess that's what comes from playing football in a dress. We asked her should we go get Mooky's mom. Ellie said no, she really didn't want to make a big deal out of it, and I appreciated her grit.

But still, her sitting there rocking back and forth, hurting, nearly crying, made me feel like I had to do something, so I knelt in front of her and with both hands I gently rubbed the area of her leg directly above her knee and around the skinned part. When I saw and felt my hands sliding over the smooth inside of her tanned leg, I felt something I never felt before, like I would swallow my heart, it felt so stuck in my throat. Then my heart started thumping like crazy. A thrill rolled all through me, confusing me because the next thing I did was really stupid and would later cause me no end of embarrassment with Mooky.

With both hands resting just above her knee on the inside and outside of her leg, I bent down and gently kissed the area right above her scrape. I could taste her salt. Raising my eyes to meet hers, I whispered, "I'm sorry, Ellie." I swear never have I felt so strong a connection with any other human than I did at that very instant. Her dark brown eyes seemed to fire an arrow into my soul, and I felt almost reverent. Neither of us smiled. Then Mooky whooped a good one, breaking the spell, 'cause that's what it was. "Junior's got a girlfriend. Junior's got a girlfriend."

"Knock it off, Mooky. This ain't funny. Ellie's hurt." I turned back to her. "Do you want me to walk you home, Ellie? You gonna be okay?"

"I'm gonna be fine, Junior," she said in a voice as soft as feathers. Then in a stronger voice she added, "Thanks for letting me play with you guys. I best be going now." She stood and straightened down her dress before slowly walking away. We watched her for a moment as she limped off. She didn't look back. I couldn't stop thinking how pretty she was and how she made me feel.

Mooky brought me back to reality. "C'mon, Junior. You want to play or what?" So we went back to our playing two way football and didn't talk about the incident with Ellie again. Still, I have thought about it and her – quite often. And kissing.

It felt so sweet to kiss her when we played spin the bottle at my birthday party. But that was just a game. That day, kissing her leg, I felt entirely something different.

I haven't talked to her about our moving away, even at my party, but I think she knows. Everybody knows everything about everybody up Harvey's Creek. So when she was ready to go home, after my birthday party, I just said goodbye and thanks for coming. She reached out and squeezed my hand, and for a moment I was afraid and hoping she was about to say something. But then she let go and just walked away.

Chapter 29

I've been spending so much time walking around these hills and woods lately Mooky's called me a "wood spook." But I can't help it. The woods is the only place I can find that stops the churning inside me. My folk's plan is to be moved out by the end of the month. Dad says he found us a new house in Ceredo, which is just to the west of Huntington but is still on the city bus line, about ten miles from here.

The idea of living like a flatlander city-slicker makes me sick, but there don't seem to be any choice to it. Still, I don't think I can stand sidewalks, cars and little yards. And how will I ever see my friends? And what will I do if I have to switch schools? Maybe I can run away, build a cabin in the woods, and live on my own.

I told Mooky about my thoughts now that I know my family is all wobbly and about to fall apart, and he was real quiet for a long time today while we were hiking up by the tree fort. Talking to him about hard things is easier than to anybody else. He listens for a long time and really thinks on things before he speaks, not like nearly everybody else, who jump right in as fast as they can with their take on things.

The black-berries are in and the woods and fields are all changing. There's still plenty of beautiful flowers to enjoy. Black-Eyed Susans and cone flowers remind me of sunsets. The flowers this time of year just seem tougher and stronger than earlier blooms. All along the roads you see ironweed purple, and even the thistle blossoms gather a butterfly or bee. Looking across the valley now you see a mix of greens, golds, and whites in blurry colors, like they're kind of out of focus, not like the sharper colors of a month or two ago. Such walking and looking makes life bearable for a while.

I told him as much as I know about our move. But that really don't amount to a hill of beans. I've never moved before. We do know that, regardless of what happens, we'll always be blood-brothers – things like that can never change. But we both know something big and important is breaking, and we hate it, and we're too young to fix it, and I'm too late in my hunting for the mistake that can't be fixed anyhow, and we don't know what it's going to look like later. His life will stay pretty much the same – same house, same folks, same hills, same school. But mine's wrapped in wavy shadows. And whatever the future will be looks like it will be without Dad.

We climbed up into the tree fort, and Mooky sat cross legged while I climbed a bit higher to my favorite spot, where three fat branches fork, making a perfect saddle, almost like a cupped hand. Then Mooky told me how he saw things. "We've got to be realistic," he said. And I thought he sounded just like his dad. I'll never say that to my own kids. It always means something bad is about to happen. "You can't live in the woods by yourself," he said. "They'll just hunt you down and make you go anyway. Grown-ups got all the power and say-so, even if they're rotten crazy."

I knew what he was saying was probably true, but still I wanted to shout back at him to drown him out. At least I knew that if I was to run away, I would have to build a new secret place and lay low for a long time. And that meant I would need a considerable stash of supplies. And still it probably wouldn't work out. "Real life ain't like Robinson Crusoe," he said, and that made sad sense. So I listened and mostly decided to do things his way.

We talked for a long time and made some decisions: Number One – from the first day of school we will go by our first names – no nicknames, no "Junior," no "Mooky." My name is Stuart: I will not answer to any other name. His name is Duke: That will be it. No baby tags.

Number Two – when we move away there'll be no crying or carrying on. We talk about it now, so we can just shake hands on that ugly day.

Number Three – we will stay in touch and visit if we ever get the chance.

Number Four – we will treat each day until I move just the same as if the move wasn't happening.

We agreed these were the important things. And then I climbed down from my perch, he stood and we shook on it. I watched Mooky shuffle off home, kicking the leaves and felt a wave of tiredness come over me.

I probably should have gone on home myself, but I really hadn't decided yet if I would ever go back. So I sagged down into the soft stuff at the base of the tree and just let everything wash over me, closing my eyes and daydreaming about how fine it would be if I was to run away.

I was so intent on my thoughts that it wasn't until I heard someone clear her throat that I opened my eyes with a start. I don't know how she found the place, but there stood Ellie, barefoot and sad-eyed, wearing a sleeveless summer dress that hung on her shoulders like a sack.

On seeing the surprise on my face she raised one hand as if to stop me from getting up. "I seen you come up here lots of times. It ain't as much a secret as you think, Junior." She maybe smiled just a little at one corner of her mouth. "I just wanted to tell you that I'll miss you." She twisted a bit nervously, like she was trying to decide something. "You're not like the other boys around here. You're thoughtful, and kind, and sorta quiet. I wish I went to your school. But that's just how it is." She stopped fidgeting.

Whatever she was pondering over, she seemed to figure out. Even if I had wanted to get up, what she did next guaranteed I couldn't have stood. She reached up under her dress and wiggled right out of her panties. "I know all about boys, Junior. Marla's told me how it is." She brushed a strand of hair behind her ear. "You gotta do just what I tell you, okay?" I just stared, but I think I closed my mouth at least.

Ellie stepped forward until she was right in front of me. "Kneel in front of me, Junior." I did. "Now, starting at an ankle, run your hands up my leg. All the way up." I felt her velvet skin up her calf, past her knee, way past where I had once kissed her. "Don't stop." She shivered a little under my touch.

My hands continued until they came to where her legs joined. "Now do the other leg," she whispered. I did as she asked. But when I tried to raise her dress, she pushed it back down. "No, I don't want you to see me. Please."

Then she took my hands and placed them on her breasts. To be honest there wasn't much there. I could tell they were starting to develop, small, soft mounds. I expected that, but what completely stopped me was when I got to their crowns. Her nipples were as hard as early blackberries. I didn't want to quit, but then Ellie stood straight up and said, "Okay, Junior, that's enough."

My whole body was just aching with wanting to keep on touching her, but if she would of told me to jump off a cliff, I swear I wouldn't have hesitated. I sagged back, sitting on my heels.

"Now then, lean back there, Junior, against that tree and close your eyes. There's just one more thing I gotta do." Then she knelt in front of me and unbuttoned the fly of my dungarees. Reaching in with one hand she found what she was looking for.

Soon I felt the familiar electric sensation overwhelming me, washing through me in every direction.

I heard what sounded like my voice calling, "Ellie, Ellie, Oh Ellie!" and then it was over. I just lay there, my eyes fixed on her face as she stood.

"I told you I knew about boys." She smiled again at me, but this time Ellie looked more confident. "Junior, I know you gotta move off Harvey's Creek, that your folks are having troubles, and you'll have to figure out what you can do about it. Like as not it'll be nothing. Maybe I'll never see you again. It'll be hard for you, but I guess you will find a way through it all."

Then she turned her back and started walking away. "Don't come down to my house to say goodbye. You can pretend today never happened." Then that girl laughed and turned to me. "But one thing I know for sure, Junior Carter, you ain't never gonna forget me." I laid there like a man shot.

Ellie disappeared behind some trees and was gone. I must of dozed some then because when I opened my eyes the shadows

Karl L. Stewart

were all angled. Supper would be ready soon, for sure. As I walked out of the woods, searching for any trace of Ellie and finding none, the thought crossed my mind that maybe I had imagined or drempt the whole thing, or maybe this was a haunt pretending to be Ellie. But I don't think so. She sure felt like the real thing.

Even writing about it now, I can still feel her with my fingers. Still, stranger things than that have happened in those woods. I guess I'll never know for sure.

Chapter 30

I just don't get how or why anybody would want to go and smash up people's lives like a car wreck. It seems to me all Dad has to do is go easy on the bottle and come home nights and not beat us up. And Mom has to give him some credit for what good he does, and cut him some slack once in a while. To my way of thinking, that's about all it would take. Then maybe they could work out any other problems.

Dad says he is taking us all out to a restaurant tonight for supper. He says he wants to show us our new house and celebrate him getting a new job in a shoe section of Corker's Department Store. So we'll all have to get cleaned up before he gets in from work. Wendy and Tootsie are still napping, the fan is humming low in the front room, Sissy's next door at McElroy's, and I hear Talulah swinging away on the squeaky swing.

I sure hope we don't have to leave the swing set behind. Dad set it all up to give us a clear view of the valley to the west, past Harvey's Creek. He set the legs in concrete so when we got the swings going high, it would all stay put and not rock back and forth.

When you kick up high on those swings, you can feel safe 'cause you know it's anchored, but that let's you feel free, like you can really turn it loose and sail right across the creek. I have rode those swings when I was younger for hours, pointing my toes up at the cotton ball clouds, feeling like I could be swinging forever, 'til I couldn't remember nothing but riding the swing, like there never had been a time before it.

One of my favorite of all time memories is of these swings. It was a gorgeous morning before I started first grade. There

196

was just the usual noises, a bob-white calling off by itself, crows hollering at each other here or there, the wheels of a car once in a while pattering down the brick road, and Mom playing the radio while she worked in the house. I was sitting dead still on the swing soaking it all in when the back door opens and Mom steps out to shake a rug.

She was wearing blue peddle-pushers, a cotton blouse, and a scarf around her head, tied up in the front. She had no socks on. I remember that as clear as a bell. But when she shook out the rug, she squinched up her face like it would keep the dust out of her nose. It looked so funny I smiled to myself. And she looked so pretty. And I surely can never forget the hours Sissy, me, and Talulah spent waxing that slide with bread bags, just to go down it a little bit faster. And how the shiny metal slide would scorch our legs on hot sunny days. And the two person glider swing that, when I rode alone could be my horse or race car, but when Mooky or Talulah would ride with me, it was a place to talk and laugh. So you see we just gotta take our swing set.

Just now Mom peeked into my room and told me to put my notebook away and start getting cleaned up before the girls rush the bathroom to start primping 'cause we got to get ready to go out to dinner. I'll finish this up when we get back.

Well, what happened tonight is what Dad calls a grand boondoggle. We don't go out much. As a matter of fact, I can't hardly remember us ever going out for dinner. Sometimes on holidays or Sunday maybe, but this was a special event. Mom hustled around getting us kids ready to go for when Dad would get here to pick us up. Wendy woke up from her nap crying and unhappy even though she is seven years old. Talulah didn't want to stop playing with her dolls, and Sissy was slow coming up from the McElroys. Only Tootsie was ready to go. But eventually we all did get set and sat in the front room waiting for Dad. Mom said as how she thought this was mighty nice we would go see the new house and all and reminded us to be on our best behavior in the restaurant.

We were getting tired and bored by the time Dad pulled up in the green Packard. Since he don't work at the fixture installers place no more, he can't use the truck. So we're mighty lucky he had bought this 1949 green Packard. It cost $50 and Mom gave him heck for wasting money on it, but now she don't say anything about it. I like it. It's very roomy and soft and feels rich.

He hollered up at us from the bottom of the hill to come on down and get in. We're running a bit late. That just started it all off wrong for Mom. She said as how he could at least come up to the house to get us. When we climbed down the steps, he was in a jolly mood and clearly had stopped off for a few beers before he got to us, just to celebrate, he said. Mom said he didn't seem to need a reason to "celebrate," and told him that now that she was getting along in her pregnancy, she could have used a hand on the steps. He leaned her way for a kiss, but she ignored him and lifted Tootsie into the front seat and climbed in beside her. Dad stood there a second, then shut the door hard.

"I love you, Daddy," Talulah said and hugged his waist.

He patted her head and said to everybody, "Okay. All aboard. Let's get this flea circus on the road," ushered Talulah into the back seat between Sissy and me, then walked around and climbed in the driver's seat. Off he drove, back towards town, ignoring Mom's instructions to slow down. "Stu, I wish you wouldn't drink so much and drive so fast."

"What do you care, Maggie? We ain't living together, and besides, I can hold my liquor. So get off my back," he dismissed her. "Okay, kids, first I'll drive by the store where I work now, so you can see. Then we'll take a look at the house. Then supper." He was fighting to have fun, but Mom with her sour face wasn't helping any.

Being with Dad when he was in a good mood was lots of fun. If he had a few beers he could make you laugh easy. And it's true; he never got in an accident, though he did drive fast enough to scare us sometimes.

One night, when I was a little kid and Dad and me were alone in the car, he let me sit on his lap and steer while he worked the pedals. "Whee," he yelled. "80 miles per hour. That's almost as fast as fighter planes go when they take off from the deck. Keep us on the road, son. We don't want to fly tonight." And he laughed.

That was fun. And I thought about it as we drove into town. Dad's new store was right downtown Huntington in a big department store, tucked in between buildings five and ten stories tall. We drove by real slow, then pulled over to the curb with the motor running.

"Wow, can we go in?" Talulah wanted to know.

"Not now. It's after five, and Corker's is closing up. But another time, I promise. Maggie, the money isn't quite as much starting out as at Robert's, but I'll be getting regular raises and commission on sales. And it's straight 8-5 and maybe overtime on weekends."

"Stu, with you it's always 'maybe, maybe.' But we gotta eat now, and bills gotta be paid now. I sure wish you hadn't been fired."

Dad hit the steering wheel with his hands. "Maggie. How many times I tell you, I wasn't fired. I was laid off 'cause of the recession."

"Yeah, that and the beer." And Dad squealed the tires pulling back out into the street.

Our gang was pretty quiet when Dad pulled the Packard up in front of a ramshackle two story old grey wood house near the end of a dead end street. "This is it. Everybody out," Dad ordered. We all were glad to hit solid ground. The air in the car had been getting packed pretty tight.

The house seemed huge but tucked in tight between two other smaller houses. It had a long screened in second story porch that ran its length, and the south half of the house seemed to tilt a bit, like it sank some and was trying to drag the rest of the house down with it. Dad unlocked the front door and we stepped in, hearing the floor's squeaky echoes.

Immediately us kids dashed up the stairs to claim our bedrooms and then I returned downstairs to find Dad showing Mom around the kitchen. "See. Even the fridge is stocked," he said and swung open the door to show her. "Aha, it has all the essentials." And he removed two beers, offering one to Mom and opening them both. "It'll feel more like home when you're settled in." She said nothing for a moment, just stood there in the middle of the room and looked around, clutching the beer bottle around its middle with both hands.

"It'll have to do. And after I clean it up, I guess it won't be so bad." she said and took a big drink from the bottle as he drained his and reached for another. "It is only four blocks from the sewing factory," she added, "so I can walk to work." Dad looked upset and about to say something but she cut him off. "Now don't you say a word about it. It's all set up. I start after Labor Day when the kids go back to school. And I got a babysitter all lined up. I was working when I met you, Stuart, and I'll be working again. I don't want to, but I can't count on you for anything. That's just the way it is. And you know it."

I didn't want to hear no more arguing so I went on out into the yard behind the house. The yard was kind of narrow but long with a new shed raised about five feet off the ground on cement blocks, separated from the alley by a sturdy looking fence that covered three sides of the lot. The question occurred to me that how would Reeko like living in the city? It was hard to see my dog there. Where would we go exploring? How would we like living in a boxed yard? Well, at least it was flat enough that you didn't have to climb a thousand steps to get in the door. As pregnant as Mom is, I'm sure she appreciates that fact. And maybe there would be nice kids in the neighborhood. But still I wondered, where do they all go to play after school?

About then Mom called us to get back in the car. "Time to go get some supper." And boy, was I hungry by then. So we all raced to the car, no dilly-dallying around now. Two things were clear when we got in: One, Dad had enough beer in him to make him kind of sloppy and quiet. Usually that means the edge of his good humor is off. Second, he and Mom had been talking and neither one liked what the other had said, because now they weren't talking at all.

I think Mom would have told him to take us home except for the facts that she didn't have anything ready for us to eat at home, we were all dressed up, and expected to go out. Quitting now would have caused a rebellion in the ranks, and also, she was so stubborn that no way would she ask him for any favor at this point.

I knew we were in for a tough evening when a stop light turned red just before we got to it, but the car Dad had been tailing just made it through. Dad exploded, "Goddam sonofabitchingbastard!" and he slammed his hands down on the steering wheel. That was his favorite of all times curse, and he used it only when he was really mad at something or someone. And Mom didn't say a word about his profanity this time.

The Golden Leaf Lounge and Supper Club sign was glowing red and orange when we pulled up and Dad turned into its parking lot. When he swung the car into a parking spot and got out, Mom asked, "Stu, can you give me a hand?" and reached up for him.

He was already growly, so he kind of pulled her out. "Don't be so rough. You're hurting me." But he didn't apologize. I'm surprised she even asked him for help. You can read his black mood a mile away, and if you can't stay away from him, you gotta try to be pleasant. I know this for a fact. I never understood why Mom don't catch on. Sissy walked ahead with the girls skipping along, while I brought up the rear.

This was only the second time in my life that I remember going to The Golden Leaf. Once before, when Dad picked me up after a movie, we stopped in there on the way home for "a cold one," and he bought me my first Coca Cola. I really like the happy feeling of the place, the sounds of voices, some quiet and then louder, a laugh, a glass clinking down on the bar, and the friendly faces.

But tonight the thing I really liked was the smell from the kitchen, like beef cooking and celery and spices and the deep fat fryer and things I couldn't name. As luck would have it, our table wasn't ready yet, so we waited at a table in the bar area. Dad had a beer and the rest of us had sodas. His mood seemed to lighten just a bit, and I tried to encourage it.

"This is really neat. Thanks for bringing us here, Dad. I think the house will work out just fine too. It's got a nice yard."

His look focused on me, and he seemed to appreciate my comment and wanted to follow it up. "And it's only a block from the city bus line. You kids can take the bus to school each day. It's only a dime. And there's an ice cream plant nearby too. You can live there 'til I get things squared away."

"You mean ice cream grows on plants, daddy?" Talulah giggled. "'cause that's what it sounds like you meant." And he smiled. I just was feeling that things maybe would work out okay when I heard familiar voices. It was Mooky and Andy, and sure enough, they were coming out to eat too.

"Hey, you guys, what are you doing here?" I asked

"Hi, Junior. Friday night fish fry," Mooky said.

Mr. and Mrs. Campbell approached. "Hi, Stu, Maggie," Earl said. "Yeah, we Catholics always find the best fish fry around. How are things going?"

Probably Earl was just making small talk, but Dad looked at him funny, like he was weighing what he said, "Just fine, Earl. Just fine. I just keep on minding my own business. How about you?"

"Just being neighborly, Stu. Maggie, everybody. Nice to see you. Enjoy your meal." And he sat at the table next to ours, behind Dad, waiting also to be seated in the dining area. I didn't know why Dad had to go and be so rude to Mr. Campbell. He'd always been nice to me. I looked over and gave a small wave to Mooky.

"Son of a bitch is always butting in where he ain't wanted," Dad said.

"Stu, watch your mouth. We're in public," Mom said and glanced towards the Campbells to see if they had heard. They gave no sign, but I thought they had to be deaf to have missed it.

I was getting worried so I thought to change the subject. "Funny we meet them here. Say, Mom, how did you and Dad meet?"

"Your dad and I met in Milwaukee, Mr. Nosy." She seemed to relax a bit. "He was a handsome sailor from Great Lakes Training Base, and I worked in a factory, a regular Rosie-the-Riveter."

"Yeah, but how did you meet?"

"A lot like tonight. It was in a restaurant."

"Restaurant, hell. It was The Avenue Bar. And your ma picked me up, J.R. Didn't you, Maggie, you little minx?" And he reached over and pinched her arm hard.

"Stop it, Stu. You're hurting me again. Please stop."

"Sure, honey. Look but don't touch. Is that the way it is now? Sure wasn't then. You and your dirty friend."

"That's enough, Stu. Shut your filthy mouth. Florence and I had just finished working all day in the factory and happened to stop for a drink on the way back to our apartment." Then she added, sounding a little sadder, "Lord, the number of times I've wished you hadn't shown up there that day."

I could see my try at making conversation clearly had gone south in a rush, so, worried, I tried another tack, a safer one. I hoped, a more neighborly one. "Well, how did Mr. and Mrs. Campbell meet? Do you know?"

Dad laughed, but it had a mean edge to it. "Earl Campbell. What a man. He was caught bouncing in bed with Kate by her dad one day. You might say Earl got married at the front end of a shotgun." At this I saw Mr. Campbell rising from his chair. He was not smiling. Dad, not seeing Earl, finished off his bottle of beer and continued, "And since then he has been working to get into your underpants. Hasn't he, darling?" looking straight at Mom, who for once either had the good sense or was too stunned to say anything.

Right then Mr. Campbell reached around and grabbed Dad by the front of his shirt with one hand and nearly lifted him out of his chair. He drew his fist back. The people nearest us, who also had heard Dad's remarks, were the only ones who noticed what happened next. It happened so quickly.

"Stu, your mouth is filthy as your mind, and you've crossed the line this time." Putting all his strength behind it, he punched Dad once on the jawbone. It sounded like a bone cracking, and it sprawled Dad out on the floor in his beer, with blood oozing from his mouth.

"Maggie, I'm sorry," Earl said, shaking his hand like it hurt. "But a man can only take so much. C'mon Kate, kids." And they all walked out, Mrs. Campbell touching Mom's shoulder as she walked by. I couldn't look at Mooky. I was so ashamed of my dad. He didn't even get in a lick. And of Mooky's dad for ambushing my dad like that. It was all confusing.

The bartender came around and helped Dad up. Dad seemed dazed and not sure what was happening. He let Mom dab his mouth with a wet napkin and asked, "Did Earl punch me? Now why'd that sombitch go and do that?"

"Shush up, you poor drunk fool. Your booze was talking again. Are you sober enough to drive us home?"

"Sure, but we're gonna eat first."

Mom threw a pleading glance at the bartender, who looked like he was about to say something unpleasant. But before he could say anything she responded, "That's okay. We've got some meatloaf in the fridge at home. Let's go." The bartender helped Dad to his feet and steadied him. She turned to us and in a low voice added, "Kids get in the car, and no fighting. Sissy, keep the girls quiet."

Sissy nodded and we all trooped out of the restaurant, hungry and amazed at what happened. None of us had ever seen anyone hit Dad, much less do it and walk away. It was an altogether amazing evening.

Chapter 31

Today was a day I hoped I would die before I would ever see. Dad showed up bright and early with the big green truck and two friends to help us move. Mom had been packing up things since yesterday in every bag or box we had or could get from neighbors. Sissy had been her "big help," she said.

But I couldn't control the way I was feeling. I didn't want to leave and wouldn't pack up my stuff. School starts on Monday, and Mooky – Duke – I have to get used to calling him Duke now – along with his Mom, stopped in for a few minutes to say goodbye before they went off to do some school shopping.

For a going away gift I gave him a penny that we had smashed one day on the way to school. We had been crossing the tracks near the swimming pool when we heard the wail of the train horn. I dug a penny out of my pocket and placed it carefully down on a rail. "Watch this, Mooky. Dad told me about this." Then we backed off and sat. As trains go, it wasn't much, just a diesel towing a string of about twenty coal cars.

We waved to the engineer and he waved back as the train rumbled by. I dreamed about sitting up in his high seat with my elbow out the window, warning everybody out of the way with my horn, bringing the world whatever it needs. When the last car rattled by we stood and approached the rail. My penny, right where I had left it, had been flattened thin as a sheet of paper, but was nearly big around as a nickel, with its edges all sharp as a knife.

"Wow! Will you look at that! Cool!" Mooky breathed, staring down at the coin in my hand. I handed it to him, and he turned it over and over, studying the expanded detail. Then he handed it back to me. "You gotta keep that forever now – for good luck."

"I might as well. It sure ain't good for anything else. Can't spend the thing," I laughed and we went on our way.

Now today I was giving it back to my friend. "Here, you keep it – for good luck." I dropped it into his hand.

"Thanks, Junior. I'll keep it sure. It ain't good for anything else." He grinned and we shook hands, then they left. With Mooky gone, I just climbed up the tree in the side yard and watched the men move us out, feeling like I got a chunk of apple caught in my throat.

So here I sit up in this old tree and for the life of me I just can't figure things out. And remembering things that matter don't seem to help much. Sometimes they even make it hurt more. Why even bother having friends? And why in the world, if Dad and Mom are divorcing or separating or whatever, does Dad help us out by borrowing Robert's truck and getting guys to move us and finding a house and stuff? And if Mom don't love him anymore, why does she let him do those things and take us out to dinner and such stuff?

Dad and his friends made two trips with the truck in the morning, and by noon whatever was left to move was piled in the front room. Our lives for all these years, piled up like that, sure don't amount to much. And after carting the last bunch down the hill to the truck, all that was left was the fridge and a couple small boxes in the kitchen.

The men had baloney sandwiches and beer for lunch while they laughed and talked about things like how tired they were and all. Us kids had jelly and peanut butter and milk. Mom closed up the last boxes and unplugged the fridge. Nothing was left. I looked in my room and they had cleaned it out. The house that used to feel so snug now felt empty as a cave.

Dad wiped his hands on his pants and said, "Well I think that's everything. J.R., will you make a final check through the house and make sure we didn't miss anything?" I didn't see how we could of, but I nodded my head and walked through the place one more time.

Hollow, that's what it was. Hollow, dingy, and sad. My room needed paint, and the linoleum was wearing through to the black backing in spots. In the attic was just a small cardboard box of some broken toys and metal pieces for some long-gone machine.

In the crawl space below the house, where we cooled in the summer or dashed in for temporary shelter when we played in the rain, was just some rusty pipes and broken flower pots. "Nothing, Dad. There's nothing left," I reported to him as his buddies were hoisting the fridge on the back of the truck and tying everything down.

Mom stood by the car holding a galvanized pail with a lily plant in it. "This I'm taking too. I can't leave all my flowers behind. Put it in the trunk of the car. And all you kids get in now. Where's Sissy?"

"She ran over to say goodbye to Danny," Talulah offered. And just as she said that, Sissy came out the McElroy's door and walked down the porch steps and towards the car. She climbed in the back without arguing about where she sat. Her eyes looked swollen and pink. She didn't say nothing.

"Did you say goodbye to Mooky, Junior?" Mom asked.

"Yeah. He came over for a minute before they went school shopping."

"Well, that's good. And you'll see him at school Monday." The truck pulled out first. Then Dad reversed the Packard and fell in behind, and we drove away from Harvey's Creek.

As I watched our home and Harvey's Creek fall farther and farther behind, I had the weirdest sensation of falling, so much so that I had to grab onto the seat edge on either side of me to keep from tumbling over. I thought of Ellie, and it hurt. I focused on Mooky and it hurt more. Finally, I turned my mind to the little rill that ran by our place and spilled into the creek. I thought of it with the purple wood violets tucked into its banks in the springtime. That calmed my stomach some. I guess I was pretty stupid to think that if I could remember the past, I could fix things. But I keep writing because when life gets all broken and crippled, the memories of beautiful things sometimes are the only things that a person can grab onto to keep from falling down forever.

THE END

Other books by the author:
Good Night, Sweet Dreams
The Legend of See Bird: The Last Long Drive
The Legend of See Bird: Devil's Backbone
The Seventh Cruise